"Isidora, you s...

His breath was warm against her ear, for he had bent his head—so that he could keep his voice low, she assumed.

"Lucien, I will go to bed when and where I choose. I have lived long enough to be fully capable of such a decision."

"Have you? I wonder, even at your age, that you do not need some guidance in that regard, or at least some inspiration?" He turned her around. "Do you *want* some...inspiration?"

At the sight of him so close, the feel of him, his eyes gleaming in the firelight...his attention focused upon her alone...Isidora had all the inspiration she could handle.

She felt dizzy. She wanted to fall into his arms. Kiss him. And beat him with her fists, so thickheaded was he. Had he no idea of the torture he put her through?

* * *

The Alchemist's Daughter
Harlequin Historical #742—February 2005

ELAINE KNIGHTON

THE ALCHEMIST'S DAUGHTER

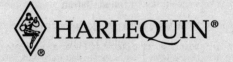

HARLEQUIN®

TORONTO • NEW YORK • LONDON
AMSTERDAM • PARIS • SYDNEY • HAMBURG
STOCKHOLM • ATHENS • TOKYO • MILAN • MADRID
PRAGUE • WARSAW • BUDAPEST • AUCKLAND

ISBN 0-373-29342-9

THE ALCHEMIST'S DAUGHTER

Copyright © 2005 by Elaine Knighton

This edition published by arrangement with Harlequin Books S.A.

www.eHarlequin.com

Printed in U.S.A.

Please address questions and book requests to:
Harlequin Reader Service
U.S.: 3010 Walden Ave., P.O. Box 1325, Buffalo, NY 14269
Canadian: P.O. Box 609, Fort Erie, Ont. L2A 5X3

To my wise and beautiful daughters, Asmara and Angela.

Prologue

The Holy Land
Somewhere between Jerusalem and Acre
Spring of 1197

"Lucien! De Brus has fallen. We must stop."

"Aye, Allan, I expected it to be so." Lucien de Griswold's heart sank as he turned in the saddle and looked back over the straggling line of weary men and horses. De Brus, who had gone with them on pilgrimage to Jerusalem only to please his lady-wife, had taken a deep sword thrust to his thigh. The attacking tribesmen, in search of plunder, did not respect the uneasy truce between west and east, no more than did many Crusaders.

The dry wind kicked up a spiral of dust and heat shimmered over the sand and rocks. This desert, this place…the Holy Land…was not a land of milk and honey, but of blood and pain and thirst. Only the Saracens, with great determination, faith and skill, were at home here.

Allan had dismounted and helped the ailing De Brus to

the shade of an overhang. Lucien left his horse in the care of a servant and knelt beside De Brus. The knight's wound was poisoning his blood. His red, sweaty skin, his leg so swollen that his foot was mottled, testified to that fact.

"He needs more medicine than the camp leech can provide, even could we get him there before he dies," Allan whispered.

De Brus opened his eyes. "Don't bother trying to spare my feelings now, Allan. I know full well I am a waste of further food and water. Just leave me here in the shade."

"Be quiet, Brus," Lucien said. He drew Allan aside. "There was a *caravanserai* going east. They may know of a physician in a town nearby. It is worth a try."

"A Saracen physician?" Allan's brows knit.

"Aye. They have the skill Brus's leg requires. I have seen what they can do. I fear otherwise he will indeed die while our leech deliberates and Brus argues with him. He won't be able to argue with a Turk."

"Very well. But be swift, for we dare not tarry here overlong. If you must go, at least take someone with you. Do not go alone."

Lucien shook his head. "To the Arabs we Franj are dangerous wild animals. A pack of us will only make them defensive. One of us may get a better result than many. And if I should fail, there will be fewer of our party at risk. No one in Acre even knows we are here, so we have no hope of them setting out to look for us."

"But Kalle FitzMalheury is due to return this way. No doubt he would come to our aid."

A surge of distaste filled Lucien at the mention of the knight whose reputation for brutality overshadowed his brilliance as a commander. "I hope we are gone long before then, for I have no wish to encounter Kalle Fitz-Malheury—especially if I need him."

"Aye." Allan rubbed his dagger hilt. "I know what you mean. He is a restless lion amongst men."

"All the more reason for me to make haste." After downing a mouthful of warm water, Lucien set out in pursuit of the *caravanserai* whose dust was still visible in the distance. It was a small procession, no more than a dozen heavily laden camels, but well supplied with guards, a mixture of Turks and mercenary Franks.

With a final burst of effort from his horse, Lucien caught up with the vanguard. He brought his mount around, just close enough for them to hear his shout. Some of the guards had already turned, arrows nocked and ready to fly.

"May peace be upon you, all honor to the Prophet!" Lucien began in Arabic.

But the guards' bows stayed taut, the arrows level; the red tassels on their horses' bridles fluttered in the wind.

Lucien took a deep breath. "I seek a *ṭābib*. Know you where I might find a man skilled in medicine?"

"Why should we help a murdering Franj?"

To Lucien's surprise, one among them replied, "Because it is the Law of God, both Christian and Muslim, to show mercy to those who ask it of us, if that is within our power to bestow."

The man rode toward Lucien, his white robes pristine despite the dust and heat. "I am Palban, known in these parts as al-Balub, a physician come from Cordoba. What is the problem?"

As he drew near, Lucien saw that whether a Saracen or

no, this Spaniard was fair of complexion and not one of the Turks by birth. He quickly explained Brus's predicament and added, "I swear to protect you and see you safely back to your escort. I can but offer you a promise of compensation, as at the moment I have nothing of value beyond my honor and gratitude."

Palban smiled. "I see you have manners befitting a prince, if not the wealth of one. And I consider the former of more worth than the latter. It would be a refreshing change to minister to a wounded knight be he French or English or German, instead of an overfed emir. Let me collect my things." He galloped back to the caravan and returned with a bundle strapped to his saddle. "They will await me here, for a few hours only, while they rest the horses."

Lucien's heart leaped with hope and he led the *ṭābib* toward De Brus. As they rode he plied the physician with questions, of medicine, of philosophy and of alchemy, an area in which he had a deep interest. Compared to this country, where such exalted knowledge was openly sought and arcane pursuits were more valued than feared, England was an abyss of ignorance.

"I seek a teacher in these arts," he confessed to Palban at last. It was a vast understatement. He longed for knowledge of beauty unseen, of words unspoken, of music unstruck. Beyond that, he owed his lady-mother a heavy debt of the heart, and realizing the fruits of alchemy had become his last hope of easing her pain…and his own nagging guilt. But as this campaign in the Holy Land had unfolded in a sea of blood and anguish, he had begun to despair of ever realizing such a nebulous dream.

"Ah." Palban smiled again. "There is an old saying, 'When

the student is ready, the master appears.' Have no worry, Sir Lucien, you will find a teacher when the time is ripe."

Lucien smiled grimly to himself. He had been ready for a long time, with no such manifestation.

As if Palban had read his mind, he said, "But in Acre, you should visit a man named Deogal. I have not seen him in years, but I think he may be of value to you."

"My thanks, *effendi,* learned one. I hope one day I will be allowed the honor of repaying this boon of your service."

"You can repay me by being of noble service to others, my young friend, that is how I was taught."

Lucien marveled that in this desert he had been guided to such a jewel among men. Then, as they drew near Brus, he swallowed against the lump that formed in his dry throat. He could not bear another pointless death and prayed that he had not brought Palban too late. "He is just over there. The sun has moved, but I think there is still enough shade."

Lucien waited while Palban remained at Brus's side until the sun neared the horizon, a crimson blaze deepening into the dusky blue of evening. At last he rose and came to Lucien, his white robes no longer pristine. "I think he can be moved to Acre now. And once there, if his wound is tended properly, he will live. But there is no time to waste. I have spoken to your comrade, Allan. He knows what measures to take in the meantime. Now I must return to my own journey."

Lucien looked to De Brus, who dozed peacefully, his lines of pain gone. "Many thanks, *effendi.* You have eased more hearts this day than you can know. I'll summon a proper escort and see you back to your party."

After a quick meal that put the final seal upon their

friendship, they set out with a half dozen men. As they left their resting place behind, a rumble of hooves met Lucien's senses. It was part hearing, part feeling and part knowing—danger approached, and would be upon them in but a few moments.

Allan looked to Lucien. "What shall we do? There is no cover."

Lucien shook his head. "We cannot outrun them, our horses are too weary. We must simply keep moving as we are and meet them when they find us. Keep Palban in our midst."

The sound of pounding hooves grew louder and the last few rays of the sun caught the helms and lance heads of a group of warriors as they neared.

"They are ours!" Allan stood in his stirrups and waved, his relief apparent. "It is FitzMalheury!"

"Then do not invite him to join us!" urged Lucien. But it was too late. Kalle FitzMalheury, who had been expelled even from the ranks of the Templars because of his extremism, came upon them in a whirl of dust and clanging metal.

He brought his horse up short and it reared. "What are you doing, Lucien de Griswold, wandering in the desert? Should you not be in the safe company of your men?"

Lucien resented having to explain himself to anyone, but decided not to argue. "De Brus needed help. I found someone to provide it and now am returning his savior to his own people."

Kalle glared at Palban. "Savior? Whom do you serve? The lords of Constantinople, or of Cairo, or of Jerusalem?"

The physician sat his horse stiffly. "I am of Cordoba, my lord. I am here on an errand, upon the request of al-'Ādil the Just, may he live forever. But I serve no one but God."

"Which God?" Kalle pressed, his pale eyes gleaming. His gauntleted fingers twitched upon his sword hilt.

Palban raised his chin. "There is but a single God. It is you Christians who are the polytheists, worshiping a trinity."

"A cursed tongue have you, dog of an infidel." Kalle swung his head to face Lucien. "You have done Brus no favor, Lucien de Griswold, by turning his leg into a pagan offering!"

"FitzMalheury, have a care as to your words," Lucien said softly, and began to ease his horse between Kalle's and Palban's.

"FitzMalheury?" Palban's face paled as if he had heard of Kalle's reputation.

Kalle sneered. "And you, Lucien, watch your empty head, lest I send it rolling along the ground as a lesson to all friends of Salah al-Din's brother."

"Allan," Lucien, his heart pounding, kept his gaze upon Kalle. "Take Palban on to his destination. I would stay here with Kalle and have it out with him to my satisfaction."

"Had you the least respect for your betters, you'd not even think of raising your hand against me. But be advised—I've seen to it that nothing remains of the *caravanserai*. And I will send this Saracen to join his friends, to be purged by the hellfire that surely awaits him."

Kalle spurred his horse forward, his sword unleashed.

"Nay!" Lucien sought to block his advance, but the heavy destrier's shoulder knocked his own tired mount off balance. Palban tried to rein his horse around to flee, but Kalle was almost upon him. In desperation, Lucien kicked his stirrups free and leaped from his saddle to land behind Kalle, on the destrier's rump. Anything to slow him down.

But Kalle's speed was beyond stopping. Palban screamed as the knight's blade flashed. A burst of red showered through the air. Then, with a snarl, FitzMalheury rammed the pommel of his sword backward and hit Lucien between the eyes.

And Lucien thought, as the blackness swooped in, *Kalle has robbed Palban of his life—and me of my honor....*

Chapter One

Acre
Capital of the Kingdom of Jerusalem
Early summer, 1197

The crunch of booted feet on packed earth and the rattle of swords echoed in the narrow, steep-walled lane. Shifting her precious bundle of glassware, Isidora hurried through the arched stone gateway into the courtyard of her father's house.

She pushed aside her linen veil and looked back. Drying fabrics streamed and billowed like pennants from windows high above, creating a serpentine play of light and shadow on the street. Below, bareheaded in the sun, as if it were not the middle of the afternoon when sensible folk came in out of the heat and dust, a group of brawny young men strode nearer.

Tall, broad-chested warriors. Franks? English? She was not certain. But they moved with bold assurance, taking up more space with their extravagant movements and loud voices than was either seemly or wise in this city of many cultures.

When the great Salah al-Din had ruled, isolated westerners like she and her father had usually been left in peace. Then the city had been retaken by Richard Coeur de Leon and King Philippe.

Little enough blood had been shed when Acre shifted hands that time, but many a Crusader did not bother to determine who was Christian and who was Muslim before striking out.

Isidora's stomach fluttered at the sight of the men with their fair heads and long swords. She swallowed her rising fear and took another peek. She had to admit they were glorious—like young, unruly chargers.

But joking amongst themselves and occupying half the lane, they acted as though they personally ruled the place.

Whatever their purpose, she should bar the gate before they drew any closer.

"Marylas, quick, help me." Isidora put the glassware down.

The serving girl was a Circassian, her face and arms heavily veiled because her flawless white skin could not tolerate the desert sun. But she was strong and willing, and helped Isidora push the heavy wooden gate. It swung a short way, met a stubborn resistance and stopped short.

Isidora's body stilled at a creak of leather and the faintest whiff of sandalwood. She looked around the edge of the thick planking. Her gaze moved from a gauntleted hand, up a muscular, linen-clad arm, and to the vivid blue eyes of the man who remained firmly in the way.

"Oh," she breathed. If the lovely Marylas resembled a

woman made of silver, this was as comely a man as could be imagined, made of red-gold. A straight nose, set in a lean, sculpted, sun-burned face, with high cheekbones and a wide jaw. Hair that flowed past his shoulders like liquid copper.

His eyebrow quirked. A charming, perfect eyebrow.

"Ma demoiselle?"

And a voice to match the rest. Resonant yet soft. Rich with nuance.

She blinked and was ready to kick herself. *What am I thinking? One bewitching stranger cannot sway me from what I know to be the truth. Fair men are perfectly capable of destroying one's life and happiness, just as are ugly ones.*

"Pardon me, do you speak French or English?" he asked, still not releasing the gate.

"Or Latin? Or Greek? Lucien knows them all," came another voice from beyond him, accompanied by male laughter.

"You are Franj?" Isidora ventured in French. His eyes were as blue as the sea beyond the walls of the city. *Beteuse! What does it matter who he is or how handsome? Tell him to go away!*

"Nay. But we need—guiding—to the, em, bathhouse. Can you help?"

His companions groaned. "Lucien—you and your hot water obsession! Why not ask where the nearest ale house is?"

Her father's voice rang out into the courtyard. "Isidora! What's keeping you?"

She glanced over her shoulder. "Nothing, my lord! Just some travelers looking for the *hammam*. It is up that way," she added, and pointed in the direction they should go.

"God speed you!" she urged the young men, but they did not depart.

Then her father, Sir Deogal, emerged, tall and spare and out of sorts. His eyes glinted dangerously from beneath his heavy gray brows. He moved in the stiff but determined way of old warriors, his faded blue robe dragging along the stones of the courtyard.

Isidora threw him a concerned look. He would still pick a fight, even though outnumbered and unarmed. Strong he might be, but men like these could cut him to pieces if they chose.

"Father, please do not trouble yourself. They are just leaving." She turned and met the handsome intruder's gaze squarely. "Are you not?"

Clutching the slender neck of a glass alembic in one hand, Deogal threw the gate wide with the other to reveal the group of four young men.

"Take yourselves off from here. Go find someone who has time to squander dealing with the worthless likes of you!"

Just this once, curb your temper, Father! Isidora's heart pounded and she balled her hands into fists as the knights exchanged dark looks and fingered their swords. All but the one at the gate, whose eyes smiled even when his mouth did not.

The stranger gave a dismissive wave. "My friends, waste not your strength upon a demented old man. Go on, I will catch up with you later." When they hesitated, he fixed them with his gaze and said but one word. "Go."

"Don't get *too* clean, Lucien, or we won't take you back." They resumed their joking and moved down the lane, away from the *hammam* and toward the closest wine merchant.

Deogal shook his flask at Lucien and its contents danced in silver waves. "How dare you speak of me thus, you sorry whelp of a—"

The young knight raised his gauntleted hand. "Sir, I could not but help notice that is quicksilver in the vessel you hold there. I have an appreciation for such things, but my friends do not, so forgive me for having discouraged them in the way that I deemed best for the situation…may I speak with you?"

"You may not. I have work to do and no time for curiosity seekers. Isidora, get inside."

As Deogal retreated, slamming the workshop door behind him, Isidora was struck by the disappointment reflected on—what had they called him?—Lucien's face.

It was similar to her own, what she felt every time her father barred her from entering his *sanctum sanctorum*. From the part of his life that mattered most to him.

This fellow did not belong here. Her father needed help, aye, but she would provide it, not some stranger off the street. As much as she resented the Work, it was indeed important, and given time, Deogal would surely let her in. She was of his flesh, his only child. Sooner or later he *had* to….

But for now, the least she could do was show the knight that manners did exist in this household. And that she was not afraid of him.

"Lord, would you like some wine?"

The knight, who she assumed belonged to Henry of Champagne, the King of Jerusalem—known to the native residents of Acre, his capital, as *al-Kond Herri*—took a long breath. He crossed his arms and seemed to consider her proposal, looking at her carefully all the while. Then he nodded, once.

She had half expected him to stalk away. Half hoped that he would. But here he remained, so Isidora ushered him into the small garden where her father received his rare but usually important visitors.

All was in order. A small fountain burbled, red-flowering vines wound around the carved sandstone columns and birds chirped, flitting in and out of the shadows.

"Please sit, sir." Isidora indicated a polished marble bench. Off to one side, Marylas stood staring, her hand clamped over her mouth. Isidora gave the girl a reassuring look and she hurried toward the kitchen.

Marylas was easily frightened by the presence of armed men. Before coming to this household, she had suffered in-dignities that Isidora did not want her to be reminded of by anyone. Even this Lucien.

He settled his elegant limbs, removed his gloves and dabbled long, strong fingers in the fountain's pool as he looked about. When Marylas returned with the refresh-ments, and hesitated before him, Isidora saw that Lucien recognized the maid with courtesy instead of treating her as an object of contempt.

He inclined his head to her and murmured something that actually made her eyes smile. No doubt he was hop-ing to lay the foundation for a future assault. He would meet with a sharp, unpleasant surprise, should he try. Marylas never went without her dagger.

Isidora poured a measure of water into a mazer, then topped it with the wine and handed it to him.

"My thanks." Lucien raised the bowl but did not drink. "Will you not join me?"

"Nay. Forgive my rudeness, I have but little time to spare."

In truth, every moment she was with him unnerved her more. She found herself staring like a foolish girl might. He was so foreign. Gleaming. Beautiful. He glowed, like a painting of a heavenly herald.

Her mind wandered, as if along the golden curves of the lettered illuminations she labored over each day. For one ridiculous, embarrassing moment she imagined him to be sent by God, to distract her from the frustration of working for her father. Working for him, but kept apart from his work. *The Work.* It was all that mattered to him.

A familiar constriction squeezed her heart at the thought. She adored her father, but the Work had become her enemy, for it always stood between them. At times she hated it, as much as one could hate anything so ethereal and elusive.

Isidora looked away, for fear the young man would see her loneliness and pity her for it.

But he did not seem to notice anything amiss at all. He took a swallow of the wine and wiped his mouth with the back of his hand. "I am Lucien de Griswold. What is your name?"

"Isidora," she managed.

"Ah. *Gift of Isis.* A fitting name…for an alchemist's daughter."

She made a small sound. At his knowledge she was truly surprised and not a little alarmed. "You know of the Work my father does?"

"Of course. It is why I am here."

Oh, dear. Isidora decided to have a drink of wine after all. She had to get rid of him. For his own sake, as well as that of her father. Deogal wanted no more outsiders, and few were likely to tolerate his deteriorating, increasingly erratic temper.

But "Gift of Isis"? Curse of Isis was more like it. Even her name was not meant for her, but only as a reflection of her father's complete preoccupation with alchemy. And now here before her was a stranger, come out of nowhere. One who, it seemed, was only interested in the Work. Just like her father.

She filled a mazer without first adding water and, sitting upon the bench opposite Lucien, gulped the wine down.

To her chagrin, Lucien's mouth curved into a wry smile. "You do not approve of me?"

Already the wine had a certain fortifying effect on Isidora. "It is not my place to approve or disapprove. I assist my father and do his bidding. Beyond that and my attempts to protect him from ill-informed churchmen or greedy fortune seekers, I have no part in it."

Lucien leaned forward and rolled the wooden bowl between his palms. He met her gaze. "I am neither a cleric nor do I seek my fortune. I would be his student, his apprentice, if he would allow it."

Nay, not another one! Kalle FitzMalheury had been fair of face and words, but he had hurt her father—and been the downfall of her mother…. Isidora would not let anyone hurt Deogal again. "What *do* you want, then, my lord Lucien?"

He looked away and the wine in his bowl shuddered. With his eyes still averted, at last he spoke. "I want the truth. I need to find the Elixir."

"I see. Then all you wish is to attain perfect enlightenment and to live forever. Nay, I would not call that seeking your fortune." Isidora had not intended for her words to sound cutting, but from the way Lucien's brows drew together, it seemed he had taken them just that way.

"I need it for someone. Before it is too late."

The sincerity and quiet regret in his voice touched Isidora despite her mistrust. Perhaps there was more to him than good looks and assorted weapons. But it was not likely to be much.

She could not help him. He was from another world and did not belong here. "There is nothing I might say to my father to make him change his mind." Not that she wished to try, in any event.

Lucien's resultant sad smile made her bite her lip. How did people as tempting as him come into being, after all?

"Nay, *Demoiselle* Isidora. If I cannot convince him of my merit, then it is not meant to be."

There came a shuffle of leather-soled slippers. "What's this—you are still here, boy?" Sir Deogal loomed at the edge of the courtyard. "Why?"

Lucien immediately rose to his feet, as did Isidora. Lucien was much taller than she. Broad-shouldered and well-made, he stood mere inches away. He smelled of smoke, horses and that elusive air of sandalwood.

In all her life she had never been this close to a man not related to her. And this man, she knew, from some secret place within her, was potent. Like mead or the red inks she used—a little would go a long, long way….

"I invited him in, Father. It is hot outside. It was a matter of simple courtesy."

Lucien bowed. "I would have returned, in any case, and waited until you gave me audience, sir."

Deogal raised his chin. "What do you want from me, then?"

"The chance to learn from a master alchemist, my lord."

"Do you, now?" Deogal came closer and waved a hand at Isidora. Her nerves on edge, she tried not to spill as she poured him some wine, after a liberal dose of water in the bowl.

He sat beside her on the bench as if she needed protection, and looked Lucien up and down. "I have had students before. They invariably proved themselves either fools or corrupt, and had to be thrown out on their heads."

Isidora closed her eyes against the flood of painful memories those words evoked. Not so many years past, Kalle, her father's last partner in the Work, had brought Deogal's wrath crashing down upon himself by his betrayal. Her father had beaten Kalle nearly to death. Then he had shoved her mother out onto the street…and lived to regret it the rest of his days. Isidora bit her lip.

She well remembered the look of rage, aye, and loss on Kalle's bloodied face. She shivered despite the warm day. He was an enemy worthy of the fear he inspired. And her father, strong as he once had been, was no match for the cunning and evil Kalle was now rumored to be capable of.

Isidora eyed Lucien appraisingly. She had to consider that he might make himself useful as a champion to Deogal, and protect him from harm in ways Isidora could not. He seemed honest…but Kalle also had sounded sincere at first.

Lucien had remained standing. "I do not believe I am particularly corrupt or all that foolish. But I cannot promise that one day you would not be tempted to throw me out, on my head or otherwise."

Deogal grunted a laugh. "We shall see, then, just how

badly you want to be my student. But do not bother Isidora, do you understand? She is too trusting by far, to have spoken to you and allowed you entrance. Sometimes I regret raising her as the Franj do and giving her such freedom, instead of keeping her hidden away."

Isidora refrained from groaning out loud. What freedom? The freedom to go to the marketplace and purchase supplies for his Work? And why must Father delude himself into supposing that a wealthy stranger might take interest in her?

After all, she was dark, and too outspoken. Often as not, folk mistook her for one of the servants. However, she knew who she was—the proud daughter of a noble house, and it mattered not what anyone else thought.

Lucien crossed his arms, as if closing a door around himself. A bastion not easily swayed. "I have no intention of bothering your daughter, sir."

Then, the rogue disproved his words with but one look. His lips parted slightly and his eyes glittered with the light reflected from the fountain's waters. His gaze swept Isidora's skin in a hot wave and made her cheeks catch fire, as if she stood naked in the public square. How dare he show such insolence!

Isidora had to force herself not to jump up and run off to hide in the house—just to avoid losing control and slapping him. But she would not give Lucien the power to affect her so, or give her father cause to either worry or question her actions.

Chapter Two

Lucien came every day after that. He spoke but little as he sat and waited for her father to emerge and accept him as a student of the Work. At first his friends accompanied him to the gate. But as time passed and he still made no progress, one by one they fell away, until he remained alone.

Leaving his sword in Marylas's charge, he would bow to Deogal but say nothing. His request did not need to be made out loud, for it seemed he was asking with his whole being.

Day by day his face lost some of its air of ruddy confidence. But he had a presence that seemed to take up more space than he did physically. He wore sumptuous clothes and his surcoat of raw, red silk and fine leather boots added to his princely air.

Despite Lucien's silence, or perhaps because of it, Isidora wanted to know everything about him. Where his home was and what kind of life he led there. But she could not bring herself to ask him directly.

He was quiet, but seemed bigger than life—as though his skin couldn't quite contain him. He made her nervous, and he might mistake her inquisitiveness about the rest of the world for a personal interest in him.

Each day she offered him unleavened bread, dates and butter, figs and honey and wine, which he occasionally accepted. But of course that was only a matter of courtesy on her part, not concern.

Lucien was polite, without ever paying her enough attention that she might engage him in true conversation. His mind was always upon his goal. He would not endanger it by "bothering" her, she was certain. But she was also just as certain that eventually he would tire of waiting and leave them in peace.

But one day Deogal emerged from the workshop, his blue robe sooty and smelling of sulphur. "Tell me again why you want to partake of this Work, boy."

Lucien jumped to his feet. "Because I must, sir. It holds the greatest fascination for me. I sense…I know—that there are worlds of knowledge waiting to be discovered through the arts of alchemy, through the patience and persistence of those who dare venture past the mundane and into the arcane. I cannot believe that my life's achievements are only meant to be what my father envisioned— nothing but breeding and a series of acquisitions by force of arms."

Deogal looked down his aristocratic nose at Lucien. "You are dissatisfied with your lot? With your enviable position of privilege, rank, honor and wealth?"

Lucien gazed at Deogal and spread his strong, lean hands. "I am not ungrateful, Master Deogal. I simply cannot bear to accept that I might miss something else, something so huge and divine and all-enveloping that I cannot see it without the guidance of a man like you. Beyond that, I cannot put it into words."

Deogal raised one shaggy gray brow. "And what makes you think I have the means to guide you? Why should I be anything other than a bad-tempered old fool puttering with substances better left alone?"

"I have heard talk…but beyond that, I felt it, from the moment I stepped over your threshold. This is the place I belong. And you are the one to teach me."

Isidora had to hide her amazement. This cool, aloof young man had such eloquence, such passion? Only for the Work, she reminded herself.

Deogal let a smile spread across his face like the slow rising of the sun. "Then so be it, Lucien de Griswold. You will take the oath revealed to Isis and swear by Tartarus and Anubis and Cerebus and Charon and the Fates and Furies. You will do as I instruct you, and you will go to your grave with the secrets I reveal—"

A numbing cold spread through Isidora, freezing her lungs, her heart… To see her father smile like that—to hear him offer his trust, his sacred knowledge, to this stranger who had only waited a fortnight for what she had waited her whole life—it was beyond bearing.

After all that had happened, how could he trust someone who might turn out to be another Kalle—perhaps even worse than Kalle? Then the numbness gave way to a fury she did not know she possessed. To a shameful jealousy, unworthy of her.

It took her off guard, like a blow from behind. Kalle's apprenticeship had never produced such a reaction. He had never won her father's love.

Isidora's body shook, she could barely breathe, and she was possessed by a sudden, dreadful hope that Lucien would collapse in fits from the glare she bestowed upon him, before leaving this house for good.

Did he not deserve it, for reducing her to such a wretched, despicable state? But he never saw her daggered look. His eyes were shining with joy and his full attention remained on her father, waiting for him to finish.

Deogal frowned at Isidora. "You, child, should not be here listening! Go to the scriptorium and find something to copy!"

"Father…" she whispered before her throat tightened beyond words. She refused to look any longer at Lucien. The hateful usurper! Her face burned as if she had scrubbed it with nettles. Yet again she was banished from all that was important to her.

But she loved her father, no matter what, and would serve and protect him as long as he needed her. Whether he wanted her to or not.

"Excuse me." She stood and forced herself to walk slowly, with decorum. But once out of sight, she grabbed her skirts and ran through the house, up the stone stairs and into her haven. In the tiny scriptorium, a sense of calm gradually enveloped her. Here was *her* Work.

Isidora blinked, sniffed, swallowed, and as her heart slowed its wild beating, she regained the control that had long stood her so well. She looked at the scrolls and piles of parchment on the shelves, the bowls and bottles of colored inks that she mixed herself, from oxgall and ground lapis and all sorts of ingredients, both rare and common.

She had produced ornate manuscripts and painted portraits that had been purchased by princes and bishops and satraps. She wrote letters for those who could not do so themselves. It was how she best helped her father, for ingots of silver and vials of mercury did not come cheaply. Nor did the gold leaf or vellum she used in her finest scribing.

Isidora slipped onto the wooden seat behind the slanted table and reached down to open the small cupboard behind it. She felt for the folio inside and brought it out into the light of day. Carefully she opened the heavy leaves.

A painting of an exquisite face smiled at her from the calfskin surface. Luminous brown eyes, skin like the petals of a dusky rose, jet hair peeking from beneath a silken veil.

Here was her treasure…an image she had created, of Ayshka Binte Amir. Of her mother, as she had once looked. Before Kalle FitzMalheury had begun her death… Before her father had completed it…. Isidora swallowed the tears that threatened.

Unlike the fabled Elixir, her art was real. People could see it and feel it. It had meaning and value. Creating it was a solitary occupation, by its very nature, but such was her lot in life. Like Marylas, who had lost everything, to hope for more, for a loving father, much less for a loving husband, or children, was to ask too much.

She had seen the suffering of the truly unfortunate. What she had should be enough. Aye, she should be grateful for the bounty she possessed. Her sight, her limbs, her very life. Enough to eat and a place to sleep…even alone. It was best that way.

Why think twice about a man like Lucien? So what if Deogal wanted him to stay? So what if he brought Deogal some companionship in his labors—was that not a good thing?

Nay, not if it is at my expense!

But it was wrong to think thus.

She had her path and Lucien had his. They would be parallel for but a short time. The inevitable divergence would come, no doubt when *al-Kond Herri* called the knight back into service, and she would be rid of his enviable presence.

Isidora rested her cheek on the cool surface of the table and gazed out the window. Just beyond the walls of the city, the sea glistened as the afternoon waned. The sail of a returning fishing boat slid by, gilded and backlit by the sun.

Isidora gave thanks for the beautiful sight and made up her mind to banish all selfish thoughts. Her father was getting old; he needed help with the Work. God had sent him Lucien, and whether she liked it or not, she had to accept it. Just as most women had to accept so many things.

She thought of her once-beautiful mother, Ayshka, ravaged by disease and now dead. The unwelcome tears stung her eyes at last. She knew passion was possible, that true love existed. Even after banishing Ayshka, Deogal had loved her with an unseemly desperation, and that was what had fueled his love of the Work. That was what still fueled his guilt.

The Work had been his lady-wife's last hope for a cure, short of a miracle or the touch of a saintly king…. The Work could provide the Elixir, and the Elixir could cure all ills. Even the worst—that which had afflicted her mother.

A dread disease that carried with it a terrible stigma of implied dishonor, which tainted the whole family. Indeed, it might be the real reason no man had ever asked for Isidora's hand.

For her mother, shamed by one man and turned out of her home by another, had been visited by God's cruelest wrath of all...leprosy.

Chapter Three

Acre
The palace of Henry, al-Kond Herri, King of Jerusalem
High summer, 1197

"My lord Henry…can you be serious? To ally yourself—a bastion of Christianity—with Sinān, the heathen Grand Master of the Assassins? It is unthinkable!" Kalle's fist thumped the table.

The company of Henry's knights and noble advisors stirred, murmuring their disapproval of this outburst. Lucien remained silent, as he had throughout the meeting, but narrowed his eyes as FitzMalheury took a visible grip on his temper. "Surely it is not necessary for you, appointed as regent here by Richard himself, to make a pact with such a one?" Kalle asked.

Henry leaned back in his great chair and stared at Kalle. "You of all men should know the value of an alliance with them. They are deadly, but capable of reason, for they pay the Templars to leave them alone—and you should have seen what took place during our conversation at *al-Kahf*. Sinān demonstrated his power—he ordered two of his men to leap from atop the fortress. They did so without an instant's hesitation and fell to their deaths upon the rocks below. I had to beg him not to repeat the spectacle…but I will ask you, Kalle—would you have shown *me* such unswerving loyalty?"

Henry tilted his head and did not wait for a reply. "Sinān offered me another sample of his skills…he thought surely there must be someone I would like them to murder." Henry leaned toward FitzMalheury and smiled good-naturedly. "I declined, but of course, dear Kalle, you came to mind as a first candidate, being commander of the garrison as well as my closest rival."

At this the company roared with laughter, but Lucien saw that Kalle's mirth did not reach his eyes. The knight cleared his throat. "You flatter me with such a designation, my lord. But how you came by this opinion is quite beyond my understanding."

He then gave Lucien a direct look. One that pierced him with its enmity and stirred his own desire for revenge. "There are other candidates for elimination. Indeed, there is a man present who spends so little time amongst his own kind, one wonders whose side he is on," Kalle said softly, still looking at Lucien.

Lucien replied, his voice as velvet as Kalle's, "And there is another present who gives his personal ambitions priority over the interests of his lord."

"Enough," Henry said firmly. "Sinān is someone I want to be close enough to that I may keep an eye on him. I need not adopt the ways of the Assassins, only learn what I may about them, to ensure the safety of others."

Kalle stood and bowed. "As you will, my lord. I am yours to command, as ever."

At Henry's nod of dismissal, the group began to break up. Lucien was halfway to the door when Kalle stopped him.

"Never challenge my honor like that again, Lucien, or I will make you sorry you were ever born."

Lucien squared his shoulders and looked down at Kalle. "Just be advised, my lord, I am loyal to Henry, and he knows it. And just because you have made an enemy of Deogal does not mean he is anyone else's enemy."

Kalle's smile struck a perilous chord in Lucien. The man was like a rabid dog. And should be dealt with as such.

Kalle continued, "I shall have to pay the old man and his daughter a visit one of these days, hmm? See what progress he has made with the Work? Or perhaps you'd like to tell me yourself and spare him the pain?"

Lucien bristled. "Stay away from them. I will cut you to pieces if I catch you."

Kalle laughed. "Of course. If you catch me. A very small likelihood. But nay…the thought of playing inquisitor with you appeals to me much more. After all, Deogal would not last more than a day or two as my…guest. And what Isidora is likely to know is hardly worth the sweat of finding it out…whereas you, Lucien, could prove entertaining, indeed. So have a care, the next shadow you see might not be your own, eh?"

Isidora wondered at the change in Lucien when he returned from the court of *al-Kond Herri*…his somber moods, his rude questioning of her servants about who they saw and to whom they spoke from outside, his pacing and restless nights....

His evident distraction even caught her father's notice. "What is wrong with him?" Deogal frowned as he dipped a piece of bread into his bowl of sauce.

Isidora shrugged. "Perhaps he is ready to move on, at last. Perhaps he longs for home."

"He cannot! Not at this stage of the Work. We are just purifying the red essence of— Never mind. Just tell him I want to see him after vespers." Deogal pushed his half-eaten food aside and stalked back to his quarters.

Isidora stared at the carved marble bowl her father had abandoned and worry yet again twisted within her. He ate less and less, looked more and more haggard. She felt so helpless. How could she stop his decline? He paid her no attention, found her concern an annoyance.

"Isidora?"

That smooth voice, from behind. Lucien. She closed her eyes and did not move. She could not quite face him with her fears still so evident. "Aye? There is food left, should you want it."

"Has all been quiet? Nothing amiss?"

"Nothing."

"Why do you keep your back to me? What is wrong?"

At last she turned around. His beautiful face was limned by the golden glow of the oil lamps, accentuating the hollows of his cheeks. He, too, was in a decline. "Why don't you tell me? You are the one who knows what is going on, Lucien. You have known for months and are making all of us miserable as a result."

Lucien put his hand to his brow and pinched the bridge of his nose. His fingers quivered, and her alarm grew. "What is it? What has happened?"

He met her gaze. "Tonight you will hear a clamor, for the city will be in mourning, as soon as word spreads. Henry is dead."

A sense of cold struck her, as if she had jumped into the winter sea. "What? How can this be?"

"He fell to his death…from a window in his palace. Kalle FitzMalheury has taken charge, only until a succession is sorted out, or so he says. I have little hope that this was an accident, Isidora. You and your father are in danger with Kalle now free to run wild."

"He is no threat to us. We have friends more powerful than he, and well does he know it."

"You do not know what he has become, Isidora. He is growing inside of himself, like an abscess of pride and corrupt power."

"Then lance him," she replied, shocked at her own bluntness.

Then Lucien shocked her even more when he caught her shoulders in a firm, warm grip. Her surprise kept her in place, as well as the dizzying effect of his nearness.

"Do not speak so," he said. "I expect better of you. I would like…" His voice trailed away and the muscles in his jaw clenched as he searched her eyes.

Her belly tightened in an unfamiliar way. She felt an invisible pull, as if from his body to hers, and the tension grew until it was all she could do not to either break from his grasp and run or throw herself into his arms. "What would you like?" Isidora prompted, and yet held herself still and stiff, and closed her eyes against his gaze.

His voice emerged in a low growl. "I'd like to be finished here. Done with this place. I need to go home."

Isidora's cheeks burned as though he had slapped her. Why did she take his remarks personally? She did not care. Indeed had she not been looking forward to the day this troublesome knight left at last? But she had more than herself to consider. "You cannot go. M-my father needs you still."

"Look at me, Isidora." When she was focused on his flame-lit, blue eyes, he continued. "We are close to the Elixir. Very close. But the slightest mishap could make us have to start all over again. I am but trying to protect him, and the Work…and you. Should anything befall him, or me, all will be lost. Indeed, I cannot think why he has not included you, to ensure preservation of our progress, but I am sworn to secrecy and must respect his wishes."

As she allowed the truth to rise within her, Isidora began to tremble. "You know, Lucien, he chooses to believe my mother yet lives…that he can still restore her to health with the Elixir. That desire is all that keeps him going. If one day he wakes up and remembers that she is dead, he, too, will die."

Then the unthinkable happened. Lucien drew her close, wrapped his arms about her and held her to his chest, as if she were precious to him. "I won't leave, unless you command me to go."

Here was the moment of his obedience…she could tell him, right now, to be gone from her home, her life, her heart. But instead she replied, "You have our thanks, sir.

My father is too proud to say it, but I say it on his behalf."
That was all there was to it. All there would ever be. Her
father and his needs.

Lucien eased away from her and bowed, his bright hair
gleaming. "I will go once more and find out the state of
things in the city." Shouldering his sword, he disappeared
out the door into the darkness. He did not return that night
or the next.

Weeks passed, then months…her inquiries met with no
results. It was as though he had been swallowed up in the
ensuing maelstrom of grief and confusion that whirled
through the streets after Henry's death became known.
Perhaps Lucien had decided to go home, after all.

But Isidora knew that was not the case. And she had a
good idea of where to go to next for answers.

Chapter Four

Lucien de Griswold, knight of the realm—sovereign lord of the village of East Ainsley, he reminded himself—and now prisoner of Kalle FitzMalheury, lay on his back in a dungeon of Acre. A Christian knight, in a Christian dungeon, in a city that lay months from home.

He squinted as a shaft of light penetrated through the wind hole, far above. Its feeble rays made his eyes ache. He had been here for what felt like forever, and time had lost all meaning. His capture had been the result of a fleeting slip of his attention...and a solid blow to his head.

What mattered now was the constant gnawing of his stomach, the thirst that made swallowing difficult, and the deep ache of his battered body.

It had been days since anyone had thrown him anything. Indeed, it had been days since he had seen or heard another human being. He wondered if Kalle had forgotten him.

Or perhaps some wild shift of fortune had caused the city to return to Muslim hands and the Saracens did not know of this small, isolated hole in the bowels of the keep?

The place was like a rabbit warren of ancient tunnels and chambers, and he doubted if any one man had ever explored all its secrets.

But he would rather suffer repeat questioning than be abandoned. FitzMalheury had not been able to beat any information out of him. He was but a student of the Work, not an adept. He was not privy to magic keys or unfailing methods of turning lead into gold. Now, silver into gold was another matter, but unlike Kalle, Lucien believed all that to be secondary to the true Work, not its goal.

Lucien forced himself to move, to raise his throbbing head and sit up. But the resultant swaying of the world forced him to seek the wall for support. And, in addition to his hunger and weakness and pain, he was so filthy he could barely stand himself.

They had doused him with latrine water to wake him up when he passed out. Apart from the murder of Palban, that indignity alone made him hate Kalle enough to kill him.

But he had to smile. Aye, even now, had he a bowl of water, he would save a bit of it to wash with. So he could not be all that close to death. When he cared no longer, then he would worry.

"Lucien?"

Footsteps on the stone floor. A feminine voice. A familiar accent, part French and part Arabic.

"Isidora?" He strained to see. There came a rustle of fabric. She peered over the lip of the pit. A thick strand of glossy black hair had escaped her veil and hung in contrast to the paleness of her face.

Her eyes widened. Warm, brown eyes that needed no

kohl to enhance their luster. "Oh, Sir Lucien! What have they done to you?"

It *was* Isidora. At this moment, the most welcome, beautiful sight in all creation. She lowered a basket to him and he amended his thought. Nay, *this* was the most welcome, beautiful sight in all creation….

He tore into the treasure and put the first flask to his mouth. Pomegranate juice…the potent liquid ran down his parched throat in a stream of pure bliss. A lemon, apples, figs, dates… Lucien paused in his ravishment of the fruit and frowned. "What are you doing here? How did you find me? You should not have come!"

"Do not eat it all at once, you'll make yourself ill, sir. And you will need your strength if I am to get you out of here."

"Out? How?"

"Never mind. Just catch hold of the rope and climb up. I have tied it to a ring set in the wall."

His mouth crammed full, Lucien could not immediately respond.

"You've had enough for now, you must move quickly!"

He eased himself to his feet. "Take the basket up first."

"I can get you more food, just come!"

"Nay, take it. I'll not have it go to waste."

"You are as maddening as ever, my lord!" she complained, but retrieved the basket on its tether.

Lucien caught hold of the rope and hoped his body would not fail him. But it was all he could do just to hang there, much less haul himself up hand over hand.

"You're not a side of mutton. Walk up the wall, Sir Lucien."

Her tone was light, but he heard the undercurrent of urgency in her voice. It was like a breeze that cleared the fog from his mind. She had risked her life to come for him. He had to get out, as much for her sake as his own.

He renewed his grip and put his bare feet to the cold, gritty stones of the wall. With agony chasing each increment of ascent, he climbed. As he topped the edge, his hands began to slip. "I can't hold on…"

Isidora caught the clothing at the scruff of his neck and pulled until she fell backward and Lucien landed on top of her, his face resting cozily on her bosom. For a moment neither of them moved.

Oh, God. What a time and place for such a happenstance. She had revived him with her basket of fruit. Only too well. She smelled clean. Like freedom. Like a woman. For one delirious, beastly instant he nearly moved against her. But even if he stank, he wasn't an animal. Not yet.

"Lucien!" She shook him as best she could. "Get up!"

He opened one eye. Of course, he had almost forgotten. She had made it clear that she wanted no part of him. He eased himself off of her and immediately wished he could lie down again.

"Oh, Isidora. I'm going to be sick."

"Not now. We have to go."

Taking command of himself, Lucien agreed. "All right." He grimaced and sat clutching his stomach.

"Here, put this on." She unfolded a garment from the bag she carried and helped him pull it over his head.

"Oh, my God." His hands smoothed the red cross sewn over the breast of the white surcoat. "Templar's garb? Where did you get this?"

"It is my father's." She hurriedly scrubbed at his face with the cloth from the basket.

"But—"

"There is no time, sir! Just do as I bid you!"

He stumbled and lurched down the corridor, sucking on the lemon as he went.

"Sir Lucien, you will have to straighten up and walk properly. If anyone sees us, keep going, as if your business is done. If they question you, just freeze them with an arrogant gaze—you are quite good at that. I will follow behind you, as a servant might. Now go left, then take the first right turning and then right again, and I will show you the passage."

The merest breath of air announced a side opening. With that hint of freshness, for the first time, Lucien began to believe this scheme might actually work. He forced himself straighter, composing his face into what had once been a habitually haughty expression, as Isidora had so kindly pointed out. But no more.

"How know you this way, Isidora?"

"Shh! I am privy to a few things worth knowing."

Lucien's mind churned. The Templars had more secrets than the Pope had ducats. So a hidden passage was not surprising. But her father, Deogal the Learned, his teacher of the arts of alchemy—was a Templar? An ex-Templar, no doubt. All that mattered now, Lucien thought, was that he had a chance to see the full light of day once again.

"Where are we going?"

"Your place is arranged on a ship to Cyprus, then to England, once you are out of here."

He paused in astonishment and turned around to face her. The expense should have been far beyond her means. "How?"

She gave him a shove. "Never mind! Just go! Get as far away from FitzMalheury as you can."

"What about you? I think I have proven myself worthless to him, but you—"

"I am staying here with Father."

A lump formed in Lucien's throat. "I will send you compensation, Isidora, as soon as I may. But I do not want to leave—"

"You must. Your family is powerful. They can help you. Father is not well. There is nothing left for you here."

Lucien came to a halt and caught her hand. It was compact but strong, her skin soft except where her pens and brushes had calloused her fingers. "How so?"

She pleaded with her dark eyes. "Lucien, what does it matter? I can help you, now, in this moment only. You can do nothing to help him, ever. So go while you can. It is what he wants. It is what he commands."

Nothing? Ever? A command to go? With the bitter finality of those words, all Lucien's other troubles faded. His studies under his beloved master were at an end, just when he might be close to the knowledge he sought…to the cure he sought…for the agony he had caused his mother…for the agony inflicted upon her long-lost daughter, his own beloved twin, Estelle. He had failed to protect her, just as he had failed to protect Palban—though at least Brus had gone home with both legs intact.

There *had* to be a way to find the Elixir, even if it meant struggling on his own the rest of his life. Or so he still hoped. Slowly he let go of Isidora's slim fingers and returned to trudging up the corridor.

Chapter Five

Wales
Saint Crispin's Day
October, 1202

"**B**y the Rood, you don't much resemble an excommunicated outlaw to me." Lucien raised an eyebrow at his friend, Raymond de Beauchamp, who sat by the central fire with a contented, plump baby in his lap.

"Nor do you look much like an overeducated horse's arse to me, Lucien, though we both know it to be God's honest truth," Raymond said agreeably, and planted a kiss on the baby's head.

Raymond's squire, Wace du Hautepont, sat cross-legged on the floor beside him, mending arrow fletches. At his master's remark, the young man looked up from his task and grinned at Lucien. The lad had filled out and looked like a grown man, nearly ready to become a knight. Lucien grinned back at him.

"Well, I must admit, fatherhood has sweetened your temper, Raymond. Has it not, Ceridwen?"

Raymond's lady paused in her refilling of Lucien's bowl of mead and glanced fondly at her husband. "Indeed it has not. But who says his temper ever needed sweetening?"

At Raymond's resultant growl of laughter, Lucien looked heavenward in mock supplication. "The pair of you make me positively ill. Such a rogue does not deserve your devotion, Ceridwen, nor your defense. As I have said before, Raymond, you are a lucky man."

"Aye, I know it full well, Lucien. Here, hold Owain while I show this wench my gratitude." Raymond stuffed the child into Lucien's arms and caught Ceridwen, neatly turning so that his body shielded her from view.

Lucien, quite unused to infants, peered into the baby's round blue eyes. The child's soft weight was unexpectedly satisfying. Black curls—obviously Ceridwen's contribution, since Raymond was blond—peeked out from the tiny linen coif he wore, and his cheeks were round and red.

The wee thing chortled, grabbed fistfuls of Lucien's hair and yanked. "Oy! What have you taught him to do?"

"Eh?" Raymond released a breathless, blushing Ceridwen, who came to Lucien's rescue.

"He ever escapes his swaddling." She swept up Owain with expert confidence and recontained him in his wrapping.

Raymond sat in his chair once again and placed Lucien's mazer back into his hands. "So, Lucien, when are you going to follow in my footsteps?"

"Steal Ceridwen away from you, you mean?"

"Nay," Raymond said gently. "When will you give up this dry path of…of metallurgic sorcery you have chosen and attend to the stuff of life? Alchemy is for old men, Lucien, who have nothing else to do—or lose. You have lands to defend, crops to grow, and it is high time you took a wife."

Lucien sighed. His bitter disappointment in his ongoing alchemical failures since returning from the Holy Land ran deep. It had been nearly five years. Knowledge of the Divine—of the Essence that could cure all ills—carried a high, painful price. He could be close, without even knowing it.

And a wife would only get in the way of his paying the debt he owed his mother… "Wives require time and attention," he said at last.

"Marriage is not the penance you make it sound, Lucien," Ceridwen said. "Even Raymond no longer believes that." Her hip met Raymond's shoulder as she stood beside him and he slid a powerful, possessive arm around her thighs.

That in itself was a small miracle, to see Raymond, so recently the terror of the marches, now basking in the glow of his lady's affection. Though no less a warrior, he was a better man for it.

"But even supposing you are right, where am I to find a woman to put up with me as you do him?"

Ceridwen gave an unladylike snort. "Lucien, I can hardly believe my ears. Do you not notice those who follow you—nay, *devour* you with their eyes—at every feast or fair or market you attend? You have but to give any of them the slightest favor. Heaven knows their fathers will be delighted to hear from you. You are a prize, Lucien. A lord both handsome and wealthy, and unlike some around here, possessed of exquisite manners."

"There you have it! From one who has *me* to compare

you against, at that—true praise, indeed!" Raymond received a nudge of his wife's knee in his ribs and grinned.

Their encouragement only sounded like a lot of effort, fraught with risk. Then an inspiration came to Lucien. If he would pursue the Divine, he could also seek its help. "I shall pray and ask God for a sign. I will let the choice be up to Him."

"Let us hope the sign is not like it was for me, finding my bride impaled on the end of my sword..." Raymond looked up at Ceridwen, who gazed back at him with sultry eyes and ran the fingers of her free hand through his thick hair in a slow, sensuous movement.

Wace's cheeks reddened and he pointedly remained absorbed in his work.

Ceridwen smiled. "Never mind, my lord, it was for the best. I would not trade my scar for anything. But look, I have caused Wace to blush, and you have bored Owain to sleep, bless him. I shall retire. Good night, Wace, Sir Lucien. Worry not, all will be well."

"I am not worried," Lucien lied without remorse as he rose and bowed to Ceridwen. "So, you feel secure here, Raymond, at this keep? Do you need any men?"

"Ceridwen's brother and I make a good team, as it happens. We have enough men. And I do not think it wise for you to fight alongside us. You are established too far into England, you might bring down the anger of King John upon your head."

"I will fight for whom I please, Raymond, make no mistake."

"Aye, I know. Just be careful, eh? Come get some rest, now. You have a long journey to East Ainsley tomorrow." Raymond cuffed him good-naturedly. "But mind you, I shall be sending Squire Wace to visit whilst the year is yet new, and take measure of your progress toward a wedded state."

"I look forward to it, Beauchamp."

Lucien sighed and lay down by the fire, cocooned in blankets of both wool and the pleasant haze of mead. He hoped, as he did every night to little avail, that his dreams did not take him back to Acre, to the nightmare of the dungeon and the inexplicable, nagging sense of something left undone whenever he thought of Isidora….

Acre

With tears streaming down her face, Isidora knelt at her father's bedside, holding his blue-veined, wasted hand. There was so much she needed to tell him, so much she needed to hear from him, and so little time.

Since Lucien's departure, Deogal's illness had worsened day by day, for months and years until she despaired of him ever getting well. He had the flux, could hold nothing down; he often did not recognize her and sometimes he raved.

But now, at the end, by the grace of God, he looked at her and spoke her name.

"Isidora…the Work…"

Even at the moment of his death, he spoke of the Work but not how he felt about her?

"My daughter, you must take the scrolls to Britain, to Lucien. My notes. And the small bundle, there, on the shelf behind the antimony…it is imperative. Promise me you will do this."

She squeezed his trembling hand but said nothing. Even

had she a way to find Lucien, she could not face his mild, brotherly regard again, nor deliver into his hands a fresh obsession that would undoubtedly drive him to death and madness as it had her father.

Deogal returned her grasp and pulled himself up to face her, his eyes burning with feeling. "You *must,* Isidora. Please…I beseech you. It is the Key, at long last…of all my students, he alone will understand its significance and bring the Work to a magnificent conclusion…"

"Why have you never shared your knowledge with me, Father? I—I might have been closer to you that way."

"Nay, it is not for lasses such as yourself. Besides, your mother, God rest her soul, made me promise not to involve you. In order to protect you. But now, I have no choice. I beg this of you, before it is too late."

Her mother made him promise? *To protect her?* Such isolation had not felt like protection! And now he would burden her with these dark arts, when all she wanted was to burn the texts in the athanor!

He loves me, even though he hurts me. Yet again Isidora felt the heat of shame for her ingratitude.

Deogal lay back, as if the effort of his entreaty was too much. "You are the only one I can trust, Isidora. This must be removed from Acre, taken as far from FitzMalheury as it can be."

Despite the tearing of her own heart, Isidora could not bear the anguish in his eyes. She could not nay-say him, whatever the consequences. She took a deep breath.

"Of course, Father. I will see it done." She pulled out the small, gilt Maltese cross she wore and kissed it. "I swear upon the Holy Cross and upon the grave of my adored mother, Ayshka Binte Amir, and upon the love I hold for you, my dear father, that I will complete the task you have set me, or die in the attempt."

He smiled. "Good girl…" He sighed. His eyes closed and his fingers relaxed completely. Irrevocably.

"Father?" Disbelief, fear, grief, rage and desolation all competed for dominance within her. She fought to breathe, fought not to weep all over again.

He was gone! Leaving her nothing of himself but an errand. Not a word of love, only his habitual, "Good girl." Just as one said, "Good dog."

Isidora wailed and embraced his body in death as he had never allowed her to do in life. The overburdened moment froze for an instant. The scent of mint rose from a bowl of water she had used to bathe him as a warm, dry breeze wafted through the small window. But it did not stir Deogal's sweat-dampened hair. Nothing could touch him now.

He was safe, beyond suffering.

Kalle FitzMalheury hurled his goblet against the sandstone wall of the castle's refectory and rounded on the bearer of bad news. "What do you mean, Deogal is dead?"

The knight, a member of Salah al-Din's own extended family, nodded gravely. "A few days ago, *effendi*. He was buried this morning."

"Then where is the book, the material? The *stone?*"

The knight shrugged. "There was nothing but broken glass and crockery to be found. It looked as though a whirlwind had passed through the place."

Kalle approached the man and sneered, his pale hair

hanging in greasy wisps about his face. "And the girl? The half-breed?"

The knight did not retreat by even a fraction of an inch. He met Kalle's chilly gaze. "She is gone, as well, *effendi*."

"Her father had the protection of the Templars, but I doubt that she does. So find her, Faris al-Rashid. Bring her back and I will see to the rest."

Faris bowed to Kalle, even as his fingers longed to grasp the hilt of his dagger. *La*—nay. Jesus Christ frowned upon cold-blooded murder even as did the Prophet. And, Faris had the feeling, even though newly baptized, that by his forbearance he himself would prove a better Christian than Kalle FitzMalheury.

He would seek out Isidora Binte Deogal, for he had his own reasons to find her.

Her head down, Isidora crept warily along the docks, avoiding the gaze of passersby. Sailors, merchants, thieves and beggars. Strangers, and dirty, dangerous ones at that.

Her heart thumped erratically in her chest. She had managed to smash what crucibles remained before she'd slipped out of her father's house—just ahead of the man who had come searching—for what?

She did not know if he was a robber or an assassin—but Lucien had been taken once, by Kalle FitzMalheury, so it was not so unlikely to think they might be after her.

Especially if they thought her father had passed on his secrets to her. Which, apparently, was exactly what he had done.

Not for the first time, she cursed the Work. She needed a way to get on a vessel bound for England, or even France.

In truth, she had little idea of how to go about it. Lucien's voyage had been made possible with the aid of her father's mysterious and invisible Templar allies.

But she had no idea how to contact them for help for herself. Her father's wretched *Work* had eaten up what remained of their resources. All but a few pieces of silver and the items she had been charged to deliver to Lucien.

Seabirds screeched and the scents of tar and the briny low tide filled her nostrils, along with rotting fish entrails. Despite that, she was hungry and soon it would be dark. What could she do?

If she managed to get aboard some galley in secret, and was caught, the ship's master might sell her into slavery to obtain his payment for her passage. Nay, she needed a better way. Perhaps one of them could use a cook or a washerwoman— A hand on her shoulder made her shriek, even as a gull cried out.

"Be not afraid—I mean thee no harm."

She whirled about and looked into the deep brown eyes of a man—one clad in a contradictory mixture of eastern and western garb. A Franj surcoat over doubled links of the finest Persian mail. A modest turban crowned his head, but he was clean-shaven. His sword was not curved, but his dagger was, the hilt crusted with jewels, as well.

She found her voice at last. "Who are you?"

"I am here to help you. I am known as Faris al-Rashid. Kalle FitzMalheury sent me— Nay, wait!" His hand restrained her instant attempt at flight. "But my mother...my mother was Ayshka Binte Amir."

Isidora chose to ignore the last part of his statement and concentrate on the first, for he still held her arm. "Please explain yourself, sir, for Kalle FitzMalheury is no friend of mine."

Faris glanced about and drew her into a doorway, out of sight. "It was the only way I could get close to you, without arousing his suspicion."

"Why do you want to get close to me?"

He caught her shoulders. "Because, Isidora, you are my sister—half sister—but my blood kin all the same. You and I are all that are left. The wars have taken everyone else close to us."

His flimsy story was hard to believe. But she saw the reflection of her mother in his eyes, in the elegant sweep of his brows. "Take off your turban and let me see you properly."

He unwrapped it to reveal wavy black locks and a central, down-pointing hairline at his forehead, just like hers. "Why now, and not before?" she whispered.

"She was widowed when my father was killed and I was sent to be fostered in one of the royal palaces. I did not know she had remarried, nor of your existence, and in my ignorance of the Franj, would not have wanted to know. In battle, I sang the praises of Allah as I cut the infidels to pieces, right along with everyone else.

"But afterward…afterward, something happened. I had a vision, Isidora. And I received instruction from an angel that my path was no longer with the army of Salah al-Din, may his great name be honored forever. For though his brother is wise and just, my heart was no longer in the *jihad*. Before she returned to God, I went to see *umma*."

"You did?" Isidora's eyes glazed with tears. She had seen her mother only once after she was taken to the house of lepers. Deogal had kept her close, isolated from others. He had been determined that Isidora not fall prey to the same disease. It had taken her much time and secret effort to find Ayshka. But her mother had forbidden her ever to return, and Isidora had not seen her again before she died.

"They say it is a judgment of God, to be afflicted thus, but she was in no pain, I swear to you. She asked me to find you and to give you this…" Faris produced a small, exquisitely carved wooden box, inlaid with ivory.

Isidora took it and carefully opened the lid. Inside, beneath a layer of red velvet, lay a beautiful but oddly crafted ring of silver. It was smooth on one edge and had rippling indentations on the other. She had never seen it before. But from her mother, it was a treasure indeed.

Faris spoke again. "She said you would know what to do with it, when the time is right. And she also said to tell you that Deogal loves—loved—you as a bird loves the air, for you were all that he had left of her, like the scent of jasmine, lingering…"

Isidora swallowed hard. Her father loved her only as a reminder of her mother? But what was wrong with her, that she could not rejoice for what blessings she had, instead of pining for what she had not?

"I—I have a brother. I am not alone. Oh…" Isidora covered her face and began to weep, as she had not done since the day her father died. Only the day before yesterday.

"Shh…" Faris held her and muffled her sobs against his sturdy chest. "We need to leave this place."

But Isidora was not done. She wiped her eyes. "How is it you can be associated with Kalle? He is a mad dog when it comes to Muslims—"

"I converted, Isidora."

She stared at him. "Not for me, please do not say it was for me."

"Nay, because of the angel's visitation, I was sincere. I am still sincere. And I sincerely hate Kalle, may the one God forgive me."

"Aye, I, too, am guilty of that. But I need to get to England, Faris, to find a student of my father's. Can you help me? W-will you come?" It was too much to ask, too much to hope for.

He grinned, a flash of white in the deepening shadows. "If I am to journey, I'll need a squire, and you look a promising lad, eh?"

At this, Isidora's heart began to feel a good deal lighter.

Chapter Six

Three months later
Ainsley Hall, England...

Lucien slouched in his great chair, absently watching his servants clear away the remains of the night's dinner. Venison—heavy—and ripe as old cheese. Such leftovers would probably choke the paupers who received them.

He missed the foodstuffs of the east. Fruit and rice and pulses. Fare that did not immediately put one to sleep. But, he was indeed grateful for what he had. None of his people were starving this winter. The hall was festooned with greenery and folk were in a state of pitched excitement, for tomorrow began the Christmas revels.

For weeks the celebrations would continue, the Feast of Fools being the highlight for those whose chief pleasures were drunkenness, dung-tossing and bawdy displays of dubious wit. The festivities would no doubt leave him exhausted, when he had much to ponder in the privacy of his solar. And such privacy was a rarity. Indeed, even now, Lucien felt a presence at his back.

"My lord."

Mauger, his not-to-be-denied seneschal. An impeccable man sent years ago by Lucien's late father, to keep an eye on him. One who had appointed himself advisor, bodyguard and chief nag.

Aye, who needed a wife with one such as he at hand?

"Sir Mauger. How may I be of service to you?"

The impressively large seneschal came 'round to face him and bowed. "Really, my lord Lucien, don't mock me thus."

Lucien smiled thinly. "How can I do otherwise? Even your plea for the betterment of my manners comes forth as an order. Dare I hope you will be chosen King of Misconduct for the Epiphany Feast?"

Mauger shook his head, making his dark curls bounce, and raised his eyes heavenward, his palms together. "I must pray for patience, Lord Lucien, for as much as I love thee, I'd see you improved as your father, God rest him, wished."

"One might think if I have not improved sufficiently yet, I never will."

Mauger put his fists on his hips. "What you must improve is your attention to the ladies who attend the revels, my lord. Your duty is clear, as is mine to remind you of it. You must produce an heir. Your uncle Conrad and ladymother are as set upon it as was your father."

Lucien shifted in his seat and avoided the seneschal's flinty gaze. As much as Lucien loved his parents and still respected his uncle, their plans for him had not taken into account his own desires. "Plenty of time for that."

"There is not. Children take years to grow, and often

don't survive. You must start now, Lucien, and your lord father charged both me and Lord Conrad to see that it comes to pass."

"Oh, and what do you intend to do? Chain me to some hapless female and instruct me step by step?"

Mauger stared at Lucien, his eyes frankly challenging. "If you refuse to cooperate, then I'll secure for you a suitable bride. Upon your uncle's and lady-mother's approval, of course."

"Not mine?"

"If you force me to such action, your approval is forfeit."

Lucien rubbed his unshaven chin with the back of his hand. "From your tone, Mauger, one might think you nursed a grievance against me."

"You nearly got yourself killed in Acre—and not in any noble, Christian cause! If you'd allowed me to go with you, no such misery would have taken place. And furthermore, had you returned in a timely manner, the marriage your father had already arranged would've taken place long ago and we'd not be having this discussion."

Lucien allowed himself a small sigh. "Ah, so it is that old complaint—I left you behind! Nay, Mauger. I needed you here, and a marvelous job you made of it. Nary a revolt, nor a shilling lost, nor a lamb or cow unaccounted for."

Mauger's ruddy face darkened even further. "Your description of my worthy efforts sounds like an accusation, my lord."

"Your worthy efforts make me nearly superfluous, Sir Mauger. I am apparently only required as a means to sire offspring."

"Indeed, look at it any way you like. You've been home

quite long enough to settle down. But there's yet another matter of great concern, my lord."

Lucien waved a hand toward a carved, leather-seated chair to his left. "Please, take a seat, Mauger. Had I known this would go on so long, I would have offered it immediately."

The seneschal sat heavily in the chair that Lucien's lady would have occupied, had he a lady. Mauger leaned forward and spoke in a lowered tone. "My lord Lucien, this unsuitable preoccupation of yours, this dalliance with sorcery—"

"Alchemy is not sorcery, Mauger. Only the ignorant believe thus."

Mauger clenched his fists. "I am not ignorant, and it *is* sorcery, make no mistake. Any art that aims to bend the course of nature to one's own will is magic. 'Tis blatant heresy, as well, Lucien, and you risk bringing ruin—aye, even damnation—upon yourself and your family by its pursuit!"

Lucien ground his teeth and narrowed his eyes. "I will not be threatened."

"I'm doing no such thing! I am but warning you of how most clerics view such conduct."

"I am fully aware of the Church and what it cares about, Mauger. As long as I am free of excessive wealth, and make no enemies of priests, bishops, abbots or cardinals, I have nothing to fear from them."

"What of the king's spies, then, Lucien? What of any visitor, with connections you know nothing about? 'Tis one thing for foreigners in outlandish places to dabble in alchemy, but quite another for a young man of good repute to do so right here in the English countryside."

Lucien gripped the arms of his chair, then rose. The seneschal did likewise and they met eye-to-eye. "Are you quite through, Mauger?"

"Nay, my lord. I am, though loath to do so, going to put a certain pressure upon you, in your own best interests. If you don't give up this obsessive study—and apply yourself to finding a bride—I shall inform your uncle and mother of the situation. Then we'll see."

Lucien's heart constricted, as if in the grip of an iron fist. It would be the death of his mother, should she learn of what he did in the wee hours, even though it was for her ultimate benefit… "What I would like to see, Mauger, is the two of us engaged in single combat, that I might be rid of your cursed interference once and for all!"

Mauger looked truly shocked. "You wound me, my lord, indeed you do. So little gratitude. *Someone* has to look after you, as you refuse to look after yourself!"

Lucien took a deep breath and crossed his arms. He knew that Mauger would no more give up this battle than a dog would a bone, for Mauger would carry out Lucien's father's wishes to the letter or die in the attempt.

"Nothing will keep me from my studies, Mauger, and you might as well face that right now. If and when I so choose, *I* will find myself a bride, not you or anyone else— so you had best leave off this well-intentioned persecution."

"Aye. But—"

"Nay. I am no longer the stripling you could browbeat into submission. You will say nothing to my uncle—or my mother—about alchemy or any other pursuit of mine that is none of their business. Or yours. If you value my respect— and if you wish to remain here as seneschal—you will agree."

Mauger gave him a long, appraising look, as if measuring the strength of his resolve. "I see. I can only assume that you, being the son of your father, will do the right thing. But—if, and when—you must choose the correct woman, Lucien. Not one you can easily set aside while you mix your—"

"Enough! Do not presume too much, Mauger. I am yet lord of this manor, so by God do not push me. Are we agreed?"

"Agreed." Mauger spit on his palm and offered his hand to Lucien, who tried to hide his distaste for the ritual as he followed suit. Mauger's face creased into a grin. "Lucien the Fastidious, that should be your name."

"And yours should be Mauger the Meddler."

"You'd best be off then, to the tonsor for a shave, my lord, and—"

"Aye, so I will do. No more advice, Mauger. Let me do this my way."

"Of course, my lord." Mauger smiled, bowed as low as his girth allowed him, and Lucien knew his troubles were just beginning.

Chapter Seven

It was more than a fortnight past Christmas, and on the ice-rimed road to East Ainsley, Isidora's horse attempted to snatch a mouthful of dried grass from a huge bundle carried by an overburdened man. She pulled back the reins with cold-stiffened fingers, but the horse was more determined than she.

"Oy!" the serf shouted.

"Your pardon. Though, as I am squire to the great lord Sir Faris, here, you should be honored to have a chance to feed my beast." Isidora attempted to wink at her brother. Somehow, pretending she was a squire made her bolder than she would have been otherwise under the circumstances.

The man grunted. "I'll feed yer beast, all right. It can be the main course for tonight's feasting!"

Isidora exchanged looks with Faris, who understood more English than he could speak. But from the blue tinge of his lips, Isidora doubted he would be speaking in any language if they did not soon find shelter.

"We seek Ainsley, the hall of Lucien de Griswold. Is it

nearby?" She could scarcely believe, after weeks of travel both under sail and overland by horse, that they might be in sight of their goal.

"Aye, 'tis so, that's where I am to deliver this load, by the lakeside, for the wounded to lie upon."

Isidora's breath caught. "Wounded? What do you mean? Is there a battle?"

"Yer no from these parts, are ye then, laddie? Well, follow me, you and yer great lord there might like to join in and get warmed up."

Faris indicated the man with his chin and addressed Isidora in French. "What is that impudent fellow talking about?"

"I do not know, Faris. But I would rather follow him than wander these foul roads any longer."

"'Ere's the shortcut."

The serf led them from the road to a lane and thence to a path that wound through thick woods. A freezing gray mist crept between the gnarled tree trunks. Everything looked the same, in any direction.

Close and still, the forest gave Isidora the feeling it was creeping up on her. So different from the long views the desert afforded…but she could not think about that now. She concentrated on guiding her horse over roots and stones, every now and again looking back at Faris.

Often as not, she saw he rode with his eyes closed, his teeth gritted together. So far, England had not suited him in the least. He needed food, and a fire. "How much farther?" she asked their guide.

"Not much," he grunted.

She could hear the faint drumming of tabors. And the

occasional swell of voices, as of a crowd shouting. After a while, a meadow opened up before them, teeming with people.

All sorts, it seemed, from high-born ladies bundled in furs to the lowliest of pig-herders. They clustered around various fires and there were ale-tuns at regular intervals.

At one end was a frozen pond—a sight at which she no longer marveled. At the other was a slope of rising land, striped fields and pastures. Past a wooden wall, presumably sheltering the village of East Ainsley, the view culminated in a rocky outcropping with a small but well-situated castle.

So this was Lucien's home. But where was he? Isidora did not know whether she dreaded seeing him or not. Her stomach churned and her heart pounded so hard that she felt quite ill.

A trumpet blast pierced the frigid air. "Hear ye, hear ye! The mêlée is about to commence! The valiant but outnumbered forces of Sir Lucien, to be faced with the Blessed Host of the Lord of Misrule! There is to be no fair fighting, no shows of bravery and every man for himself!"

At a great shout, to Isidora's astonishment, two hordes of jubilant men poured onto opposite sides of the ice-covered pond, bearing all the accoutrements of battle as well as of farming. The smaller group seemed to be better dressed and equipped, but throughout were swords, spears, flails, staffs, clubs, forks and even digging tools.

Some rode stick horses, others had bones strapped to their feet, which seemed to allow them to glide over the ice faster than those who merely slid around in boots or shoes.

Isidora was completely baffled. Had they all gone mad?

"Knights, to the fray!" With a roar, the smaller force surged toward the center of the pond. Their opponents fell back at first, then rallied and soon the battle was fully under way. Isidora picketed the horses and coaxed Faris to warm himself at one of the fires while they watched the spectacle.

A red-cheeked young woman smiled at them. She was dressed like a troubadour, her head capped by a jaunty hat with a turned-up brim. "You're not joining in the fight?"

Isidora bowed. "*Demoiselle,* we are strangers here, and are unfamiliar with this custom."

"Oh, it is the tradition! The Feast of Fools is the one day of the year when serfs and servants are the equals of the master and his men. They battle out on the ice, and Lord Lucien is as apt to be beaten as any other. There is no fear of reprisal, and all are allowed to participate."

"That sounds—" Isidora had been about to say "barbaric," but amended it. "Entertaining."

"Aye, indeed it is. My lute teacher is out there, giving as good as she gets, I'll warrant."

Faris asked, "Which is Lord Lucien?"

The girl raised up on her toes and peered at the mêlée. "Aye, there he is—on his knees, doubled up, with his arms over his head. Taking quite a thumping— Oh dear!"

Isidora's jaw dropped at the sight of several rough-looking men belaboring their lord with wooden rods. These English had to be mad! Then a massive fighter came to Lucien's rescue and tried to drive off the attackers with a flaming torch. But yet again, the mob surged toward them.

Panic surged through Isidora. She had witnessed bloody, lethal fights in the crowded streets of Acre on the heels of *al-Kond Herri*'s death. This looked no different. Lucien was about to be killed and she could not stand by and watch. She ran toward the pond.

"*La!* Isid—boy! Stop!"

Isidora heard Faris shout after her, but paid no heed. She bounded across the icy surface, only realizing her mistake when she found she could *not* stop, nor indeed even stay upright.

Her feet went skyward and the impact knocked the air from her lungs. She sprawled onto her back, spinning and sliding until she rammed something larger and heavier than she was. Then she knew she had made yet another mistake, for she had no weapon.

The recipient of her skidding blow was about to deliver one of his own—a fist aimed at her face. Lucien's eyes blazed like blue flames and she squeaked in terror.

"The devil—*Isidora*?" he breathed, frowning, and then lowered his arm. "Good God!"

"Hold!" Faris shouted.

There came a thunder of hooves. Her brother was coming to protect her. "Nay, Faris! Stay back!"

Lucien looked up and his face paled. The horse landed on the ice and an ominous groan sounded.

"Everyone off the pond! Now! The ice is breaking!" Lucien scooped Isidora into his arms and made his way with amazing speed to the safety of the shore.

But he dumped her there only to go back out onto the ice, his skill with the bone-clad boots making him swift.

Faris had jumped clear and was attempting to help his floundering horse out of the hole he was in. Some men were racing back to land, others were still so caught up in the mêlée they had not heard the warning.

Lucien grabbed the burning torch from the huge man who wielded it and shouted until he had their attention. "*Oyez!* Listen to me—the ice has cracked and is broken in places. Make your way back as lightly as you can. Spread out, and do not run or cause any more vibration than you have to. If you must, slide on your bellies to spread your weight, do you understand?"

Isidora watched, her heart in her mouth. The men, common and noble alike, slowly regained the shore, leaving red patches on the ice where the fighting had been fiercest. When all were safely in front of them, Lucien and the big man followed.

Faris's horse lunged, found its footing and scrambled out of the water. Then, with a shriek beyond anything Isidora had heard before, a gash ripped the ice open like a strike of lightning. The black water swallowed Faris up as if he had never existed. Only an echo of his cry remained.

The Persian mail! With so much metal weighing him down, he might as well have held a boulder in his arms and jumped in. She felt helpless, as if a tide were sucking the last remnants of her life away. This nightmare could not be true....

Lucien raced to within a few feet of the ice's edge, then lay on his stomach. Wet and half frozen himself, he scooted to the brink and held the torch over the water. The stranger might have a chance to surface, if he knew which way was up. If his eyes could yet see...

All were silent. The only sound was the irregular creaking of the pond's crust. Then came a small splash and Lucien grasped an ice-cold hand in his. A dark head emerged, and the stranger gasped for breath.

"Mauger, hold on to me! Get someone to pull us out with rope!"

His men quickly formed a human chain and tied something to Lucien's belt. It took all his strength to hang on to the drowning man's hand. Then his wrist. Then both wrists, and he came slithering out, as if newborn from the waters.

"Come, you can make it," urged Lucien.

"Mâshallâh!" croaked the fellow through chattering teeth, and Lucien nearly let go of him in surprise. *An Arab?* A handsome devil, no less, and obviously high-born. But what was he doing here?

"My mail, *effendi.* S-see to it, I b-beg of you."

Lucien blinked in confusion. Then the Arab pulled down an edge of his surcoat to reveal the shiny links.

"Of course, I will not let it rust. But let us get away from here first."

"Shuk-r'n."

"I only do as God allows, my friend."

A gust of freezing wind skittered across the pond and the Arab began to shake from head to toe. Lurching and slipping, Lucien guided him until they regained the shore at last.

Lucien wrapped a cloak around the man and helped him back onto his steaming, shivering horse. He tried to untie the rope from his belt, only it was not a rope, but a long length of cloth, and his stiff fingers could not undo the wet knot.

Climbing up behind the man, Lucien took the reins and halted the horse before Isidora. "This Turk belongs to you?"

She nodded, her face white even with the snow as a background. "He is not a Turk. But, aye, that is his turban. I gave it to your men, for there was no rope."

"Larke!" Lucien called out, his gaze sweeping the crowd.

The troubadour girl came running. "Are you all right, Lucien? Is the man all right? And the horse?"

"Aye, aye, have no worry." He indicated Isidora with a nod. "This is my friend. Take her to the hall and get Mauger to go with you. Isidora, my sister, Larke, will attend you. Kindly do as she says."

Isidora stared. "You have a sister? And in all the time with us you never told me? What is the matter with you, Sir Lucien?"

"Never mind, we'll talk later. This man needs to get warm, and my cuddling him atop his horse is not going to do much good." Lucien then turned to address his people. "This was but a minor mishap. All the revels will continue as usual, and I congratulate the fools who routed us!"

A cheer rose and Lucien breathed a sigh of relief. At least this farce was over for the year. But Isidora? In England? With a Saracen escort? He needed some hot mulled wine before he could take on such a puzzle.

Isidora sat before the fire in Lucien's solar, sipping warm wine from a wooden bowl that still rattled against her teeth, she was yet so cold. As was Faris, no doubt.

He dozed in Lucien's bed, dark against the white linens. No wonder Faris was exhausted. He must have found the strength of many men, to have risen in the water despite the mail coat he'd worn.

She felt a stab of fear for him, that he might be singled out and targeted by someone for the color of his skin. But so far, though many had stared, no one had said a word against the guest of their lord. He was yet safe, his sword but an arm's length away.

And, his mail now hung from a rod, Lucien having made certain it was dried and oiled. Faris would be glad.

But to her, the situation was utterly overwhelming. The journey, the dangers, the weather, the English themselves, and now this place, Lucien's home. It offered slender comfort, by eastern standards. Though clean enough, it was rudely furnished and only vaguely warm despite the roaring fires. Still, in any event, she did not belong here. Did not want to be here.

But perhaps he was merely a land baron now, and no longer possessed by alchemy. Perhaps she need not give him the things she had come so far to give him. Things she did not understand and that were certain to be dangerous.

"Isidora."

Lucien's voice, smooth and rich and heady. He was here with her, as if summoned by her thoughts of him, just as spirits—and devils—were summoned. Despite his coming up behind her, she did not jump in startlement.

Instead she was suffused by a flood of warmth. Nay, this was all wrong! She must stay strong and keep her heart her own....

"Isidora?"

The weight of his hand upon her shoulder. She closed her eyes. She would not speak, would not move, was glad she was already sitting. Maybe he would go away.

"Isidora, I do not know why you are here, or why you are garbed as a man, or who this person in my bed is to you, but…"

The intensity in Lucien's resonant voice made her open

her eyes. Now he was on his knees before her. His eyes shone in brilliant blue contrast to his blood and dirt-darkened skin—indeed, his face appeared little better than it had the last time she had seen him, but was still so handsome that he was almost painful to look upon. She shifted her gaze to the bed where Faris lay heaped with furs.

Lucien plucked the bowl of wine from her fingers and engulfed her cold hands in his even colder ones. "You shield yourself in silence, Isidora. It is not necessary."

"Is it not? Silence reveals much, if one is patient."

"But you must have news...an explanation?"

"I am on a grim errand, Lord Lucien. I will explain it when I am ready. Not before."

He gazed at her, searching her eyes. "Isidora, you have come a long way, and I...I am not sorry you are here."

Before she knew what was happening, he had pulled her into his hard embrace. Her cheek pressed against his wet surcoat, his heart pounded beneath it. She could scarcely breathe, he was squeezing her so tightly.

"I thought I would never see you again," he whispered. "I was afraid that Kalle might have— I should never have left."

"Nay, Lucien—I wanted you to go. You know that."

Despite Isidora's words, he did not push her away. And for reasons unknown to her, she did not try to escape.

Then the solar door creaked open.

"My lord?"

A young woman's voice. One sounding confused, perhaps even dismayed.

"Goodness, Lucien!" That, Isidora knew, was Larke's amiable, if surprised, response.

"Unhand Isidora, you Saxon!" A man's growl—that

of Faris. The hiss of metal being unsheathed. That of Faris's sword.

Lucien cleared his throat and eased Isidora from him. He looked at her as if he had just awoken from a deep sleep and could not believe where he found himself.

"*Effendi,* by God, that is my sister, not some camp follower!"

"My lord Lucien, who is this woman?" the unknown young lady asked, her voice quavering.

Isidora remained silent. Only her eyes questioned him.

Lucien cleared his throat and stood. "Lady Rosamunde, allow me to present Isidora, daughter of Sir Deogal, a brave knight of Acre." He gestured at Faris. "This is Faris, ah—"

"My half brother," Isidora supplied.

Faris nodded. "Faris al-Rashid, great-nephew to Salah al-Din the Magnificent, may his name be bathed in eternal glory. I am a Christian knight, even as you are, Lord Lucien. But I hold my sister's honor more dear than do you, it seems."

Isidora saw that it took Lucien a moment to take in this information. But he recovered quickly, only to deal her a blow for which she had no defense.

"Isidora, this is Rosamunde d'Artois. Daughter of the Count Hardouin. My betrothed, as of this New Year's Day just past."

Chapter Eight

Mauger marched into the solar and took in the scene at a glance. "Milady Larke, kindly take fair Rosamunde back to her quarters to await Lucien's apology." Once they had gone, he rounded on Lucien and shouted, "What in the name of all that is holy has been going on here?"

Lucien sat on his bed, to whence Faris had retreated, and sighed. "Should you not be supervising the Mass of the *Festum Assinorium,* Mauger? There will be much more to disapprove of there in the chapel than here."

"Aye," growled Mauger. "But a bunch of drunken peasants dancing naked in church with a donkey is not as serious as the Lord of East Ainsley kissing strange Saracen lads before the very eyes of his intended!"

"Even on Feast of Fools day, when all must be forgiven?" Lucien offered. "Besides, I was not kissing a lad. I was not kissing anyone at all."

Mauger's green eyes bulged and he glared at Isidora. Lucien winced as she rose to his defense.

"I am not a boy, my lord Mauger. I can prove it, if you like. Nor am I a Saracen. But for that you must take my word."

Lucien shook his head. How could anyone mistake Isidora for a boy, no matter what garb she wore? "For God's sake, Mauger, leave her alone. It is not her fault."

Isidora drew herself tall and raised her chin. "Indeed it is my fault, Sir Lucien, for I have placed myself within your reach. You did not kiss me, but you might have done so without censure, because I owe you my gratitude for saving the life of Faris."

Lucien put his hand to his brow, then looked at her through his fingers. "I had God's help. But, I thank you for your courteous speech, Isidora."

Isidora bowed her head and her dark tresses fell in waves about her face. Through a gap in the curtain of her hair, Lucien saw that a tiny smile graced Isidora's lips.

Full, pink lips that he had not just been kissing.

He hurriedly looked at the fire. A conquest by an invader from Acre? He thought not. It had merely been a slip of control. She had surprised him, when he had not held a woman in God only knew how long.

Lucien indicated the door. "Sir Mauger, please go see to Rosamunde's comfort. She requires your subtlety and decorum."

Mauger's face reddened. "What of this knight in your bed?"

Lucien shrugged. "Oh, I daresay he will keep his hands off me. Will you not, Faris al-Rashid?"

Faris grunted incoherently. Lucien suspected—and hoped, especially since the man had drunk a great deal of mulled wine—that he did not fully understand the exchange.

With obvious reluctance, Mauger withdrew.

"So, Isidora. I…" Lucien tried to keep his voice light, as if he cared not one way or another that she was here. But her presence brought forth waves of memories—of hot nights, of the scents of jasmine and roses—and burning charcoal—and sulphur.

Of the excitement of discovery in Deogal's workshop, of secret knowledge and solemn dedication and joyful, mutual understanding, all lost to him now. One did not often meet such a skilled and highly principled master of the Work as Deogal.

Lucien wanted to catch Isidora in his arms again and hold her, to try to regain some of what he missed so much. But instead he turned to her and asked, "Why have you come, Isidora?"

"To see you, Sir Lucien."

"A long way, just to see me. Tell me the truth."

She looked up at him, her brown eyes soft and serious. "I cannot. I am not ready to tell you. You must give me time."

"Very well."

She played with the lacings of her tunic. "Are you truly going to marry that girl?"

"Isidora…"

"Are you?"

His composure slipped and clawed for a purchase. He forced himself to answer. "I have promised."

"Then that makes my task all the more difficult, for now I must consider her well-being in addition to yours."

"What are you talking about?"

Isidora tipped her head to one side. "Are you still an alchemist, my lord?"

Lucien blinked. What else was he, if not that? "Aye. Not a very good one, perhaps, but I am yet trying."

She gazed steadily at him. "I see."

"You are driving me mad, Isidora. Speak your mind!"

Isidora strolled around the brazier, jabbing at the coals with a poker. "Have you told her yet? Does she know of your unnatural delight in lead and quicksilver and acids?"

"Well, nay, I have not mentioned it. But why do you call it—"

Isidora interrupted him, waving the iron stick in emphasis. "You must tell her, Lucien. Otherwise it is just as if you wed her without mentioning that you already had a lover you were unwilling to give up."

He stared at her as if she had grown an extra head. "Not so! I will not be allowing her near the Work, in any event."

Isidora's smile was anything but humorous. "She will find it sooner or later, my lord, and right or wrong, she will draw her own conclusions."

His belly muscles tightened. "I cannot give it up."

"Then you should give *her* up."

Lucien jumped up and began to pace. "You do not understand."

Isidora threw down the poker with a clang and crossed her arms. "Then explain it to me, so that you might in due course explain it to her."

He stopped before her, wanting to shake her for such impertinence. "What gives you the right to come here, without warning, and tell me what to do?"

The liquid look she gave him then, of pain, and yearning, and love forsaken, was enough to make his own heart begin to ache. He took her hands in his once again and drew her to a wolfskin-draped bench before the brazier.

She sat stiffly and gazed at the red glow of the coals. "I have no right. Forgive me, my lord."

Lucien straddled the bench and leaned toward her, his elbows on his knees. "Tell me what has happened, Isidora."

She still did not look at him and, one by one, great tears began to slide down her cheeks. "Father is dead, Lucien. He went mad and he died."

Lucien's heart convulsed, as though it had been crushed by the careless blow of a hammer. "Oh, Isidora. I am so sorry. It must have been difficult for you."

She grabbed up the poker again and stirred the coals into a seething mass of heat and sparks. "Difficult? Oh, aye! To watch him being eaten alive by the Work. To know it would only be a matter of time before Kalle FitzMalheury tried again to gain his secrets. But Kalle was too late, may fleas infest his nether parts! And it was too late for me, too. Father died thinking of *you,* Lucien. Of you and the Work and my mother. That is all he ever thought of."

Lucien sat back, chastened. He remembered. Isidora peeking into the workshop and being driven away. Isidora serving him and her father food and drink as they spoke, watching and listening, but never included. Clever, inquisitive Isidora, always kept apart from what was truly important to her father, and to him.

She gently set the poker down. Her slender shoulders began to shake and she turned her face from him.

"Come, Isidora, it is all right." Lucien shifted closer, wanting to do something to comfort her, but not sure what she might accept. Then his body took over where his usually reliable mind stumbled. He drew her into his arms, so she was between his knees, and hugged her. "Shh, don't cry."

She wept all the harder and her body trembled.

When he rubbed her back with his palm, she turned to him. She pressed her wet face to his chest and neck, wrapped her arms around him and hung on as if he were her only refuge.

He swallowed against the closing of his own throat. "I miss him, too, Isidora."

"I know," she whispered.

Lucien found her shining, black hair beneath his hand and carefully squashed the urge to stroke it. To tip her head back and kiss her... He cleared his throat. "You had best go to bed now. The women's quarters—"

"Please, Lucien. Do not send me away."

Her whispered entreaty cut him to the quick. "You cannot stay here with me. It is improper."

"But I am afraid, Lucien. For the first time in my life, I am afraid, and I feel so alone. Next to you, I feel that much closer to how things were when Father was still alive."

He was helpless to deny her. She had come so far with nothing but false hopes, and had nothing to return to. "You are a brave lass, make no mistake. And you are not alone."

Isidora pulled herself upright, away from his warmth, and looked into his eyes. "You say that because you feel sorry for me. But you are still going to send me away. Aren't you."

"Not tonight. After all, it is still the Feast of Fools."

Her heart beat faster. "Must I be coy and deceive you about how I feel, like an English maid might?"

"I wish you would, Isidora. It would make it less painful for me. But you are still cold from the pond. If I shove your brother over a bit, you can get into the bed between us. I will remain awake, on the outside of the covers."

A tiny spark of heat ignited within her. "And if Sir Mauger comes in?"

A corner of Lucien's shapely mouth quirked. "I will tell him there is no room for him to join us."

Isidora smiled. "No wonder he is so vexed with you. But are you not supposed to go give an apology to Lady Rosamunde?"

"Aye."

Lucien's coppery hair gleamed in the firelight as he gazed at her. She wondered what Rosamunde would discover in him, and do with him, and if he would be happy married to her…indeed, what would it be like for any woman to be wed to Lucien de Griswold?

His eyes narrowed. "Isidora, you are thinking thoughts you should not be thinking."

She sniffed. "If you know what they are, then neither should you be thinking them."

Isidora felt the tension rise in his body, and slowly, Lucien eased farther from her and stood.

"This is all wrong, Isidora. You never should have come here. You must go home as soon as the weather allows."

With his warm strength now out of reach, she hugged herself instead. "I cannot leave until I do what my father bade me do."

"And what is that?"

"I cannot tell you."

"Why not?"

Now Isidora got to her feet and looked him squarely in the eye. "Because I must first determine if you are truly worthy."

His jaw muscles tightened. "Of what? Who appointed *you* my judge?"

"My father—your master—did! He asked me to bring you a gift. But I will not give it to you until I am convinced you are ready for it."

"What makes you think I want any such gift?"

"Oh, I know you do, Sir Lucien. You want it as much as you want your next breath of air."

He grew still and she could see a pulse pounding in his neck. "Do not tease me, Isidora, or I swear I will make you sorry for doing it. Tell me the nature of this gift."

The brazier's glow seemed to increase, perhaps because they were both breathing so hard. "It has to do with the *Tabula Smaragdina...*"

Lucien's eyes grew wide. "The Emerald Tablet?"

Isidora nodded. "...'It is the power stronger than any other power, because it can overcome—'"

"'—every subtle thing and penetrate every solid thing,'" Lucien finished for her, then put his hand over her mouth as if she had continued the utterance herself. "You must never, ever speak of such things to anyone. Anyone but me. Do you understand, Isidora?"

His hand remained over her mouth so she could not reply.

"What do you know of this? Were you paying heed, all that time, to the bits and pieces available to you? A little knowledge is like a little fire, Isidora. It can do good or it can get out of control and destroy everything in its path. Oh, had I known!"

He released her and began to pace again.

"What would you have done, cut out my tongue?"

"Don't be stupid."

"I know enough to see that the Work consumes men, like flesh is consumed by a wasting disease. I know enough to see that nothing I can say to you will stop you from this folly."

Lucien stopped and rounded on her. "Tell me what your father sent me."

"Nay." At her refusal, his eyes blazed so fiercely that she took a step back. "Not until you have proven yourself to me. I trusted Kalle once, did you know? And he betrayed me, and my father and mother—all of us."

Lucien took a deep breath. "What do you want me to do?"

"When I know, I shall inform you. I must allow the Divine to guide me in this."

"Right. In the meantime, allow *me* to guide you." He scooped her up, strode to his bed and set her down upon it none too gently. True to his word, he pushed Faris to one side to make room for her. "I will be back once I have spoken to Rosamunde. When I return, I want to see that you are asleep."

His arrogant regard for her well-being both annoyed and warmed her. "As you will, my lord Lucien."

Lucien swept out of the room as if he were an outraged king, not just an angry man. An impossibly handsome, excessively intelligent and altogether overwrought man.

Isidora lay still, with the furs draped over her exactly as Lucien had placed them. Then she turned and curled up on her side. Why had she come? *Because I promised Deogal.* But Deogal was the one who had faith in Lucien, not she. And here she was, in his care, at his mercy.

Chapter Nine

Lucien approached the women's solar with dread seeping higher and higher in his gut. He hated scenes, and he had already had too many women weep over him, whether pining for his attentions or nursing his wounds.

Rosamunde had appeared on Christmas Day, accompanying a group of his guests. She had stood in the hall, surrounded by greenery, haloed by candlelight, fresh and glowing and oh, so willing to obey her mother and father, who had apparently sent her, their youngest, to catch the eye of the wealthy Lord Lucien.

When she smiled, everyone else in the vicinity faded by comparison. Lucien was not smitten. Nay. But he knew a good thing when he saw it. A pretty lass, biddable and easy to handle, one who would not ask too many questions, and one who, once she was got with child, would be too busy with her own concerns to bother about his. Aye, she was the perfect solution.

And he was a heartless, mercenary horse's ass to even think of marrying an innocent maiden when he felt nothing for her, no matter what Mauger had to say about it. But it would not be the first time he had broken a woman's heart. He steeled himself and knocked on the door. "It is I, Lucien, *mesdames*."

A servant opened it, to reveal several women, including unwed female guests and a few who were married but chose to spend the night with lady-friends instead of their husbands.

A wide bed with its curtains parted provided seating for some, others rested on chests or four-legged stools. Gowns of varied hues and fabrics were draped over a wooden bar suspended from the ceiling beams.

Lucien experienced an uneasy instant of feeling that he had just gained entrance to a harem—one not his own. No doubt he had spent too long in the east. He bowed to the ladies, received a soft chorus of well-wishes, and a small pack of lap-dogs scrambled to him, wiggling their bodies and trying to lick his fingers.

He could not accommodate them all, so he bade the dogs be patient, and they settled back down. Rosamunde sat stiffly by the fire, her face white and her hands clasped in her lap. To Lucien's surprise, Mauger also sat nearby, stroking his dark beard, fidgeting, and his face shone with sweat. He looked extraordinarily uncomfortable.

"You took your time, Lucien," he growled.

"Aye, I had good reason. You may go, now, to your well-earned rest."

"Nay," Rosamunde said. "I wish for him to stay. He does not frighten me the way you do."

Lucien could hardly believe what he was hearing. He glanced at their rapt audience then back to the young lady.

"Em, mayhap we should have this conversation in a place more private, Lady Rosamunde?"

"Nay. What I have to say might as well have witnesses."

Now Lucien was thoroughly taken aback. "I frighten you that much? But I have not so much as—"

"Not in that way." Her eyes grew round and bright with tears. "It seems to me you are here, Lord Lucien, and yet you are not. Always, I see your mind is churning with thoughts—about what, I cannot fathom, but I know that they are not about me, nor are they anything you will ever share with me. You are not a man one can get close to. I do not want a husband who will make me feel that I am alone even when we are together."

Lucien swallowed. So, he had been in error about her. She was pretty *and* perceptive. "I see. I beg your pardon, Lady Rosamunde, for my inattention."

She rose from her cushioned chair. "That is not necessary, my lord, for after tonight's display of passion, I see no reason for me to stay, even if my parents punish me for returning. I will not marry a man who lusts after boys."

The resultant gasps and titters made Lucien want to crawl into a hole. "But—"

"And especially not a man who shows absolutely no remorse or shame about it, Feast of Fools notwithstanding."

"I can assure you, Lady Rosamunde—"

A spot of color appeared on each of her cheeks. "I need no assurances, sir! If you had embraced *me* in such a blatant and…and…lewd—manner, I should not be half so offended! But as it stands…"

Her lower lip began to tremble and Lucien braced himself for a flood. But yet again, the girl surprised him. She bit the tremulous lip and took visible control of herself.

Mauger opened his mouth to speak, but Lucien scowled and threw him a quelling look before going to one knee before the beautiful Rosamunde. "My lady, even if you will not accept me, please accept my heartfelt apology for what you witnessed this night. I can explain, but I fear you will like the real truth no better than what you have mistaken for the truth."

She looked down at her hands and must have heard his sincerity for she spoke in a small voice. "I know it was not a boy. I only said that because the thought of you wanting to hold another woman was so unbearable to me. I know what life is like for a woman whose man strays. My mother…"

Lucien stood and took her hand in his. "What does your heart bid you do, then? For I cannot, in good conscience, wed you merely to please your family. Or mine. I want you to be happy."

She took a deep breath. "Then release me from this betrothal. I can see only heartbreak in it, Sir Lucien. For you think too much and are far too attractive. I should marry someone older, plainer, someone who would feel absolutely blessed by my acceptance. Then I might shower him with bliss and feel his devotion for me alone."

Rosamunde glanced at Mauger, who shifted yet again, as though he had just landed in a pile of gorse. Lucien raised his brows. Mauger coughed and squirmed some more. "Indeed. Mayhap Sir Mauger has proven his charm to you?"

"He certainly understands women better than you do, my lord."

An inexplicable wave of relief swept Lucien. He was

free again… "I release you, Lady Rosamunde, and I wish you much joy."

Mauger got up and shrugged himself into order. "You and I shall have a talk, sir, on the morrow."

Lucien bent over Rosamunde's hand, which he still held, and kissed the backs of her white fingers. "I hope, my lady, that you do forgive me. But I fear you are wise to refuse me. I am indeed selfish and preoccupied."

"Oh, Lucien!" She choked on a sob, then said with admirable calm, "Good night, my lord. God keep you well."

"And you, my lady." He bowed to her and the assemblage, then retreated as quickly as politeness allowed.

Mauger took a bit longer.

Chapter Ten

"Did you listen, Faris, or are you truly asleep?" Isidora asked, looking at the back of his dark head on the feather-stuffed pillow. Even with all her clothes on, she was yet chilled.

"I listened," he admitted, and turned to face her. "And I will tell you, Isidora, this knight, this self-proclaimed *alchemist,* will break your heart in the end. I advise you to come away with me, and let us return to Acre. This was a fool's errand."

Isidora sat up and drew the bed furs about her shoulders. "My father was no fool! If he sent me here, it was for good reason. And I will not fail him. You go home if you like, but I am staying."

"I will not leave you here with Sir Lucien. From what I have seen thus far, his morals are worse than those of a Franj, which perhaps he cannot help, for he is a Franj and a Saxon combined." Faris punctuated his statement with a sneeze.

"So you would have preferred that he did not risk his life to save yours this day?"

Faris punched down his pillow. "It is a measure of his

own foolishness that he did. For he should realize that I will not stand by and allow him any further liberties the like of what I witnessed earlier. And that after he had pledged himself to another!"

"You know nothing of what you speak, Faris. Had I thought you would make yourself so disagreeable, I would never have allowed you to accompany me here!"

Faris gave a long-suffering look toward heaven. "As if you could have stopped me! And had I the least bit of sense, I would not have allowed you to leave Acre in the first place. I have many friends, strong, well-favored knights, any one of whom might have made you a better husband than this fellow."

"Who, pray tell, has ever suggested that Lucien be my husband? Thus far, only you, my lord brother, and I would thank you to keep such remarks to yourself in future!" With that, Isidora turned her back on him and scooted beneath the furs.

With a creak of old wood and iron hinges, the door swung open to admit Lucien. Lord of this place. Lord of many female hearts, no doubt. But not hers. She squeezed her eyes shut so that he might not see anything beyond her exhaustion.

Only when she felt his weight settling next to her did she open them. Here Lucien lay, right beside her, but he might as well have been across the room, he felt so distant.

But she could see that a strong pulse beat in the hollow of his throat. His cheek was ruddy and smooth but for the stubble of his beard. His red tunic, of soft, thick wool, had intricate embroidery along the neck and seams. Griffins and wolves intertwined in fantastic combinations of lapis and gold thread.

Who could afford such expensive clothing? He could,

apparently. He blinked, a slow sweep of thick, dark lashes, and then turned his blue eyes upon her.

"You are supposed to be asleep."

"One cannot order another to sleep, my lord. One must be taken upon the angel's bosom in its own good time."

"What does that mean?"

"It is what my mother used to tell me. That to sleep was to be carried through the night on the bosom of an angel. It made me less afraid of the dark."

"I never knew you feared the dark."

"There is much you do not know about me, my lord."

"So, your coming after me into Kalle's dungeon took great courage."

"Nay. I needed no courage for that. Something else carried me that day."

Lucien swallowed and his voice grew husky. "I have never properly thanked you for helping me."

"The fact you are alive is thanks enough."

"Isidora, such talk makes me ill at ease. I feel as though you want from me something I do not even possess, much less can give."

She propped her head up on her hand. "Sir Lucien, you are ever searching outside, but there is a wealth of treasure within you as yet undiscovered. Have you not learned that in any of your studies?"

He looked into her eyes, a piercing, poignant look that spoke of a terrible yearning. "Nay, you are wrong. I am still empty. I have yet to find the—the touchstone that would fill me, and save my….save what is dear to me."

Isidora felt her heart catch. "Is that what the Work means to you, then?"

"I see you know me little better than I know you, after all." His tone was flat with disappointment.

She almost reached over to touch him, to reassure him, but it was too soon. For her, as well as for him. "Given time, we might each learn a great deal, my lord."

"Ahem." Faris was awake. Indeed, so awake that he sat up in the bed. "I wish you two would be silent. I prefer not to listen to such a private conversation, especially one I cannot properly understand."

Lucien gave Isidora a wry smile. "Your brother is indeed mannerly, is he not?"

"Aye," she agreed. "And had I a longer acquaintance with him—beyond these recent few months at least—I would feel more at ease telling him to stop trying to protect me!"

"I think Faris is to you what Mauger is to me. Mayhap the two of them should not be allowed to communicate. God knows what well-meaning horrors they would come up with for us were they to get together."

Faris bristled. "You, sir, are as close to single combat with me as you'll ever be and still live to talk about it."

Lucien was off the bed and on his feet faster than Isidora would have thought possible. Cold fury poured from him and in a panic, she threw herself back against Faris.

"Hold, both of you! Faris al-Rashid, I humbly ask that you offer an apology for this affront to our host. And Lucien de Griswold, please overlook my brother's ill-considered words."

Faris, looking only mildly repentant, said, "May God forgive me for such rudeness."

Lucien relaxed a fraction. "I do not know about God, but I am willing to let it pass. We have no quarrel, Faris al-Rashid. I have no designs upon your sister. She is beyond reproach."

"Your behavior is not!"

Isidora lay back down. "I am going to sleep. Surely you two can find something more important to fight about in the morning?"

But Faris was not finished. "You cannot change the subject so easily, Isidora Binte Deogal! I want assurances from you that you will behave as befits a daughter of the house of Salah al-Din, may his name be emblazoned upon the heavenly firmament for all eternity!"

Isidora threw a helpless look to Lucien, who seemed to have understood Faris's outburst of Arabic perfectly. He awaited her response with his arms crossed upon his chest and one eyebrow cocked.

She took a deep breath. "Very well. Sir Lucien, I forgive you for your intrusion upon my person. And I am sorry for the way I felt about it, as well as for the way it seems to have made *you* feel."

Lucien shook his head slowly and half turned from her. "I will find somewhere else to take my rest. This situation is most unseemly. I cannot remember a time when I was more mortified, unless it be a short while ago, while explaining this same infamous *behavior* to Lady Rosamunde." He bowed to Isidora and Faris. "I will send a guard to sit before your door, with instructions to allow no one entrance, not even me."

With that he swept out of the solar, leaving a faint scent of sandalwood in his wake. Isidora turned a furious eye upon Faris. "I hope you are satisfied, brother!"

"I am, at that. The Saxo-Franj has been humbled at last."

Isidora grabbed the majority of the covers and jerked

them over to her side, then changed her mind and tossed some back. "I do not want you snuggling against me for warmth in your sleep."

"No need, sister, for your anger throws off enough heat for me to keep my distance and still stay warm."

She ground her teeth and no angel came anywhere near for her to settle upon its bosom.

Lucien stalked his keep like a restless wolf. Women! If ever had there been a king of fools on this feast day, it was he.

Rather than risk disturbing his guests who slept in the main hall, he threw his mantle about his shoulders and went out a side door into the still, frozen night. The moonlight showed him that the narrow stone stairs were slick with ice, but he made his way down without mishap until the reassuring crunch of the bailey grounds met his feet.

Across the yard were the mews. Aye, horses were the best company he could keep just now.

He stepped into the dark warmth of the stable and soft nickers greeted him. He could just see a groom dozing in a pile of fodder. Careful not to wake the lad, Lucien took several handfuls of dried grass for each of his beasts, as well as the horses of his guests. The resultant contented munching soothed his heart. At least these creatures were well satisfied with him.

But his uncle would not be. Indeed, he never had been. At least, despite providing him with the best of everything, the stern Lord Conrad had never told him so.

Lucien sat down on an old, folded horse blanket and prepared to put himself into the contemplative state Deogal had taught him.

Unum in multa diversa moda—one in many manifestations. The Great Work. The distillation, reduction and ultimate fixation of the many into the Perfect One.

Nigredo, albedo, citrinitas, rubedo…black, white, yellow, red, stages of separation of every particle of dross from the impeccable substance that constituted the essence of purity—the Elixir. Omniscience and eternal life…a cure for all evils.

What made him think he, Lucien of the Grey Forest, had the character, much less the right, to pursue such divine knowledge, such power? Deogal must have been mistaken in accepting him as an apprentice. Such things were not meant for such as him, men who used their brawn as much as their brain…were they?

But was that not the point? Were not ordinary men capable of ultimately achieving unity with God, just as base metal might be transmuted into pure gold? Mauger was right about at least one thing—the very idea was Gnostic—and utter heresy.

Lucien sighed and put his head into his hands. All he could do was to keep on struggling. Alone. As ever. Aye, on the morrow he would rid himself of all these guests.

Including the estimable Faris al-Rashid *and* his sister.

Chapter Eleven

Isidora kicked at the bed furs. She envied Faris his sound sleep. By the sliver of light on the floor, the moon had moved halfway across the night sky and she still lay wide awake, staring at the brazier's glow, listening to the occasional pop of the coals.

How many times at home in Acre had she observed her father at his athanor, the clay furnace in which he heated the metals to their various states? It had seemed an endless, pointless task. Dry and dusty and inexplicable.

What was he doing? And why? It broke her heart to see him so absorbed. At times she was certain if she had dropped dead before him, he would have merely stepped over her body to reach his tongs and alembic or whatever crucible he needed.

Isidora hugged her pillow tighter. If only her father were still alive, she would gladly suffer his unwitting neglect. Glancing at Faris, bundled with his back to her, she wished the brazier in Lucien's solar threw off more heat. It would be a long time before she got used to the English cold.

Indeed, she hoped she would have the opportunity to get used to it.

"Milady? I am Larke, here to see you."

The soft voice reached Isidora from the other side of the door. Rather than risk waking Faris, she slipped out of bed to greet the young woman. Her bare feet alternately met wolfskins and wooden planking as she hurried across the chamber.

The girl was wearing a voluminous, white nightdress, and with her wild, red-blond hair cascading about her shoulders, she resembled some kind of escaped denizen of the heavenly firmament.

"What brings me the honor of your presence, Lady Larke?"

"Oh, but I am not a lady, just ask Lucien!" The girl grinned and caught Isidora's hand in one of hers. "Are you comfortable? I thought I'd see for myself, as I cannot rely on my brother to know enough to provide adequate blankets and so on."

"Well, I—" Isidora glanced over her shoulder: Faris yet slept on "—he is certainly comfortable enough. In fact, Lucien piled us with furs. But I am still a bit cold."

Larke raised the candle she held and peered into the solar. "Ah. Your Faris was the most handsome man at the mêlée, I trow! But come with me, my quarters will be more to your liking, perhaps."

Isidora felt a small thrill. To think that Larke had troubled herself to seek her out—what a joy, to have a friend in this place! "That sounds lovely."

Then she started as she realized a man stood in the shadows, but a few feet away, with a pike in his hands.

"Larke…who is that?"

"Oh, that is but Jager of Cumbria, whom Lucien sent to guard your door. I gave him a penny to let me by, but he will let you out for nothing—won't you, Jager? Come on." She gave the guard a smile as she towed Isidora past him.

Wood had long given way to rough stone beneath Isidora's feet and she wished she had donned her shoes. Larke led her around the perimeter of the central hall's upper expanse to a door set into the corner.

Larke ushered her into a small chamber, nearly filled with a bed and brazier, and much warmer than Lucien's solar.

"Now climb in and get under the covers," Larke ordered. "Just elbow your way in if those vixens won't move over," she added.

Isidora saw the bed already had at least two other occupants. The "vixens" giggled and made room. She sank into the feather bed with gratitude, and Larke followed.

"Now," her hostess began, "we can talk properly. Isidora, these are Brannwenn and Eyslk, cousins to the Lady Ceridwen, who is wife to Lucien's ally, Raymond de Beauchamp."

"Aye, the very same," chorused the girls.

"They are fostering here, and my task is to keep them out of trouble until they are wed. No small challenge, that! But the important question, Isidora, is what think you of our Rosamunde?"

"Oh, well, she is very beautiful, of course."

Larke snorted. "Of course! But is she good enough for our Mauger? *That* is the question!"

At this, Isidora could only open her mouth in surprise.

* * *

Lucien woke to something warm and heavy in his lap. Nothing that purred or licked his face, but it had its arms and legs wrapped around him in blatant invitation.

He opened his eyes. He had slept in the mews. And now this girl—delightful creature that she was—had climbed atop him. "Daphne? What are you doing?"

She yawned and snuggled closer. "Nothing, more's the pity."

"Get off of me and find someone else to do nothing with, then."

A lass from the village, Daphne was a luscious temptation, though one he had never succumbed to despite her best efforts. But why not? She was comely, reasonably clean, and more than willing…as willing as his own body apparently was. But that was beside the point, and she had made no move to obey him. "Get off. Now."

Something in his low tone must have gotten through to her, for she sat back, her pale, tousled hair haloed by the dawn. "My lord?" She quickly disentangled herself and got to her feet, her eyes wide.

Lucien followed and gazed down at her. "Who did you think I was?"

"I—I, forgive me, lord. I did not mean to make so bold with ye."

"Of course you did. But you should take more care in the dark, Daphne. You leave yourself far too vulnerable. You might have woken to find someone much more unpleasant than I between your legs. I could have been anyone."

She twisted her hands together. "Nay, you are like no other, Lord Lucien. Everyone says so…"

"Says what?"

"T-that you'll bring bounty to those who can get near enough to touch ye."

That nonsense again! "Do not listen to idle gossip, Daphne. And do not let me catch you in the mews in future, for any reason. Horses are no more toys than are men."

"Aye, lord." She curtsied and ran out, her breath clouding the cold air.

Bounty? Someone had had too much to drink and nothing better to do than to make up such a story. It had started upon his return from the east. Folk had begun the irritating habit of laying hands upon him with the flimsiest of excuses. Especially women. All ranks and ages.

With the horses clamoring for someone to break their fast, he woke the stable lad and headed out into the bailey.

Mauger approached, his long strides looking far too energetic for the early hour. "Ah, there you are! I saw that wench fly out the gates and I wondered."

"Wondered what?"

Mauger stood with his arms crossed over his chest. "If she fled your inevitable rejection, of course."

Lucien walked right past Mauger toward the hall of the keep, where his guests still slept, as he wished he were doing. "Aye, Mauger. I must keep myself pure for the Suitable Bride. But, as a matter of fact, the winsome Daphne only wanted to make use of me as a talisman, by touching as much of me as she could, all at once. That is my sole appeal, apparently. So I sent her packing."

"Hmm." Mauger caught up and fell into step beside him. "I wonder what started such a ridiculous notion?"

Lucien shrugged. "The summer drought ended when I

returned. We had a winter of few losses. The lambs and calves were born healthy and the cows' milk stayed sweet. And there have been no raids upon us."

"So they give you credit for all that?"

"And so they should! I sold my soul to my near name-sake, Lucifer, on their behalf."

At Mauger's look of dismay, Lucien had to laugh. "My good sir, please, you must know by now when I am jesting."

Mauger shook his head. "With all that goes on behind closed doors here, I know less than I ought, I'm certain."

"Do you wish to observe my operations, then? Do you want to become my assistant?" Lucien challenged him.

"Nay! I have no desire to be tainted with the vapors of such deviltry. It is bad enough we must send the Lady Rosamunde back to her family."

Lucien halted. "I thought she expressed an interest in you, Mauger. What of that? Surely such beautiful prospects do not often cross one's path?"

"She knows nothing of me. I was but a ready ear for her troubles. She likes to think I might grovel at her feet in gratitude for her attentions."

"And would you not?"

Mauger hesitated a fraction too long before his denial. "Nay…"

Lucien grinned. "Of course not. She will flee your 'inevitable rejection' as Daphne did mine."

"And what of this Saracen and his outrageous woman?"

"Isidora is his sister, Mauger. And Faris is not a Saracen, but a Christian, even as we are. But, I would see them return to the east as soon as possible."

"Why did she come all this way? It had to be important."

"I—"

At that moment Isidora emerged from the hall, looking pale but lovely in a blue-and-silver over-gown that Larke had been given but never worn. The sun struck gold on some small ornament around her neck—the Maltese cross she wore, Lucien recalled.

Behind her, Larke and Rosamunde emerged, as well, and Lucien's sense of being outnumbered went far beyond their three to his one. He bowed to them and nudged Mauger, who was staring stupidly at Rosamunde, to do the same.

"I bid you good morning, ladies. Glad am I to see you have made such cordial acquaintance." Indeed Lucien was not glad at all. Such an alliance could prove his undoing, in ways he no doubt could not as yet imagine. "Are you preparing to journey home, Rosamunde?"

"She is staying, Lucien," Larke announced. "Isidora and I believe you and your household may benefit from our continued presence."

"How?" Lucien blurted.

"If one stays, then so must both, Sir Lucien," Isidora said, as if he were a witless dolt. "A young lady alone in residence at your hall is a scandal. Two young ladies, and it is merely a happy gathering."

"But why should either of you—"

"My lord!" Larke surprised him with her sharp tone. "Isidora has reason for being here, the awkwardness of it caused only by your stubborn refusal to cooperate. She has explained everything to me. And I have decided that helping her is the least I can do, for by doing so I will also help you."

"Cooperate? What have I refused to do? I need no help. Pray enlighten me."

Larke stood upon his steps like a queen on high, declaring a proclamation. "Rosamunde tells me Mauger had much to say whilst they were closeted awaiting you last night. And Isidora, who could sleep no more than could I, came to me, as well. Rosamunde has decided, as your former betrothed, that since she has thrown you over, you should wed Isidora instead."

Lucien remained speechless for a moment, then turned to Mauger, who was still staring. "What did you tell her? Nay. You will not command me in this, nor in any other thing! None of you!"

Fists clenched at his sides, Lucien climbed the stairs to where the women were. Rosamunde backed off a step, making him ashamed of being so obvious in his anger. But better that they see it rather than feel it. He pinned Isidora with his gaze. "What say you to this grand scheme of Lady Larke's and Rosamunde's?"

Though her color was now high, Isidora remained steady. "She flatters me with such an impossible suggestion, my lord. Well do I know you have no intention, much less desire, of keeping me underfoot any longer than you must. I am unwelcome here, and I beg your pardon for arriving unannounced with my brother."

"I never said you are not welcome, Isidora."

"You did not have to say it, it is obvious."

"Oh, then it was not you I embraced, after all?"

She blushed and looked at her feet. "Let us speak of it no more. Please, show me where you do the Work, my lord," she asked.

"Why should I?"

"It will help me decide about the gift I yet hold in trust for you."

An unreasoning panic rose within Lucien. "I will not show you, for it is none of your concern. It is a private place and a private endeavor."

Rosamunde put her hands on her hips. "And had I continued with the betrothal, you would not have told me of this endeavor at all, no doubt?"

Lucien began to feel like a cornered beast. "No doubt whatsoever."

At last Mauger found his voice. "Em, ladies, let us amuse ourselves in some way other than baiting Lucien, here, shall we?"

"Aye, why do you not take them out on a ride over the fells, Mauger? Go hawking. Play hoodman-blind." Lucien waved a hand vaguely. "Or something."

"Many thanks, but no," said Rosamunde, as if he had been serious. "I would not like to leave your other guests behind."

"What will your lord father say, Lady Rosamunde, when he learns of this turn of events?" Mauger asked.

She smiled, revealing a mischievous charm Lucien had not seen before. "He will probably come here to give Lord Lucien a thrashing in person. Then he will agree to whomever I have my heart set on."

Lucien fumed. "Oh, that is something to look forward to, indeed! Who do you have as an alternate, then?"

"Why, Sir Mauger, of course. I thought I had made that clear already."

"Just to be certain, lady," Lucien said weakly. He exchanged looks with Mauger. It was one thing to avert the whim of a maiden, but quite another to avoid the will of her powerful father. Just as his own father's will could not be denied, even from the grave.

Perhaps he could help Mauger escape Rosamunde's trap, in exchange for being left unfettered himself a while longer. "What say you, Mauger?"

Mauger opened and closed his mouth, then bowed over her hand and uttered the fateful words, "Lady Rosamunde's will is my command."

Lucien pulled the seneschal aside. "What are you doing?"

Mauger turned a hard gaze upon Lucien. "I know how your mind works, my lord. If I can marry, then so can you. Our agreement remains intact and I need not summon your uncle."

So, Mauger thought to sacrifice himself, his independence, to bring Lucien to heel? Nay. "You want her, in truth, Mauger, admit it! You are lusting after a highborn maiden, as you ever have urged me to do."

Mauger stole a glance at Rosamunde. "There is more to her than meets the eye."

"Such as her father and brothers and uncles, I trow!" Of a sudden, Lucien remembered he had spent the night in a horse barn. He looked down at himself. Straw, dirt and wisps of dried grass adorned his mantle and leggings. He was hungry and cold.

"I need to gain the sanctity of my solar, Mauger. I will have no more talk of marriage this day, to anyone or about anyone, but I promise you I will think upon it. Let us first see to my other guests."

Mauger nodded his assent and Lucien was relieved he did not have to shake another spit-besmeared hand.

Isidora watched as Lucien returned from his private consultation with Mauger. He did not look any happier, but nor did he look angry. He paused before her and she gazed up at him.

A nimbus of light from the morning sun crowned his head. Except for a black eye from his beating on the pond, he looked little different than he had the first time she had seen him on the street in Acre. Just as handsome, just as lordly. Why did she care, when all he showed her was indifference?

Aye, he had held her close. But now he returned her gaze with a look of puzzlement. Not affection, nor concern.

Merely an expression befitting a man who has discovered something wholly unexpected at his door and knows not what to do with it.

"Isidora…"

His voice, so smooth, saying her name…

"We needs must have a talk."

Her heart sank. "As you will, my lord."

"After nones, then, once I have seen everyone off."

"Where?"

He hesitated. Swallowed. Then took a deep breath. "Meet me in the chapel. From there I will take you to my *laboratorium*."

Before she could show her appreciation for the enormity of his offer, he had stalked away ahead of her up to the hall.

Chapter Twelve

The midday meal was long over and most of the guests from the revels had departed. Head to head with Faris, Mauger was attempting to win a game of chess. Lady Rosamunde cast him glances as she worked her embroidery by the wintry light of a small window.

Isidora did not know exactly when nones was, but thought it better to be early than late. She declined Larke's offer of a maid or servant to accompany her on her supposed quest for fresh air and made her way out of the hall.

Even with a woolen mantle drawn about her face, the chill air bit into Isidora's nostrils and seeped through to her skin. What a place. She missed the warm breezes of the east, the graciousness and easy affection of the people. Small wonder these English were so hard, having to live under such conditions.

By the time she reached the chapel she was shaking with the cold. A vine, its leaves tinged with red, climbed its walls, creeping toward what light and warmth it could find. Isidora admired its tenacity.

She touched the door's great round, iron handle, wondering if she should go in or wait outside. A crunch of footsteps came closer. She turned to see Lucien, walking about as if it were not a frozen, uninhabitable place he lived in. Beside him lumbered a large, shaggy hound of some sort.

"Your hand will stick to that if you don't wear gloves in this weather."

"I have none," she admitted.

Lucien stopped before her and took one of her chapped hands into his leather-clad ones and examined it. "Larke will give you some. But for now, wear mine."

Before she could either accept or object, he had doffed his gloves and slid them onto her hands. The leather was fine, they were lined with soft wool, and so large on her she could scarcely keep them from falling off.

But they were wonderfully warm. From the heat of his body. To her own dismay, she shivered again at the very thought. "M-my thanks, sir."

Lucien frowned and swept his mantle from his shoulders to hers. She closed her eyes for an instant. Now she was wrapped in not only his heat, but his scent. Elusive, smoky sandalwood...

He jostled her with his elbow. "Are you going to sleep? Come. It is not here."

He walked away, as if Isidora's following him was inevitable. Only the dog had the courtesy to pause and look back at her. She trotted to catch up.

"What is this dog you have? It seems an unlikely companion for one such as you, my lord. I would have thought an elegant gaze-hound to be more of your liking."

Lucien grunted his amusement and scratched the beast

behind its ears. "You have some odd ideas about me, Isidora. But this wolfhound was given me by my friend Raymond de Beauchamp. One does not refuse such a princely gift. Not from Raymond, at any rate. He adores its sire and considers my having the pup as strong a bond between us as if I had wed his sister, had Raymond a sister."

"Pup?"

"Oh, aye, he will be twice this size before he is done."

"Heavens. What have you named him?"

"Raymond named him Gawaine. Though I have not noticed his strength increasing before noontide."

"Ah. Well, let us hope he has some of Sir Gawaine's other characteristics, then."

Lucien brought her to a wall covered in the same leafy vines as was the chapel, into which was set a low, arched door. He unlocked it with a stout key and shot the bolt free. Its heavy hinges creaked and the nails studding the wood were set in the shape of a triangle. After the briefest hesitation, he motioned her through.

"Watch your head."

"I thank you, Sir Lucien." Isidora ducked as she entered and, with a fresh shiver, looked about. The chamber was built into the thickness of the wall itself, lit by windows high up, so one could not see in or out, except the sky. The walls were white, plastered stone, which reflected even more light.

But drawn upon them, by a skilled hand, were all manner of signs and symbols. Suns, moons, stars, runes, dragons and animals and humans…nothing like her father's stained and smoke-smudged workshop.

Where his had been a jumble of whole and broken

crockery and glass vessels, bowls and jars of unlabeled substances, discarded failures and hopeful but incomplete experiments, Lucien's *laboratorium* was a place of order and clarity.

Crucibles were arranged by size, tongs and tools hung neatly on racks. He had an immaculate balance, with brass weights, and each of his containers had a label—though not decipherable to the uninitiated.

Dominating the space at one end was the athanor, the smelting furnace, where each metal endured a trial of purification by fire. But it was unlit, and if possible, the chamber was even colder than outdoors.

The whole of it filled her with both dread and longing. She missed her father so much. And with all her heart, she did not want Lucien to travel that same desperate, impossible path to nowhere.

There was one thing written on the wall that she could read. *Ora, lege, relege, labora, et invenis.* Pray, read, reread, work, and you shall find. She turned to face Lucien, who stood in the only shadowed part of the room. Watching her every move. "I did not know you could draw, Lucien. These figures are quite marvelous."

"Is this enough for you, Isidora? I would rather we leave now." His voice was low, emotionless, yet she knew it had cost him much to bring her to his secret place.

"Sir Lucien, from what I have seen here, your approach to this is a bit skewed."

"How so?" He stepped toward her, a challenge in the set of his broad shoulders, in the elegant tilt of his head, in his velvet voice.

She blinked. "Oh…no doubt I am mistaken."

"Finish what you were going to say."

Somehow he now had her backed up against one of the tables built along the wall. "Perhaps, my lord, you are too…too aggressively methodical. Alchemy requires method, aye, but it also requires intuition, subtlety and inspiration."

"This you learned from Deogal?"

Isidora started to nod, then shook her head. "I learned it from the texts."

Lucien put his hands upon her shoulders. "And those are…?"

"The ones I took from Kalle FitzMalheury's dungeon."

"What? You did not!"

"I did! His guards had found a pile of scrolls in an alcove, they were burning them to stay warm at night. I had bribed them to let me pass and I saw symbols of the Work on one of the scrolls they had not yet touched, and others had marks like what one sees in Egypt. I picked up a couple of them and hid them in my skirt. I made a joke about putting good use to worthless old letters, and continued on my errand—to free you—without giving them back."

Lucien's fingers tightened on her upper arms. "Fitz-Malheury would have skinned you alive, had he known. But they probably are indeed worthless, and you should not have taken such a risk!"

"Well, I did have cause to regret it, because a few days later I saw those same foolish guards hanging from the curtain wall. At first I assumed it was because they had allowed your escape. Then later, once I had had a closer look at the scrolls, I thought perhaps it was because Kalle had found out they had been burning a long-lost library full of ancient secrets."

Isidora wondered at Lucien's hold on her, even though she was certain he was barely aware he had her in his grasp. For once again, she saw that look in his eyes. The faraway look so familiar to her she would recognize it in her dreams. The look of an alchemist who has only molten metal on his mind.

By God, she wanted to slap it right off his face.

Instead she pushed herself away from the table edge and impulsively threw her arms around his middle. At this assault, Gawaine, who had been sitting patiently all the while, stood up and barked, the sound echoing in the cold *laboratorium.* Isidora buried her face against Lucien's chest. Warm. Fragrant with his unique scent. "Do not ask me to show them to you, please."

He had not put his arms around her, but nor had he pulled away. "You must, Isidora."

"It is too dangerous. They are incomplete. You yourself told me what danger a little knowledge presents."

Now he did step back from her, the better to look her in the eye, no doubt. But he still loomed over her, holding her hands, and his voice was quiet and stern.

"A little knowledge to one who has none to begin with is dangerous, aye. But to one who already has much, it could lead to the final piece of a vast puzzle that has been painstakingly assembled for years on end. Knowing your father's struggles, knowing mine, how can you even consider withholding this from me?"

Isidora did not know what to say at first. To be so near Lucien, in such a short time, after such a long while, and after so much bitterness was like drinking too much wine at once. She felt his warm hands move around her waist, to settle at her back, and the words came at last. He deserved the truth from her, if nothing else.

"Because, Lucien, I do not want you to take what you believe to be that final piece and have it lead you astray to madness and death, as it did my father. So, do you see now? I killed him! It was my fault, it was my bringing him the scrolls that pushed him over the edge into the abyss."

"Oh, Isidora, do not think such things of yourself."

"It is the truth."

"Your father was a brilliant man, devoted to the Work. It would take much more than some moldy old scrolls to bring ruin upon him. Put your mind at ease."

She withdrew from him. "Let me see your hands, Lord Lucien."

"Why?"

"Just give them to me!"

He held them out and she took them into hers. They were strong, shapely hands, with long fingers and broad palms. They also had black stains of various degrees of intensity, along with rusty red ones, nicks and abrasions and a few blistered burn marks.

"Look at the abuse these have suffered, all for the cooking of mercury and antimony!"

"Anything worth having bears a price."

Isidora looked into his eyes, still holding on to his hands. "You would not want to pay the price, if you knew just how dearly bought is the Elixir. There are worse consequences, much worse than sore hands."

To her surprise, Lucien's fingers squeezed hers in a gentle caress, and he spoke in a voice to match. "Do you not understand the nature of the Elixir, Isidora?"

A vision of her father came to Isidora, as he staggered and fell in his madness, unable to eat or sleep, his body withering, his mind a wasteland… Her eyes brimmed, her throat closed, and she could not answer.

"Let me tell you…just as it can turn base metal to gold, it can cure all ills. *All* ills, Isidora. Body, mind and soul. Do you realize what that means?"

She shook her head. She did not want to know.

"It means that even if all the afflictions you spoke of were visited upon me during the course of the Work, a single minute speck of the Elixir, mixed in a barrel of water or wine and a sip swallowed, would effect a cure. That is how powerful it is."

"B-but, Lucien, all it takes is the smallest misstep in its preparation, perhaps months in the making, requiring certain seasons to aid specific processes—aye, I know these things—and there would be no Elixir. Just a worthless puddle of disgusting elements. And that is all your efforts will ever come to, do you not see? If my father, the great Master Deogal, could not do it after years of effort, how can you ever hope to succeed?"

Lucien straightened and released her hands. "You came so far, by land and by sea, to tell me that? I do not believe you, Isidora Binte Deogal, and I do not think you truly believe it yourself. Elsewise you would not be here."

"Nay, Sir Lucien. I am here because my father charged me to come with his dying breath. But I do not know what is worse—breaking my vow to him or giving you what I fear will lead to certain death."

Lucien put a hand to his brow. "Do as you will, then. I will carry on, no matter what. With or without the gift you brought. Come, let us take our leave of this place, as it obviously brings you no joy."

With a heavy heart, Isidora went back out into the fresh air and waited while Lucien relocked the door. The frost on the tree limbs sparkled, birds chattered and she even heard an occasional drip, as if some hidden warmth was melting the ice from the eaves of the workshop.

Gawaine stationed himself in front of her and gave her a toothy grin, his tail thumping the ground. She knelt down, stroked his head gingerly, and he rewarded her with a generous lick to her mouth.

"Ugh!" She hurriedly stood and wiped her lips with the back of her still-gloved hand. It hardly tasted better.

Lucien faced her with a grin even more charmingly idiotic than his dog's. "Better his kiss than mine, eh?"

"I would not go that far, my lord. But then again, I have no idea what your kiss is like."

The smile vanished from Lucien's face and was replaced by a raw, hungry, dangerous look. He would not allow such a challenge to go unmet.

He stayed his ground.

And for once, she stayed hers.

He clenched and unclenched his jaw. "What would you have me do, Isidora? I scarcely know whether to flee before you or to throw you on your back and—"

She stared at him. "Pardon me? Is there not some course in the middle you might consider, my lord?"

Lucien's eyes darkened. She heard a growl—either from him or his dog—and in the next moment he caught her in a hard, breathless embrace. His mouth moved over her neck, burning along the curve of her jaw, across her cheek and at last to her lips.

Lucien. His blood, heating hers. It was bliss. As close to pure happiness as Isidora had come in her life. Her heart pounded, expanded and soared with delight. She abandoned herself to his kiss. It might never happen again. Indeed she could not allow it.

But his arms bound her so tightly, with her feet barely touching the ground, she could not have escaped even had she wanted to. Though she had first met him as a knight, she had had no idea that the Lucien she had come to know—the scholar, the alchemist, the landlord, could also be the impassioned man who held her now.

Then, just as suddenly as the kiss had started, it stopped. Lucien, breathing hard, eased her down and away from him. It felt as though she had been torn from a comfort she could not live without. Her eyes welled with tears against the loss.

He looked at her, aghast. "I should not have done that. I am sorry, I—"

The hurt grew to an unbearable pain. "Nay, you misunderstand. I am glad of it, Lucien, truly."

"Nay, that is not right."

"Why not?" She could contain herself no longer. "Are you so heartless, my lord, or merely blind?"

He stared, now astonished. "Obviously, I must be both, if you are asking."

"For one with such a keen intellect, you are woefully lacking in powers of simple observation, my lord."

"Oh, indeed. Tell me what I have missed, then, Isidora.

The fact that you hound me with your gaze whenever we are together? That your cheeks flush whenever I so much as flicker an eyelid in your direction? That you hang on my every word, and can doubtless quote back to me every pearl I have spoken since I first walked through your door in Acre? That you adore me from the safety of your self-imposed inferiority?"

Isidora gasped. She knew that a truly highborn woman would have slapped him for saying such things, or at least tried. But it was not in her. And, the only reason she had to slap him was that everything she had goaded him into saying was true. Yet her pride could not allow him the last word.

"Oh, you are worse than any *advocatus,* my lord. I pity the woman you finally marry."

"Indeed?" His soft tone told her he doubted the truth of her second statement, not her first.

She shivered, all alone inside his mantle. "I mean, she had best keep her wits about her."

Lucien crossed his arms and nodded his agreement. "She will need them, and more besides. And the same goes for the poor besotted fool who takes *you* to the marriage bed."

To her own pathetic surprise, Isidora found herself encouraged by this. "So, you do not consider my being wed one day a possibility beyond the scope of mind or magic?"

"Not entirely." He gave her the smallest of smiles and, once more, for that moment, all was right with her world. Then, with his next words, he put it all to ruin again.

"I should tell you, Isidora. I think I should give up on Mauger's idea that I must be wed. He has threatened to expose my activities to my uncle, but I am coming to the point where I would rather have Lord Conrad put me under siege than make me marry against my will. Or, as you have pointed out to me, inflict my heresies upon some unsuspecting woman."

Isidora bit her lip as a terrible, wonderful idea formed in her mind. "Your uncle, Lord Conrad, is on his way?"

Lucien shrugged. "Maybe not now, but he could easily be, once the roads dry a bit."

"Then consider this, Sir Lucien. What if you were to present me to him as your choice of bride? All we would need do is convince him until he leaves. Then I could be called away by my family, decide to become a nun, or even conveniently die, and you would be free. Especially if I died, you would be in mourning for some time, would you not?"

"Oh of course! What an idea, Isidora. The very thought is absurd. We would fool no one. And he would still want me to produce an heir."

She lifted her chin. "That would all depend upon how convincing we were."

"But what of Mauger, and my people? They would surely see through such a farce. It would hardly be fair to you, either, Isidora. The risk to your reputation would be awful."

"How badly do you want to continue the Work? You are lord here, no one would dare question you. As for my reputation—is it of any concern at all? I have no family beyond Faris. I am an orphan. No one cares if I become a harem girl or even a whore."

"I care. And, I would hope, you care. I will not use you in such a way, Isidora. I must simply face my uncle's anger as it comes."

"Why will you not let me help you?"

"I do not need your help, Isidora. I know you mean well. But it is not proper."

She dug her nails into her palms. "To hell with what is proper!"

Lucien's face paled. "This has gone far enough. You must return to Acre before you are entirely ruined."

"You are mistaken. I am already ruined, Lord Lucien!" *I see no one but you. Nothing but your face in my dreams.* "I have nothing to return to. Only a shell, for Kalle's men have destroyed my father's home in search of the Elixir. I will end my days scribing merchant's contracts in the marketplace."

He turned partly away from her, as if he could not bear to face her pain. "I know your fear, Isidora. My yearning for forbidden knowledge has separated me from much I might have been blessed to be a part of. But there are some things I cannot explain, cannot put into words. It is like trying to describe the taste of honey to one who has never had it. Or love… Do you see?"

"How can I? If you know this, then you are simply mad to continue. Perhaps you have truly earned your loneliness."

"I never said I was lonely!"

"Oh? Then why is it you kiss me and hold me as if you were a drowning man?"

"That is different. You…you beguile me. I cannot help myself. Yet another reason you should be away from here." He rubbed his arms. "Let us go back to the keep. It is too cold yet for such fresh-air dalliances."

"You should take back your mantle. Here." She started to unpin it.

"Keep it, I pray you. I know how long it took for me to

get used to the cold again, once I had returned from the east, so you must be suffering the same."

Aye. My suffering has not changed at all. I am still alone as ever despite people all around.

Chapter Thirteen

"But, my lord…to go so far, when the prize is not certain…?" Earm's big hands shook as he poured wine into the silver goblet upon the table in Kalle FitzMalheury's refectory.

Seated in his great chair of carved, imported oak, Kalle curled his lip in a way calculated to make his would-be advisor, Earm, cringe even more than was his wont.

"England, far? To one who has pirated the coasts and trampled the peasants of half the known world? It is my opinion, Earm, that your hesitation to return to your homeland is due to the fact that I've explained you'll be hanged if anyone recognizes you, not because it is 'far.'"

"If you say so, my lord, then you will of course understand if I do not accompany you—"

"That is all the more reason for you to accompany me! I will wring from you every last drop of the servitude you owe me, Earm, but I will also protect you, and in the end, make you a wealthy man. Trust me."

With that, Kalle curved his sneer into a grin and Earm's face turned a gratifying shade of pale gray.

"B-but, how do you know the girl took anything of value with her when she fled?"

"Because, my dear fellow, nothing of value was found when my men searched the *laboratorium!* Deogal had reached a critical point in the Work. I felt it in my bones—that is why I left him alone for so long. When he died—and damn his timing—who else did he have to confide in but that impertinent girl of his? His old Templar comrades? Hardly. But she slipped away, despite Faris being sent to hold her.

"And now he, too, is gone. So, Earm, I have two things to accomplish in England. One is to recover the Key to the Work, and the other is to punish Faris for his treachery. No one escapes having once betrayed me. You'd do well to remember that yourself."

"Aye, milord."

Kalle took a closer look at Earm. The man was sweating! A mass of quivering, terrified flesh that had once been a bold soldier of the cross. Perhaps he'd been too harsh of late. Aye, he needed Earm to at least be able to sit within a lance length of him and not shake like a maiden on her wedding night.

"Go and relax in the baths, Earm. It will do you good. I'll have Shunnar send Lina herself to attend you."

Bewildered gratitude spread across Earm's face. He sagged with apparent relief.

"Go! Before I change my mind."

Earm rose and straightened his broad shoulders before bowing to Kalle FitzMalheury.

Earm sank up to his neck in hot, silken water. Rose petals floated upon its surface and curls of steam wafted their perfume to him. Lina, a lovely Berber woman whose sorry fate, like his own, was to be part of Kalle's household, rubbed Earm's tight shoulders with practiced hands.

She paused for a moment. "You are unhappy tonight, my lord?"

"Every night, Lina."

"What misfortune dogs your steps, then? It seems you have the favor of the master, to be here like this."

"That is like having the favor of the devil. I am damned, with or without his patronage."

"Why do you say that?"

Earm turned his head, so he could see her face as he replied. "Do you know, Lina, 'Earm' is not my true name? It is a name *he* gave me, as a jest. It means 'wretched.' And he was right."

"What then, is your birth name, *effendi?*"

Earm shook his head. "I was struck down in battle. I do not remember my name. I know nothing about myself, save the unpleasantries which Lord FitzMalheury tells me."

She slid her hand over his shoulder and gave his chest a slow, light caress. A tremor ran through him, much different from those he had experienced earlier in the evening. Her voice matched the touch of her fingers.

"You should speak no more of these sad things. I will give you another name, one that will make your heart shine anew. It will be our secret."

Earm found himself smiling. "Truly?"

She put her cheek next to his, and whispered, "Nadir. *Beloved.* That is what you shall be, from this moment forward."

"Why show me such kindness, Lina?"

In one graceful movement she was in the water, facing him, her bare legs straddling his and her chemise afloat and billowing. He could scarcely breathe for the swift effect she had produced. Lina caught him around the neck.

"Because, Nadir, I see in you a champion, and I have great need of a champion. I wish to leave my lord Kalle, and I can help you do the same."

"Aye," he murmured, already becoming lost in the waves of her loose, dark hair. He cupped one of her lush, round breasts and kissed it through the wet fabric. She arched her back and wrapped her legs around his middle.

From a dark doorway Kalle watched Lina work her magic on the hapless Earm. As a tester of men, the girl was priceless. To know the weaknesses of those he used was always wise.

And to know that he himself could resist her potent charms—indeed, resist those of any woman at all—gave him a well-deserved sense of superiority. The benefits of a pure bloodline, brutal training and high rank would ever outweigh those of love. Only the weak fell prey to fleshly pleasures.

And yet…something stirred in him at the sight of their impassioned embrace. Not lust…nay, it was far worse than that. A despicable sense of yearning…it occurred to Kalle that he had not felt a kindly intended human touch in more years than he could recall.

Ayshka… Even now, he wondered if she had kept his gift…. He closed his eyes against the sudden pain.

There was no profit now in wanting something so vulgar and common as love. He ground his teeth and turned away. Let them have their moment together. It would not last.

Nay. The only thing of permanent value was the Elixir—and the gold it would bring. Brother Deogal had been close, very close. His daughter was not as stupid as she pretended.

And Lucien, the one who had taken *his* place—the one he had not been able to break—now, mayhap there was one capable of finishing what the old man had started.

He would find them both. And take from them what was rightfully his—for might, of course, made right.

Chapter Fourteen

Hoofbeats thundered over the drawbridge and Lucien's stomach tightened into a knot. In the cobbled bailey, he straightened from his examination of a slight puffiness in his palfrey's foreleg. Aye. No one made such a noisy arrival as his lord father's brother, Conrad.

"Mauger!" Lucien bellowed. "Get you down here and tell me you did not send for Lord Conrad."

The seneschal ran down the stairs to the courtyard, quick on his feet despite his size. He halted before Lucien and crossed his arms over his massive chest. "I did not send for Lord Conrad."

Lucien stroked his horse's shoulder and nodded to a groom to lead the beast back to the mews. He met Mauger's hard gaze, then glanced at the heavy beams of the gate, opening even as they spoke. His heart sank.

"Oh, God. What do I tell him? I swear, Mauger, you must decide this day whether you serve him or me. You cannot do both." For an instant, Lucien caught a flash of sympathy in the seneschal's usually frowning countenance.

Mauger uncrossed his arms. "Never will I lie to your uncle. But nor will I ever reveal to him anything that I do not honestly believe is important to your ultimate welfare."

"In other words, you will play the same game you ever have. Keep me on the edge of torment while trying to satisfy him."

"Lucien, that is not—"

Mauger was cut off by the clatter of hooves into the bailey. As one, he and Lucien turned and bowed to Lord Conrad as he trotted to them, his retinue following, all clad in the red and white of his household.

"Lucien!"

His uncle jumped down and caught him in a hard embrace. Lucien froze, not certain how to respond to this unexpected overture.

"My lord, I hope the journey was not difficult."

Conrad shook his head and actually smiled through his close-cropped, gray-streaked beard. "A bit, but no matter. Your mother is coming, too, a few days behind me."

At this, Lucien could scarcely gather his wits to speak a coherent sentence. "What brings such favor from you, my lord? I did not expect a visit until full spring was upon us. I fear I am not yet prepared to honor you properly."

"Come, my boy, you need not be so formal!"

Lucien narrowed his eyes at Mauger. Since when had his relationship with his uncle ever been anything *but* formal? Though the thought was terrible to contemplate, there remained the possibility that Mauger had lied right to his face. What might have brought his uncle here, with a smile on his lips?

Mauger slowly paled under Lucien's gaze, but Lord

Conrad did not seem to notice. "The pigeon arrived in good time, Mauger. Bearing good news, for a change! So, Lucien, I would meet your Rosamunde right away."

Mauger studied the buckle on Lord Conrad's reins. *Later, sir,* Lucien promised with his eyes. "Uncle, please have some dinner first, it is getting on toward evening."

"Surely she will be dining with us?"

Lucien could not let this go on. "My lord, there has been a misunderstanding. Rosamunde—"

"Rosamunde is no longer amenable to the proposal," Mauger blurted. "But there is an alternate choice."

Lucien had to make a conscious effort not to grab Mauger and shake him. The announcement of such a turnaround should not be received by Conrad on an empty belly. What had come over Mauger? Was he *trying* to make things worse?

Then, at that moment, they became so, without Mauger's help. For, no doubt having heard the noise of the new arrivals, Isidora, Larke and Rosamunde all emerged into the bailey and approached them.

Before Conrad could respond beyond the deep frown he had assumed, Mauger said, "Here she is now. Ah, Lady Isidora! How good of you and your companions to brave the cold."

Lucien bit his lip. Isidora and Larke looked at each other, then Isidora smiled and curtsied before Sir Conrad.

"Good evening, my lord."

Conrad threw a sharp glance to Lucien and cleared his throat. "What a charming accent! It sounds almost Byzantine. But of course that is absurd."

"Ah, well, my lord, my brother is of late from those lands, and we are so close, his ways rub off on me."

She raised her brows at Lucien. What did he want her to do? He and Mauger were up to some game, that much was clear. But Mauger stared at his own feet, his face pale and his brow furrowed.

Lucien gave her a forced smile. "Allow me to introduce you to my uncle, Lord Conrad, lady."

Conrad interrupted with a wave of his gloved and be-ringed hand. "Surely if this be your choice, it is her father I would meet."

At this Lucien's jaw looked hard enough to split a rock. His nostrils flared and his mouth set in thin line. Isidora was afraid if she mentioned her father was dead, she would merely increase his ire.

Finally, Larke spoke. "I hope, my lords, that you might wait until our lady-mother arrives before conducting any marriage negotiations."

"Aye, let's do," growled Lucien. "For I have made no 'choice,' as you well know, Uncle."

Conrad glowered. "Indeed, there will be no choosing beyond what I and your mother agree upon. Such a matter of import cannot be left up to you alone."

At this something very like a sneer curled Lucien's lip, then vanished. He met his uncle's gaze.

"It is too cold to stand out here talking." Lucien led the way back inside, not seeming to care whether anyone followed or not. But the return to the relative warmth of the hall was a relief.

"We will settle this when your mother gets here." Conrad threw his sword and dagger down onto the table with a clatter.

Isidora felt the situation spiraling out of control. Now

that this man of immense power and influence had arrived, no one's will but his mattered. Not even Lucien's.

Within two days Lucien's hall was overflowing with nobles. His uncle's retainers, friends and hangers-on, all hoping for a moment of Lord Conrad's attention. In addition, a bold and well-favored young man, Wace, who hailed from Raymond de Beauchamp's household, arrived on the heels of the rest.

In the midst of such chaos, Isidora wondered what Lucien's mother would be like. She herself had long been without one. Leaving her respectable widowhood to marry Deogal had cost her own mother her life and her honor.

Apart from Ayshka's family's rejection was the subsequent shame of leprosy. The Franj believed that leper women had loose morals, were lustful and full of vice. And that God had made his judgment upon them painfully obvious.

Isidora wondered…how could Faris have found the woman who was their mother and not taken Isidora to her? Was it only because of the terrible disease—or was there reason beyond that? She should ask him.

She found him in the solar, looking at various books and scrolls Lucien had there—more than she had ever imagined existed outside a monastery. "You are recovered, Faris?"

He casually set aside the manuscript he had unrolled. "I am, thank God for his mercy."

Isidora approached him and put her hand over his. They had spent many long hours in the saddle, aboard ships and afoot. Too many for there to be any lies between them.

"Faris, tell me, could you not have brought me to see our mother, one last time?"

He looked at her, then out the narrow window that allowed light into the small space. "She forbade it, Isidora. I could not disobey her. And, in truth, I was more concerned with my own questions…I asked her who my father was."

"Oh, Faris. That is hard, indeed."

"She would not tell me, other than that he was of the house of Salah al-Din. She said the risks were too great." The corners of his mouth lifted. "But, her gift to me was knowledge of you."

Isidora's heart rose like a feather on the wind. "A gift?"

"Aye." His smile faded as he met her gaze. "I was in the service of Kalle FitzMalheury, Isidora."

"So you said before." But she wished it were not true.

"He sent me to search your father's workshop—the *laboratorium*. All I found was rubble and an empty house. So I came after you. But I swear to you, Isidora, that never would I have robbed you, nor harmed you, no matter what Lord Kalle had ordered."

"Harmed me? Why would he order you to do that?"

Faris cast his gaze about, as if in search of something that might ease his shame. "He did not. But he expected me to find you and…question you. I would never have done so in the manner he questioned Lucien."

"Of course not, Faris."

"By the holy shoes and beard of Allah—nay. But Fitz-Malheury surely knows by now that I have betrayed him. He will come after me. I should not remain here any longer, for it is only a matter of time, and I would not draw him to you."

Isidora's hand tightened over Faris's. "But, if he wants

to punish you and to 'question' me, then what difference does it make if we are together? And, no doubt, he wishes to reacquaint himself with Lucien, as well. Should we not try to make a united stand?"

"Against whom?"

Isidora dropped Faris's hand and whirled about to face Lucien. She had not intended her actions to resemble those of a guilty person, but she was aware that so they must appear.

"My lord Lucien, you startled me."

"My apologies, lady. Sir Faris, do you feel stronger now that you have had rest and food?"

Faris bowed. "I do, and many thanks. Isidora and I were speaking of Kalle FitzMalheury and his inevitable pursuit of me."

The sight of Lucien's grave, beautiful face made Isidora lose the thread of her thoughts. Indeed she scarcely heard his next words.

"I have a thing or two to discuss with Kalle, myself. I will welcome him to my hall, should he come so far."

The undercurrent of menace in Lucien's tone took Isidora by surprise. "Please, stay clear of arguments with him. He is ruthless and deadly. A sorcerer."

Lucien smiled without humor. "He caught me when I was off guard. I will not be so easy to catch again. Indeed he may find himself in an uncomfortable situation one day."

Faris said, "Do not make him more of a foe than he is already. Let him think you have learned your lesson. Be wary. Be prepared."

"Aye, have no worry on that account. I bid you excuse us, Faris, I would have a word with your sister."

Once they were alone, a hard hand gripped her arm. "Isidora." Lucien's voice was low but serious. "Do not create any more lies about you and I being wed or betrothed. I command you in this, as I cannot command Larke or Rosamunde."

"Why not?"

"Because such lies do not make it—"

"Nay, why command *me?*"

"You are not under anyone's protection but mine whilst you are in this country. Faris has no power or influence here."

"Except for what he enjoys by the mere fact of his being a man."

"Aye, as do I."

"But he is my brother."

"Do you obey him, any more than Larke obeys me?"

"Nay, but I have only known of him these few months."

"That does not matter, he still should have authority over you—if you truly believed him to be your brother."

Isidora's breath caught. "If I did not, would I have been in the same bed with him?"

Lucien smiled wickedly. "You were with me."

Isidora sniffed. "You have never posed any threat to my virtue, I think."

"You should be glad of that, Isidora."

But was she? Well, if she did not know for certain, then he had no business knowing, either. "Aye, so I should," she replied firmly.

"Which is precisely why I am telling you not to play any games of pretense with my uncle. He has no sense of humor when it comes to matters like my marriage."

"You are fortunate to be of so wealthy a family you need

not wait for an inheritance or marry an heiress to have your own household."

"Aye, so I am. But that does not mean that they keep any less a grip on their purse strings."

"What do you want, then, Lucien? To be free of the prospect of a woman and children of your own?"

Lucien raked a hand back through his hair. "My mother expects me to marry, she is counting on it, for I am her only son."

"But will you?"

"Aye. I will. But on my own terms."

Isidora could not help but smile. "It will interest me to meet your lady-mother when she arrives."

Lucien scowled and did not reply.

Chapter Fifteen

His lady-mother did arrive soon thereafter, borne in a curtained litter like some eastern queen. In the women's solar, with her ladies out of earshot, Lucien took his mother's cool, slender hand. She looked up at him, her eyes liquid with feeling. With love. But she said nothing at all. He would have felt less guilty had she ever even once ranted or raved or shouted or ordered him beaten.

But no such thing had ever happened. Sometimes he wanted to shake her, to jar free the anger he was certain still lurked beneath her long-suffering surface calm.

As if in compensation, his father had rarely revealed anything but a stern acceptance of Lucien's expected successes, whether at learning to play the lute or to smash an enemy's skull with a mace. And Lucien's uncle was of much the same mind as his brother, Lucien's father, had been.

In that, and in the way he gazed at Amelie, betimes… No, that could not be so. Could it?

Lucien looked at his mother's head, now modestly bent as she worked some kind of stitchery in her lap. The linen of her coif was white, pure and clean and soft. Just as she herself was. If only he could get past that purity and reach her, without destroying her...

"*Mere...*"

She did not look up, but her hands grew still.

"*Mere,* I am sorry, you know that, do you not? I will be sorry for the rest of my life." Lucien got on his knees beside her. "I would do anything for you, anything at all. Just ask me."

Then she turned and met his gaze with hers, blue and fever-bright. "Marry the girl, then. Marry Isidora of the dark eyes. That is what I wish of you."

Lucien blinked and tried to calm the sudden roar in his head. "May I ask why?"

"Why? B-because someone must be happy! If not me, then her. You must please her. You must!" Amelie burst into tears.

Lucien was horrified. But he did what instinct told him and caught her close to his chest, wrapping his arms about her until her sobs dwindled.

Her women gathered around and Lucien gave her up to their care. Once again, she was childlike, allowing them to guide her to bed, saying nothing, not even a farewell as Lucien headed to the door.

Bewildered and discouraged and dismayed, he excused himself and ran down the stairs. Women! Who could possibly bear them, much less understand them?

As he rounded a corner he nearly collided with Mauger, and blurted, "I am stifling here with so many folk about, all wanting something from me. I am going for a ride."

"I'll accompany you."

Lucien aborted a dismissive gesture. "I am telling you as a courtesy, not as an invitation, Mauger."

"And I am telling you I'm coming along, not asking permission. There are still too many unsavory leftovers from the revels hanging about the woods."

Lucien decided to ignore Mauger, since the man did not listen to him, much less obey him. He strode out into the bailey, but Mauger was the one who ordered up the horses.

With relief, Lucien mounted his big gray courser and took up the reins. He guided the beast out the gates and across the narrow, ice-slick drawbridge.

The afternoon sun had crept in a low arc across the pale, watery sky. Now it hung just behind the beeches and oaks, silhouetting their bare limbs. The great wood lay silent and waiting, in a dark blanket beyond the stubble of the fields.

"Don't go in there!" cautioned Mauger.

"If that is the only way to escape you, perhaps I will," Lucien replied. Though he shared some of his friend Raymond's dislike of the woods, it was more of a vague uneasiness than outright fear.

But he kept his horse to the muddy path and patted its warm, rough-coated neck. "I do not want to be continually butting heads with you, Mauger. I have more of a problem now than I did but a few days ago. You have helped create it, and I expect you to help solve it."

Mauger pursed his lips. "All you need do is obey your uncle's wishes."

"Has he informed you as to what they are?"

"My lord Lucien, you speak as though he and I are in collusion against you. We only want what is in your best interests, and those of the family."

"Aye, of course." Lucien cocked his head and listened. The small noises of the surrounding fields and coppiced hedges had dwindled. He halted his horse, the better to hear, but nothing seemed amiss.

"Mauger, let us turn back. I feel uneasy."

"As you wish. The horses do seem a bit twitchy."

Lucien reined his horse around, then paused and leaned an elbow on the pommel of his saddle. "Do you truly want her, Mauger? Do you want Rosamunde?"

The seneschal's strong jaw tightened and released. "If her father agrees."

"Nay, Mauger, listen to yourself. I am not asking if you want to marry her. I am asking, do you want *her?*"

Mauger's mouth pursed into a rueful smile. "I might ask the same of you in regard to Isidora. But, aye, Lucien. I want Rosamunde. No doubt I'll live to regret it, but I do."

Lucien nodded and allowed his horse to move forward. "I will help you then. For I would see you well content, Mauger. The happier you are, the less shall you pester me."

Mauger grinned. "You may be right. But you have my thanks, for lending your support to my cause."

"Oh, don't think it is out of the goodness of my heart, Mauger. Well do I know, you are a man of prowess, and I want to avoid making an enemy of you."

"Lucien, you are not even aware of the depths of your own heart, so speak not to me of its goodness or lack thereof. It shall be tested, and then you'll know."

Lucien took a deep breath. The goodness of his heart. It had already been tested. And failed.

* * *

Having met Lucien's mother, Isidora saw from whence he got his purity of skin and coloring. Much younger than Isidora expected, Amelie was like a delicate flower, her head bowed modestly and the fragrance of roses about her. Lucien and his uncle both fell over themselves to please her, though she seemed to ask for little.

Isidora sat in the hall by the fire, opposite Lady Amelie, who stared into the flames but said nothing. Isidora's heart ached for the woman, who seemed so frail and all alone. What was wrong with her? And why did Lucien not speak of it?

There was a rustle of the heavy curtain that blocked the draft from the anteroom and Lucien entered with Mauger behind him.

Lady Amelie came to life, turning to face her son, yet still she did not smile. He came in, smelling of fresh, cold air. He bowed first to her, then to Isidora, took a seat beside his mother and he, too, said nothing.

Then, without warning, as she sat between them, Amelie caught Isidora's and Lucien's hands and put them together. Isidora stared first at Amelie, then at Lucien, whose face was now as red as she had ever seen it. But, to her immense gratitude, he did not jerk his hand from hers.

Instead he swallowed and, with a flicker of a look toward his mother, leaned toward Isidora.

"Em, my lady, this—" he gave her fingers a squeeze "—is how it is to be between us, from now on. Lady Amelie has expressed her desire that I have you. And I am agreed."

Isidora nearly choked. Lucien had agreed to his mother's desire that he *have* her? As *what?* "Pardon me, my lord, but I do not understand. Just what does *this* signify?" She returned his subtle squeeze.

Amelie broke her silence. "He will have you. You will have him. Be glad of it."

We will be wed? Isidora's heart felt like the froth on a mazer of ale. Light and heady. Full of intoxicating promise.

Then, daring to be bold, she looked into Lucien's eyes.

And felt as though she had been slapped. They were not joyous or loving. Just a steely blue. Determined. And they held no promises at all.

The cold, terrible truth crashed into Isidora like a warrior into a shield wall. He was not doing this because he loved *her.* Of course not. He was doing it because he loved his mother. And because he felt guilty about something.

"Isidora." Lucien held on to her hand as she tried to pull away. "Not now. Please."

He was right. Why should she be upset? Husbands and wives were not meant to love each other with passion.

Moderation was in order. Propriety. Conserving one's strength for the trials ahead. Good wives gave their love to God and obedience to their husbands.

Look what happened to those who loved with abandon. Look what had happened to her own mother!

Isidora bit her lip. To hell with good wives! She would never be one. But she could not bear the thought of being a bad one, either. Bad for wanting more from Lucien than distracted glances and his duty to provide her with children…she wanted him, heart and soul.

For poor, wounded Amelie's sake, Isidora gave him a false smile in return. Aye, soon enough Lucien would have to face his bride and just how she felt.

Chapter Sixteen

Lord Conrad cleared his throat as he approached them. "Let me escort Lady Amelie to her quarters."

He held out his hand for her to take, and for the first time Lucien saw something he had never before noticed. His mother looked at Conrad. With glowing eyes and trembling lips, blushing cheeks and quickened breaths.

The way a woman in love looks at a man.

Lucien stared at her, then at his uncle, who immediately frowned. But not quite fast enough to hide a flash of longing. *My God!* How long has this been going on?

They are in love! Lucien backed away, both from the thought and from his mother.

The two of them slowly mounted the stairs. Nay, this was crazy. And so was he, to agree to wed Isidora, the alchemist's daughter, just to please his mother! But was that not what every son and daughter was expected to do?

To obey their parents and accept whatever choice they made for them in regard to marriage? It was. Who was he to question it?

Never mind that most matches took months, if not years, of negotiation and planning. That they were arranged when the principals were children, not fully grown and fully capable of making their own choice, were they allowed. But a man was always a son to his mother. And Isidora had no one but her brother—*Faris!*

Lucien's heart jolted. Important relatives who were left out of the consent process—the bride herself notwithstanding—might be so insulted that they did violence to whomever they felt had slighted them. Especially a proud warrior like Faris, with a most traditional bent of mind.

Lucien turned to Isidora. "We must tell your brother on the instant."

She eyed him, her face already turning toward the door. "Oh, aye, it is a fine thing, to tell him after the fact. He will appreciate your consideration. As do I."

Lucien caught her arm as she was about to flounce away from him. "You and I will discuss this later. Accompany me or not, but I will speak to him now." It was imperative.

"Faris!" Lucien called as he made his way upstairs.

The wooden steps shuddered as Mauger ran after him. "Lucien, let me come, too. We will explain your lapse together."

"I would not have him think we are mounting an offense against him."

"Nay, we are showing him the respect he deserves, by the both of us addressing him."

Isidora followed them and Lucien did not try to stop her. They found Faris making ready as if to go out. He wore his Persian mail, a heavy surcoat and woolen mantle. His dark hair was combed back; hollows shadowed his cheeks.

"Sir Faris. You look as though you are missing your homeland," Lucien offered cautiously.

Faris jerked on a gauntlet. "So I do. I like it here, surprising as that may seem, but I fear I may have stayed too long already. While at first I had my doubts, I see now that Isidora is safe here, among friends."

"That is what we wish to discuss with you, Faris. My, em, family wants me to take Isidora to wife. I would ask for your blessing."

Faris stared. "What does Isidora have to say on the matter?"

"I—"

Lucien cut her off. "She is well content."

Faris pulled his other gauntlet on and flexed his fingers. "As I have said before, your courting customs are unseemly by our standards. I believe you have taken liberties with Isidora and that her honor has been jeopardized. In fact, had you not made your announcement just now, I would have insisted upon it before taking my leave."

"But—" Isidora began again.

Faris held up his hand. "Nay, Isidora. You must listen to me. You have nothing to return to in Acre. You are much better off here, with these English and Welsh. They are more amiable than the other Franj, I think."

"But you cannot go now," Mauger said. "The roads are not yet decent. At least wait until after these two are wed, which cannot be long, because it must take place before Lent begins."

"Please stay, Faris," Isidora pleaded.

He looked at her, into her eyes, and she saw pain and

regret in his. She held out her hand to him, but he turned from her and addressed Lucien once more.

"*Effendi*—Sir Lucien—it is best that I leave. I cannot explain further. My journey has been long, but it must end with my return to Acre. You have my thanks for seeing to my health, and for taking charge of Isidora Binte Deogal. I wish you many long years of happiness and many fine sons to make you proud. Fare well."

Isidora clenched her hands into fists to stop them from shaking. Bit by bit, her world was crumbling….

"I will escort you to the borders of my land, then, Faris," said Lucien.

"That is not necessary. I can take care of myself. This land is a garden paradise compared to some places I've been."

"Then take my gray courser as your own, he will see you past many dangers, with more grace than any other horse I have."

Faris smiled. "I am honored by your gift, sir." With an elegant gesture of finality, Faris strode past Mauger and Lucien, headed for the stairs. Then, just as he was about to pass out of sight, he halted and turned. With a crook of his finger, he bade Isidora come to him.

She had to stop herself from running, from begging him to take her home. Away from these merciless English…

"Isidora, forgive me," he whispered. "Do not lose the box I gave you from your mother, eh? Keep it as a remembrance of me, will you?"

She nodded, any words she might have uttered were locked behind the tightness in her throat. Despite her efforts to prevent them, tears began to stream down her face.

With Faris's departure, she lost not only him, but all con-

nection to everything that had once been so familiar…warm sandstone, sunny blue skies, the flowers and
birds and refined subtleties of manners and chivalry she
had always taken for granted. Now she understood how
rare they were.

Faris raised his hand and, with the back of his gloved
forefinger, wiped her cheeks. "No tears, *habibti.*"

She swallowed hard. "Faris, grant me one boon, if
you will."

"Name it."

"Find Marylas, the Circassian woman who served in my
father's house, and make certain that she is safe and happily situated."

"I will. Have no worry for her."

"My thanks. Go with God, Faris al-Rashid." Isidora
watched him descend the stairs to the main hall, Mauger
at his heels. Somehow she feared she would never see
Faris again. She felt more alone than she had ever felt at
home, even with her father paying her no heed.

Then, just as she was about to turn and run, warm hands
settled upon her shoulders. Lucien's hands. She held herself still, not wanting to give in to the immediate sense of
safety his touch brought, however fleeting. Nay, it was not
fair at all. She would not be pitied by him, or used.

There was always a nunnery as a choice…

"Isidora, it has been a trying day. You should go to bed.
My mother is already settled in the women's quarters."

His breath was warm against her ear, for he had bent his
head—so that he could keep his voice low, she assumed.

"Lucien, I will go to bed when and where I choose. I have
lived long enough to be fully capable of such a decision."

"Have you? I wonder, even at your age, that you do not need some guidance in that regard, or at least some inspiration?" He turned her around. "Do you *want* some…inspiration?"

At the sight of him, so close, the feel of him, living, breathing, a pulse beating in his neck, his eyes gleaming in the firelight, his male scent proving his nearness…for once, his attention focused upon her alone…Isidora had all the inspiration she could handle.

She felt positively dizzy. She wanted to fall into his arms. Kiss him. And beat him with her fists, so thick-headed was he. Had he no idea of the torture he put her through? What was the matter with him? She could not ask.

"Lucien, this should wait."

"What should wait?" He slid his hands from her shoulders to the small of her back, drawing her even closer. His eyes had darkened and his lips parted in a small, beguiling smile.

Apparently helpless to do otherwise, Isidora's arms wound around his waist. She took one last glorious look at him, then shut her eyes and tilted back her head. "*This*, Lucien, God help me. Yet again."

"He will not," Lucien whispered in a low growl. "He cannot. Not now."

"Blasphemer. Then He should help *you*."

"Aye, by making you stay quiet for a moment…"

His hand roamed lower.

"Oh!" Isidora could tell he was truly smiling now. Indeed, he nearly purred. She wriggled at the warm expanse of palm against her backside. That small movement brought her body to his, his mouth to hers, in a hard, hot and all-consuming kiss. A mingling of breath and essences, of scent and skin, an illusion of unity that gave her such pleasure she could not describe it.

It was not until he withdrew that she opened her eyes, was able to breathe, and realized her thigh had climbed his during the encounter. She felt blood rush to her cheeks and quickly put her foot back on the floor. "My God, Lucien!"

"Eh, He *was* quite helpful, after all…"

"Stop this!" She pulled her arms back to her sides.

"You mean the same 'this' we were just doing?"

"Aye, the very same."

"Why? Did you not enjoy it?"

She would not lie, but she would indeed sidestep. "You toy with me. If you intend to marry me, then you should have a care for my honor."

A look of stunned bewilderment crossed Lucien's fine features. "Of course I care for your honor. How could you imagine otherwise?"

"You are not indifferent to me, true, but you allow lust to be your guide, my lord. That is what must wait. I should not even be having to say such things to you."

Lucien's hands fell from her waist and the loss of their comfort brought an ache to her heart.

Of a sudden his color rose. "Indeed, you should not. But, lest you fall victim to my…lust…again, mayhap you should keep to your quarters, or do not roam about unescorted."

"I will not be made prisoner here, just because you cannot control yourself."

His jaw tightened. "Oh, Isidora, if I am such a threat, then so shall you be kept safe from me by the same God that brought you here!" He turned on his heel and stalked away.

Now what had she done?

Chapter Seventeen

What have I done? Lucien crossed the cobbled bailey in the night, kicking bits of stone as if they were himself as he went. He had tried to seduce a woman to whom he was betrothed but did not want to marry? Where was the reason in that? Had he lost his mind?

Never had he intended to hurt Isidora. There was simply something about her that made him want to seize her and—and what? Kiss her? Bed her? Aye, both. But it was not her fault. And she deserved more—and better—than that.

By the dim flicker of the oil lamp he held, Lucien made his way to the *laboratorium*. It had been days upon days since he had last seen to the Work. It was all that was truly right and real in his world.

Dropping his mantle onto a hook in the wall, he lit the candles in their sconces and the lamps upon the workbench. He looked about. Dust coated the glassware and crucibles. One should have an assistant to keep such annoying impurities at bay, he thought.

With a sigh, Lucien took a bit of rag and began to rub

the bubbled, green-glass surfaces clean. The pure drudgery of the task was soothing in a way. He picked up a flask, still laden with the liquid, silvered remains of a failed effort.

Nay, he would not give up! He could not…not if Amelie's happiness meant anything to him, and as far as he could see, she had none. That was what he must remedy, his debt to her—atone for the death of his sister, a tragedy that had broken his mother's mind.

His fingers tightened around the flask and it shattered in his hand. Pain burst into his consciousness. A heavy, curved piece of glass had impaled his palm at an angle, and shards were scattered all over, mingled with spilled mercury. Lucien pulled the glass out, cutting his other hand's fingers in the process.

He pressed the rag to the wound, then looked at the mess of discarded quicksilver. The heavy liquid ran over the stone table's top, its racing metallic edges crimson in the firelight. It seemed to have a life of its own, pooling here and continuing there…at last it came to a stop.

Lucien stood, his eyes wide, his bleeding left hand forgotten. The liquid had formed a shape. Like the graceful, gray body of the horse he had given Faris. There was even a suggestion of a rider upon its back. A splotch of red disturbed the image. Then another.

Shaken, Lucien clenched his dripping fist and wrapped the rag tighter. Something was wrong. He should never have allowed Faris to leave as darkness approached, much less unescorted. Knight or no, one man was not always enough. He grabbed his mantle, extinguished the lamps, slammed, bolted and locked the door before running back to the mews.

Gripped by a sense of urgency he could not explain, Lucien did not wait for a groom. His wounded hand left him clumsy, but he managed to saddle Mauger's palfrey, a fine Andalusian, for apart from giving Faris his gray, he had sent his other courser to cover a mare at an adjoining estate.

Lucien was nearly out the gate before remembering he had not brought his sword. He halted the long-maned, restive horse outside the portion of the keep that provided the barracks and armory for his men.

"Oy, are any of you lads awake in there? Or is Daphne visiting?" he shouted.

A blond head, perpetually touseled, to Lucien's observation, preceded the emergence of a tall, strikingly fair but solidly built man.

"Milord?" he rumbled.

"Jager, you're here. Good—" It struck Lucien that Sir Jager looked even more pale than usual. And stiff.

Then another body emerged through the low doorway from the dark confines of the men-at-arms's quarters.

"Oh, hullo, Lucien!" Larke smiled cheerily as she straightened to stand beside Jager, only reaching the man's shoulder. She was garbed in her usual inappropriate attire—a long hunting tunic, torn leggings and a voluminous, muddy woolen mantle.

Jager did not twitch a muscle. Indeed, he seemed frozen to the spot. Lucien breathed in deeply and released the air slowly, until the blood stopped pounding in his neck. He could not fault Jager for succumbing to his sister's persuasive and persistent ways. "Larke, go back to the hall."

She frowned. "Whatever for? Sir Jager is just about to show me where the orb of Venus is to appear tonight. I was going to bring Isidora along later, so she can see it, too. And Rosamunde."

Lucien took another deep breath. There was no point in shouting. "Jager is needed. Venus will still be there tomorrow night. Or ask Mauger where it is."

Larke brightened. "Oh, indeed, a splendid thought, Lucien. Jager, I thank you for your time." She swept the man a bow, as if he outranked her and she were another man.

If she wanted to behave thus, then she could make herself useful, as well. "Larke!"

She turned on her heel. "Aye, Lucien?"

"Bring me Isenbana."

A flicker of darkness passed across her face and her smile vanished. "Aye, Lucien, at once."

Jager's eyes moved to follow her departure, then he closed them briefly. "Lord, I meant no—"

It was becoming more and more difficult to rein Larke in. She needed a husband. Soon. Lucien raised his hand. "I know, Jager. Never mind. Just find another two men, I need an escort."

By the time Jager had readied himself and his men, Larke, too, had returned, bringing Lucien's heavy sword to him. Isenbana. *Ironslayer.* An ancient thing, but well had it served him. He strapped it about his middle.

But, confound her, Isidora had followed Larke from the hall! No doubt to see why Gawaine was barking so loudly, tugging against his chain.

"Let's go." Lucien urged the courser forward, ready to simply ignore the young women rather than argue with them about their being left behind. Besides, he did not want to tell Isidora that he feared for Faris's safety.

With Jager mounted, his men, afoot and bearing torches, fell into step beside Lucien's horse. At the gate, as the porter opened it, Lucien risked a look back. There stood Larke and Isidora, their breaths clouding the air, looking forlorn and abandoned.

If only Larke had the sense of a pea-hen, things might be all right. But she was far too clever for her own good.

Isidora watched as Lucien and his men ventured into the evening mist. She put her hand on Larke's arm. "I don't like this. Did he say where they are going? Or why?"

The girl shook her head. "Nay. But we can find out, if we dare."

"Dare what?"

A mischievous grin lit Larke's features. "Well, you have your mare and I have mine. We could follow them."

Isidora looked about, at the red glow of the sun's last rays as they tinged the bellies of the clouds. At the black rooks lining up along the battlements of Lucien's fortifications. The forest swayed and creaked in the wind. It was far too cold and late for any such adventure.

But she had not come all this way to simply stand by while Lucien rode off into the night for no apparent reason. She could follow him, as Larke suggested, for she still had her clothing from posing as Faris's squire.

Faris! The pain of his departure was but hours old and not hers alone. She had seen a bond form between Faris and Lucien. Isidora turned to Larke. "What if Lucien has decided to pursue my brother, to bring him back? Or to find him, that he might accompany him past his borders, after all?"

"It is just the sort of thing Lucien would do, after the fact," Larke declared.

"They do not have much of a start on us. If I could see Faris even one more time, it would be worth your brother's ire."

"And I, too, would like to see *your* brother one more time."

"Why? What do you mean?"

"I told you, he was the most handsome man at the mêlée on the pond. Except for Lucien, of course. Nothing like what I had imagined a Saracen to be—no pointed teeth, or scales, none of that. One does not get to see such sights as Faris often. So dark, yet so brilliant—"

"He is not a 'sight,' Larke, nor a Saracen any longer, but a man. A good man, whom I love and might not ever see again myself."

Larke bit her lip. "I know."

Isidora frowned. "What is it?"

"Nothing. He is not married, is he? Or if he is, does he yet have his full contingent of wives?"

"Larke! Of all the foolish notions! He is not married. But if he were, it would be to a Byzantine princess or one from the family of an eastern Frankish king. He has no ties to England, no reason to ally himself here."

"I never thought you capable of such…such elitism, Isidora. I thought you were my friend."

"Oh, Larke, so I am. I but want to protect you from heartbreak. Did he show you any interest whilst he was here?"

"Nay. I do not think he even noticed my existence."

"So for that, you would place your heart at risk?"

"I never got to say goodbye! I made him a good-luck charm."

Larke sounded so earnest that Isidora was moved to co-operate. What a pair of fools they made! "Very well, Larke, but we must tell someone we are going."

After her initial smile, Larke's brow creased. "Not Mauger. He would be most vexed. But…we could tell Rosamunde."

Isidora tucked her chin to her chest. She wanted as little to do with Rosamunde as possible, for both their sakes. The whole situation was a stew of dishonor.

"Come!" Larke strode into the stable, barked orders to the grooms and walked with Isidora back to the hall.

"But, Larke, if Lucien thought it prudent to take three men along with him, what about us? I have my bow, but…"

"Oh, what bother! Our darling Lucien is always over-prepared, for anything he does. We can bring Gawaine along, he'll protect us! You're not afraid of the dark, are you?"

Isidora met Larke's clear, fearless gaze. "Aye, I am. The dark holds the unseen. And the unseen are not to be taken lightly. This I know…"

It was how her mother had been saved and cursed…starving and stumbling in the dark, until she received help from those who were not supposed to be out amongst the ordinary living. Nay. Ignorant folk believed that lepers were no longer fully human. But some of the afflicted had more compassion than many a sound-limbed man.

"Well, Izzie, dear, I trow there's nothing like a warm horse between one's legs at night to chase the devil away, eh?"

Isidora put her hand over her mouth and stared at Larke. Then they both burst out laughing.

"What's all this?" Mauger's deep voice put a quick end

to their mirth. He moved toward them, just as a bear might amble toward an object of interest. Faster than one might expect and just as impossible to stop.

"Em, mere speculation, sir," Larke offered with a winning smile that obviously had no effect upon Mauger, who crossed his arms. "You should be in bed soon, Lady Larke. Night is nearly upon us."

Larke put her hands on her hips. "I beg your pardon, Sir Mauger, but I am no longer an eight-year-old. Kindly address me as befits my station. And yours."

Mauger cleared his throat and pursed his lips. "As I said, my most esteemed Lady Larke, you should be in bed soon."

She stood up on tiptoe and peered over his shoulder. "What of Lady Rosamunde? Should you not be seeing her to bed, as well?"

The resultant crimson of Mauger's face was not pleasant to behold. He uncrossed his arms, bent to Larke's level and lowered his voice to a hiss. "If she is behind me, and heard, Lady Larke, I swear upon my grandfather's beard, your hind parts will have cause to regret the indiscretions of your fore parts!"

Isidora thought Lucien's sister an outrageous minx, but her next move topped all those heretofore witnessed. Larke caught Mauger's broad face between her palms and planted a noisy kiss on his lips.

"Nay, Rosamunde is not behind you," she announced. "Elsewise I would not have done that. I *am* fond of you, despite your grumpiness, Mauger."

He straightened and backed away. "By God, young woman, you have much to answer for!"

Larke smiled sweetly. "I'll just tell Rosamunde you will be up shortly to see her."

Isidora could have sworn she heard Mauger growl.

Chapter Eighteen

A short while later Larke and Isidora slipped through the hall and out to the mews where their mounts awaited them. Gawaine had to be admonished, so that he did not entangle himself amongst the horses' legs.

Larke carried a horn-paned lamp, which was not enough to see by but better than nothing. Isidora was so intent upon climbing atop her horse, she nearly fell off at the sound of yet another authoritative male voice behind her.

"Where are you two going at this hour?"

She righted herself in the saddle and looked down at the speaker. Wace, the squire from Wales, though he himself was not Welsh. Good-looking and arrogant, Wace had hair of dark auburn and a clear-eyed gaze that missed little.

Before she could reply, Larke did. "What business is it of yours, Wace du Hautepont? Your master did not send you here to nursemaid us, did he?"

Wace grinned. "Had Lord Raymond known how badly you needed it, he might have, Lady Larke. He has tamed much wilder women than you!"

Larke raised her chin. "Do not speak to me of taming, sir, if you wish to be my friend. You *do* want that, do you not?"

"Em, well, aye, I suppose."

"Declare thy intentions convincingly or be gone!" Larke commanded with a flourish.

Isidora could see Wace's resolve harden before her eyes. But his response was not a capitulation, as she expected.

He crossed his brawny arms and stood with his weight on one leg. "Why do you behave like a child, Lady Larke—now before me, and especially, before your brother? You know better."

Larke placed one hand upon the other on the pommel of her saddle. "But *he* expects me to act witless! Perhaps he knows I am not, but he is more comfortable having his expectations met. He has much on his mind, Wace. I love him and I want him to be happy."

Wace snorted. "Has it occurred to you that he might be happier if he did not have to always worry about what you next might do? If he could count upon you to behave properly, as a modest maiden should?"

Larke gave Wace a withering glare. "Mayhap that is what would make *you* happy, Wace? Do I shame you?"

"You shame yourself, when you behave like an imbecile!"

At this Larke urged her horse around, so that Wace was forced to step out of the way. "You, sir, have much to learn about how to address a lady."

"And you have much to learn about acting like one."

An icy void of silence spread between them, then Larke proved his point by declaring, "Oh, go dunk your head in the tanning vat!"

To his credit, Wace did not fall prey to her taunt. "Not

before you've told me what you are up to. Dragging Lady Isidora out into the freezing night."

Larke looked to Isidora, who replied, "We are on a quest, Squire Wace. To guard Lucien's back."

"What do you mean? Where has he gone?"

Larke snugged Gawaine's leash tighter. "We do not know. But he needs us."

"Then so do you need me. I am coming with you."

Larke rubbed her chin, as if considering his statement. "Very well. But I am in charge. And on no account must you tell Mauger or anyone else."

Wace grinned again. "Of course not. Where would the fun be in that?"

Larke beamed from ear to ear as Wace collected his horse.

When they approached the gates, the porter challenged them. "What's this, milady? Yer goin' out?"

Larke winked at Wace and whispered to Isidora, "I am a much better liar than you, so let me do the talking." Then she replied to the porter, "Aye, 'tis but a game, nothing to worry about. Squire Wace is going to show us how to night track certain wee beasts. We will be back soon."

The man cranked the portcullis up with shrieks of protest from the iron chains.

"You need some fat in there, porter!" Larke called as they trotted through. Once outside and across the drawbridge, the dusk-befallen fields and woods spread before them in a misty array of muted greens and browns. The air smelled of wet leaves and woodsmoke, and cattle grazed upon the common, with a herdsman beginning to gather them up for home.

The lane skirted the forest for some way, then once past

the pond, dove into the cover of the trees. A shiver of dread coursed through Isidora. These woods—so dense, so close, even in daylight. And at night…

Gawaine howled and Isidora started. Her horse jigged, and Larke's lamp swayed and bobbed like a cork on the sea. The shadows danced to the motion of the swinging light, as if the trees were beings fully aware of their passing.

They progressed farther into the forest, then the path forked. The mud was hoof-marked in both directions. Larke turned to Isidora and Wace, her eyes wide. "Em, how do we know which way they went? The right turning goes back to the main road, the one you came on, no doubt. The left goes to another village, down the valley."

"It is your wood. I am merely here to protect you, not lead you," Wace said coolly.

"Stay right," Isidora said, not knowing why she said it.

But Larke reined her horse to the left, as if she had not heard. "I think they went this way. Lucien has no sense of direction."

Farther and farther they went, the trees moaning as the breeze quickened, until Isidora was shivering with the cold and the darkness had become nearly impenetrable. "What is that ahead? That flickering?"

Larke halted her horse and peered forward, but Gawaine leaped against his lead and jerked it from her hands. He bounded toward the golden light ahead, barking as he went.

"It must be Lucien he's sniffed!"

"Nay, Larke, we should not go any closer!"

But Larke urged her horse on and Isidora had to follow. She half expected to see a fairy ring—she had heard such things were common in England. The place was so strange and eerie, anything might manifest. But the sight that met her eyes when her horse stepped into the clearing was beyond anything she had imagined.

A striped pavilion had been erected in a meadow and a fire burned off to one side, with a cook pot suspended from an iron tripod. A wagon had a pair of carthorses tethered to it, and picketed beyond them were a fine bay palfrey and a chestnut rouncy.

Blue and yellow pennants hung from a cluster of lances propped together in a circle. The device on them looked familiar… *I must be mistaken.* Isidora's stomach curled at the possibility she was not—

"This looks welcoming, eh? Hello!" called Larke.

A short, stocky man walked out of the darkness, bearing an armload of wood, and stopped at the sight of the riders. Another, tall and dark, came out of the tent, a frown upon his face.

"These are strangers and we are not a welcome surprise, Larke," Isidora whispered. "Let us turn around and go."

"But they may have seen Lucien. At least let me inquire. Your pardon, sir, but—"

Larke went quiet as yet another man, far more imposing than the first, emerged from the pavilion and straightened to stand before the fire to warm his hands. He, too, was tall, but fair-haired and grim, with strong, sculpted features and startling gray eyes that barely spared the women a glance.

"Bon soir, Isidora," he said softly.

She swallowed back a sick, rising fear. She had not been mistaken. "Good evening, Lord FitzMalheury."

"Earm, kindly provide the young man and these *demoiselles* with some hippocras."

"Our thanks, but no," Isidora said. At the moment, even the thought of drinking sweetened wine, warmed and spiced, made her ill. "We must be going. Perhaps some other time."

Kalle glowered at them. "You would refuse my hospitality? Have you already forgotten how civilized people behave since you came to this godforsaken country?"

Wace's hand rested on his sword hilt and Larke looked at Isidora. "You know him?"

Isidora nodded. "Please, Larke and Squire Wace. I will handle this." A flash of anger speared her and sweat trickled down her sides, even though she was cold. "My lord, I have forgotten nothing of your hospitality toward Sir Lucien."

Larke's brow creased. "Lucien knows him, too?"

"Shh!" hissed Isidora.

Kalle laughed, a deep, rich sound. "What a pretty pair of doves you make. All a-flutter. What think you, Earm?"

The dark man inclined his head. "I think whatever you command me to think, is that not so, my lord Kalle?"

Kalle's gaze narrowed into icicles of light. "It would seem everyone is forgetting their manners tonight."

Larke stirred and sat up straight in her saddle. "Oh, indeed not, sir. I bid you come to our hall and make yourselves comfortable."

Wace and Isidora looked at the girl in dismay.

"They will be outnumbered there," Larke whispered.

"A fair enough invitation," Kalle said. "Earm, tell Cooke to dump that mess out of the pot and pack up."

With a careful glance at Kalle, the short man set his wood down and bowed, as if begging to be spared.

Kalle ignored him while he pulled on his gloves. "I will

ride along with these *petits oiseaux,* Earm. No doubt you can find the way yourself."

Earm brought Kalle his palfrey. "Aye, God speed, milord."

Isidora clutched her bow, little use that it was in such close quarters. She had only ever shot at targets, not at a living being. And Kalle…he was so hard, and no doubt surrounded by protective spells of some sort, the arrows would probably bounce off him.

Kalle mounted his horse, which shook its head and pawed the ground. He brought it alongside Isidora and leaned on the pommel with one elbow, the picture of relaxed detachment despite the beast's restlessness.

The knight smiled, ever so subtly. "So, Daughter of Deogal. Shall we call a truce, until we can meet on trodden ground, as it were? I do not want you fleeing into the wilds on account of me."

Isidora stiffened and her grip on her bow grew even tighter. "You mock me, sir, with such a suggestion, and flatter yourself. I am not my mother, may God forever bless her innocent soul."

At this Kalle's smile and easy manner vanished. A seething cloud of rage and pain seemed to surround him. "In that you are indeed correct," he snarled, his teeth flashing white against the tan of his face.

Larke cleared her throat. "Em, Isidora, good sir—let us be on our way before we freeze. You can best sort out any differences at the hall."

Isidora had to force herself not to do just what Kalle had said—flee into the wild at a gallop, to put as much distance as possible between them. His presence brought back an unbearable burden of wretched memories.

Of her father, his fists bloody, the night he nearly killed Kalle. Of her mother, weeping, forced out onto the streets because of Kalle. Of herself, screaming, being restrained by servants to keep her from running after her mother.

But in truth those memories remained a part of her, whether Kalle was present or a thousand miles away. He was a danger, aye, to Lucien for one set of reasons and to herself for another. And Lucien? What was he to her?

Something, for certain, elsewise she would not have come chasing after him into the forest at night.

Kalle spoke again, this time addressing Larke. "So, I take it you are not Isidora's servant, though you've dressed the part." He scrutinized her profile and she nudged her horse, putting Wace between herself and Kalle.

Isidora understood her apparent desire to hide, but had to remind her, "Larke, you have the lantern."

The girl held out the light to Isidora. "Take it, please. I would not have him look at me thus."

Wace leaned over and caught hold of the lantern's bronze handle and the flame flickered precariously in the growing darkness.

Kalle chuckled. "Ha, no matter, I have it now. You are the young sister of Lucien, but no longer a child. Aye, I learned a great deal about our Lucien whilst he was in Acre. He had another sister, as well, did he not? His twin? And he let her die cruelly at the hands of vicious outlaws."

Isidora stared, first at Kalle, then at Larke. What was he talking about?

Larke looked over her shoulder. "You, sir, are cruel, to bring up such a thing. I pray you do not speak of it in my presence again. Nor in Lucien's, if you value your life."

Kalle's eyes crinkled at the corners. "I see he has not mentioned it to our Isidora. But all in good time. Then shall you have the full measure of your precious Lucien."

A stick cracked. Out of nowhere, a horse and rider loomed ahead, barely visible in the gloom, but Isidora knew the set of those broad shoulders and, as they approached, the familiar gleam of coppery hair.

Gawaine whined and broke free of his leash yet again, to roil toward Lucien as Jager and the other two men brought up the rear, carrying torches.

Isidora felt a pang that was a mixture of alarm and relief. "Perhaps you may have his full measure *now,* FitzMalheury."

Again, Kalle's teeth showed white as he grinned. A cunning, predator's grin.

"Sir Kalle." Lucien held up his empty right hand. "Somehow it does not surprise me to find you here. But leave these women out of any business that only belongs between you and me."

Kalle shook his head, like a lion shaking his mane. "Have no fear for them, Lucien. I am but escorting them home from their ill-advised outing. But why you allow such delicates to roam at night is beyond me, especially with all the wild animals in the woods. I came across quite a ferocious specimen earlier, in fact. He got away even after I wounded him, but I expect he's finished by now."

Isidora felt rather than saw Lucien stiffen in response. The atmosphere went even colder than it already was. Still, it was strange, how the shared experience of captive and captor created such intimacy between the men. Strained to its limits, no doubt, but intimacy nonetheless.

Lucien frowned at Larke and Isidora, and scowled at

Wace. "Fascinating. But these three shall hear from me upon that score. Later."

At this ominous remark, Isidora exchanged a glance with Larke, who, for once, said nothing, and Wace's look of utter calm did not ring true.

Lucien continued. "Jager, Wace, light the way for the ladies. FitzMalheury, ride alongside me, if you will. I know you have not come all this way to kill me, you could have done that long ago."

Kalle laughed in his mirthless way. "You have more use to me alive than dead, Lucien. I do apologize for having forgotten about you in my dungeon, but of course, that is the purpose of an *oubliette*. You were indeed fortunate that our Isidora decided to pay me a visit sooner rather than later."

Isidora's heart lurched. If Kalle said another word...

"Oh, aye, *our* Isidora is quite the resourceful one," Lucien agreed, as if he knew all about it. But the very quietness of his tone made Isidora more uneasy. She would have to talk to him. Not that it was any of his concern. She had saved his life, was that not the important thing?

"Em," Larke squeaked. "Lucien, can we hurry? I'm hungry!"

Lucien did not reply. Not to her, nor to any more of Kalle's baiting, for the rest of the ride home.

Chapter Nineteen

As they entered the gates of his keep, a black stew of hatred boiled within Lucien, begging for release. Begging to be visited upon Kalle FitzMalheury's arrogant head. He dismounted, gritted his teeth and kept his hand well away from his sword hilt.

It was he himself who had failed Faris, and if he was hurt or dead, Lucien could not place the blame on anyone else. Jager and the others knew to keep an eye on Kalle, for the moment. Lucien looked at Isidora, still atop her horse, her face pale even in the red-gold glow of the torchlight. He went to her.

The loss of Faris would be a terrible blow. But by God, she needed a leash more than did Gawaine! Or his own fiendish sister! Riding astride, through the woods, in the dark— And Wace! That boy had much to answer for.

"Get down, Isidora. It's icy. I will catch you."

Rather too meekly, he thought, she kept her gaze downcast and swung her right leg over the high cantle and the horse's rump, and deftly kicked her other foot free of the stirrup as she went. Halfway to the ground he caught her about the waist and turned her around, more roughly than he had intended, and his wounded hand began to hurt again.

"What were you thinking? I expect such idiocy from Larke, but not from you. Have you any idea the sort of wicked folk who inhabit those woods?"

"I do now," she replied. "But you forget, Lucien, I traveled all the way from Acre, and have ridden through many such woods."

"Aye, with Faris at your side to protect you. A battle-hardened knight."

Her eyes widened and glittered with sudden tears. "Faris…he told me he worked for Kalle."

Lucien's grip on her waist tightened and he glanced over the horse's back. Lord Conrad had come out of the hall and was speaking to FitzMalheury. "Is that why Kalle is here? To meet with Faris?"

Isidora shook her head. "I do not think so. I think Faris loathed Kalle."

"As do many others. I had a bad feeling, Isidora. I went to look for Faris and provide him escort. But we did not find him. I am sorry."

Isidora looked up at him and her face was such a picture of pain and regret that he wanted to make it all go away. To kiss her and kiss her some more, and then—

"The animal! The wild animal!" Isidora cried, and tore herself free from Lucien's grasp. Dagger in hand, she ran across the bailey toward Kalle, who caught her easily even as he disarmed her.

Lucien followed and felt a fresh stain of anger spread through his heart at the sight of Kalle's hands upon Isidora.

"Let go of her!" he snarled.

Kalle locked gazes with Lucien and smiled, but did not release Isidora. He casually began to toss her dagger into the air, catching it by the handle each time.

Conrad stared at the spectacle. "What is this? Has this woman lost her wits, Lucien, that she should attack Sir Kalle? Confine her, by God, or I will do so!"

Lucien fought down his inclination to challenge Kalle to a fight. "Let her go, FitzMalheury." Lucien pulled Isidora away from Kalle. "She merely has had a touch of moon madness, my lord."

"Nay, I am not mad! He has mur—"

Lucien clapped his hand over her mouth. "Not now, Isidora. Come with me." He looked for his sister, who was still holding her horse's reins, staring at him and Isidora. "Larke! Get yourself up to my solar. Wace, I will speak to you later."

Larke jumped, then hurried to obey, Wace at her back.

Once upstairs, behind closed doors, the servants dismissed and a goblet of wine quaffed, Lucien wished—not for the first time—that Larke had been married off at a very young age to some unsuspecting knight of sturdy constitution. As it was, she would see him to an early grave.

She and Isidora huddled together, sitting side by side on a chest.

"What came over you, Isidora?" he asked, weary of ever being the inquisitor and disciplinarian.

She gave him a soulful look. "I merely acted upon the impulse you yourself have been stifling, Lucien, is that not so?"

He would not lie to her. "Aye."

Isidora took a shaky breath. "I believe Kalle came here to kill Faris. And I think that is what he meant when he spoke of wounding an animal in the forest. He looks at Arabs in that way. Even those who have converted to Christianity, I trow." *Except for my mother...* She twisted her hands together.

"You may be right. I hope not." Lucien did not want to admit to her that he himself had rushed into the forest on the strength of what seemed to be a sign.

Larke, who now showed no sign of contrition, peered at Isidora. "Here, you've bloodied Isidora's lip, Lucien! How could you?"

Momentarily shocked, Lucien knew not what to say. "I did not mean to."

Isidora touched her mouth. "Nay, I am not hurt. I think it is you who are hurt, Lucien. What is that soggy thing wrapped around your hand?" She got up to see, with Larke following.

Lucien backed away. "It is nothing. Just a cut."

Isidora looked at him, her brown eyes serious. "It is more than that. Else you would not try to hide it."

Lucien pointed to the door. "Larke, leave us now. Go to our mother and reassure her."

Larke, who obviously wanted to stay and hear more, reluctantly withdrew.

With the heavy, timbered door closed after her, Lucien continued. "I broke a glass vessel from the *laboratorium*— Larke does not know all that I do there. My blood spilt and formed a shape along with the quicksilver, and I had the foolish thought that it meant something I could remedy. I was wrong."

"Oh, Lucien. Every man who comes near me seems to end up either dead or in harm's way, sooner or later."

Lucien smiled a little. "Nay…that is simply the way of the world, not you. You are not *that* powerful a force to be reckoned with." *Or was she?*

"Do you believe Kalle has killed Faris?" she asked.

"There is little I believe without seeing it for myself." Now, seeing the hope in her eyes, he was ready to lie to her, after all. "Nay, I do not believe it."

She gazed at the floor, her dark hair coming over her shoulder in a thick, shining braid, and he knew she struggled not to show what she felt. Just as he did. Right now.

With his fists and teeth and gut clenched hard, the only way he could think of to keep himself from envisioning her…Isidora, of the east, naked, fragrant and willing…in his bed, an invitation in her eyes, his name upon her lips…her body, supple and warm, beneath his—

"Lucien, I must tell you something, about me and Kalle."

His fantasy shattered. "I don't want to hear it. Not now. I must go down to see what is taking place. Kalle and my uncle seem to be on friendly terms. For all I know, Conrad may be selling Larke to him at this very moment."

What could be worse than that? The thought of Isidora in Kalle's embrace? Was that what she wanted to tell him? Nay. He would not let her, even if it were true. She could save that for her confessor.

"I will go down with you," she said.

"Nay."

"Please, Lucien. I have a right to be privy to this. And I should apologize to your uncle, if not to Kalle. Do not treat me like you do your sister."

She pleaded with her eyes and something inside Lucien cracked. He had thought himself angry, frustrated and longing for solitude. But with Isidora here before him, he only wanted to touch her. "Not like my sister? What do you want, then? This?"

He drew the back of one finger along her cheek. She shut her eyes and her lips parted slightly.

"Or this?" His hand slid around to stroke her neck, then moved down and around to bring her up against him. She still said nothing, but her lips trembled.

"Enough of that," Lucien said in a voice he himself barely recognized, so hoarse was it. He looked upon the fresh, pure skin of her face, at her eyes, now open and searching his. Brown and gold and beautiful. He took her mouth, in a savage, sweet kiss, drawing from her a moan—of pleasure, he hoped.

"Do you want me, Isidora? Say you do." He did not wait for an answer—could not wait—and kissed her cheeks, her brow, her throat. Her arms wound about him and her whole body began to quiver.

"Lucien, I—you m-must stop."

"Why? Are we not to be wed?" He held her closer and spoke into her hair.

"No one has asked me. I have been told, that is all."

An icy pang struck Lucien's heart. Why had he assumed she must love him? "I see."

"I doubt that very much, Lucien. You see only what you want to see, what you shape and create to your own design. You are used to having your way, to being obeyed. And I, I am used to being obedient. But I do not want that any longer, Lucien. I want to be free."

Slowly he pulled away from her so he might see her expression better. "Free? But you are!"

"Nay, not when I must come when you call, sit when you tell me to, sleep when and where I am told, my movements restricted, my choice of clothing, of food, of husband, dictated by someone else. All my life. Either by my father, his relatives, or Kalle, or Faris, or you, or Mauger, or your uncle, or even your mother."

"But…but that is the way of things. For the good of everyone, yourself especially."

"Oh, Lucien. Do not be so thick. I will not be your shadow, forced to watch you as you pursue the Work, to aid you in its pursuit when it will only consume you and leave me more alone than I was to begin with."

"But what about…" He kissed her again, tenderly at first, then relentlessly, until she opened to him and he could taste her desire.

With a small cry she pushed him away. He stared at her, like the dumb animal he was at the moment.

She shook her head and her braid began to come loose. "Nay. This shall not be the way of it. Not until I say so."

"Oh, God." Lucien sat heavily on the edge of his bed and wanted to roll into it and go to sleep. But he still had to go downstairs. "Give me a few moments and I will leave."

"Why do you need any time? It would be best if—"

"Isidora, I do not want to be seen—in this state."

"What state?" She looked him up and down, turned pink, and stammered, "O-oh. I am sorry."

"I am not. Nor should you be, though priests will tell you otherwise. It is the one thing you can do to me that I cannot control. So, if you want power over me, you have it already."

"Doesn't every woman have that power?"

Lucien found this amusing. "Of course not. Not over me, at least. Not when I am conscious, anyway," he added truthfully, remembering Daphne in the barn.

A small furrow formed between Isidora's brows. "I do not understand."

Lucien caught her hand in his. "Whether I care or not makes a difference, Isidora. Does it not do the same for you?"

She pulled her hand back. "I—I do not know. You see, my mother, it seems, had this same effect upon Kalle."

"What?"

Isidora hurried on. "Though I do not believe she cared for him. And if he felt something for her, that does not mean it was her fault, does it? But if he has grown bitter over the years, and hurt you and Faris because of it, I could not bear that."

"Isidora, what Kalle feels or felt about your mother has naught to do with what I feel about you or you feel about me."

"But it does! It is all tied together. Lust or love—there seems to be little difference—caused my mother to be cursed, my father to be damned, and Kalle, who, believe it or not, was once much like you, to become wicked and cruel. I cannot be a part of any such disaster again."

"There is a difference between lust and love."

"Is there? Can you prove it to me? Like the knights of old, who for the sake of love, freely allowed their lives to hang upon their lady's merest pleasure? With no hope of reward, beyond her smile or a fleeting kiss?"

"That was not love, but lunacy. What could you expect from Provençals, anyway?"

"Kalle is a Frank."

"Even worse. Not only French, but an uneducated boor, no doubt."

"He was once not only a Templar, but a priest, Lucien."

"Good Lord." Lucien wiped his face with his palm and took a deep breath. "You know more about him than do I."

"When he lived with us, I was but a child. But I heard a great deal. More than I should have. More than I wanted."

Lucien put one hand to his thigh and stood. "I am going down now. I do not think it wise for you to accompany me. Let me find out what Kalle wants. I will convey your regrets, and you can make amends properly later, though in truth I don't see why you should. I will take you to my mother and sister on the way."

"You are angry with me."

"Nay, Isidora. I am angry with myself, for being such a blind, prideful fool."

Isidora gave the slightest of shrugs.

"Oh, so you agree! And, no doubt have the same opinion of every other man of your acquaintance."

"Some are worse than others," she admitted, and a tiny smile dimpled one cheek.

"Come, let me take you out of here before I do something I'll regret."

Grateful she did not argue, Lucien left Isidora with Larke and his mother in the women's solar before heading down to face his enemy.

Chapter Twenty

Earm put his shoulder to the back of the wagon and shoved—with all his might and all his rage. He had put up with a great deal, in the service of Kalle FitzMalheury, but doing the work of a beast of burden, up to his ankles in mud, in the middle of the night, was beyond the call of any such duty.

"Cooke! This is futile. We will leave the damned cart and continue with the horses."

"But, sir, Lord Kalle will have my head, should I fail to meet his request, or lose the implements we've brought so far—"

Earm caught the cook by the front of his tunic. "*I* will have it, by God, long before Kalle, if you do not help me unharness these beasts! You can carry your pots and pans on your back if you like, but do not look to me!"

"Nay, do not speak so, sir!"

"Then do as I say or I will leave you to find your own way." Scum of the earth, were kitcheners and the like, thought Earm. He felt unclean even having touched the fellow's greasy clothing. But Kalle had such a fear of being poisoned, he ever dragged his own cook about with him.

But the people he had ridden off with—the woman called Isidora had seemed familiar, as had the knight called Lucien. The others, the girl and lad, were complete strangers to him. Earm ground his fist against his head as a searing pain shot through his temples. Not for the first time, he wished Kalle had simply left him to die on the plain of Hittīn.

If, of course, that was indeed where Kalle had found him, because he himself could remember nothing. Nothing but waking up in a clean bed in Kalle's household, finding his wounds bound and Lina feeding him sweetened, watered lemon juice.

What he had never understood was Kalle's dual capacity for both kindness and cruelty. It was as though a demon sat on one shoulder and an angel sat on the other. Ach, but this was not the sodding cook's fault. "Come on, then. I will tell Kalle that I made you leave the cart behind, eh?"

"You have my thanks, sir." The cook staggered forward, a copper vessel balanced on his head.

Earm rode the rouncy and led the two carthorses. Cooke had never put a leg over a horse in his life, and if he preferred slogging through the ice-cold mud to trying it now, that was his affair.

"So, Cooke, what was Kalle hunting while I was mending harness? Did he tell you? Or did you sneak it into the pot he had you dump?"

Cooke puffed in order to keep up. "Nay, nay. I have no idea. I never saw a thing. Never heard a thing."

"What good fortune for you." Earm chewed his lip and

tried to warm his hands, one at a time, between his thighs and the saddle, as if that might make his brain work a bit faster. What had Kalle gone after, to be that smug about it? But he himself was so cold and tired, it was all he could do just to concentrate on which way to go. Whatever had happened, it was bound to be something unpleasant.

Faris al-Rashid! the voice in his head called, louder and louder. His mother's voice...at last. Faris opened his eyes and admitted that he was yet alive.

But it was still dark. Still freezing, and he was soaking wet. Kalle's powerful arm had sent an arrow that ripped through his mail shirt and pierced his side, as no arrow had done before.

He had known it would only be a matter of time before Kalle found him. That it had happened on this night, on this lane, in this dank forest and in this foreign country, were merely details of inevitability. But the fleet gray courser had saved him, outrunning Kalle's heavier horse.

He must have passed out and fallen off. He did not know how long he had lain here or where he was. Now Lucien's horse nuzzled him, with warm, hairy lips and steamy, grass-sweet breath. That was a comfort, to not be alone. Faris felt for the arrow and found it was broken off, several inches from where the fletch end had been.

He ran his hand along the horse's jaw and up until he caught a fistful of mane. The animal obliged him by raising its head and thereby helping him get to his feet. He sagged against the warmth of the big body, then, fighting the weakness that made him want to lie down again, hauled himself back into the saddle.

He knotted the reins loosely, then dropped them, giving the courser its head, and whispered, "Take me where thou wilt, oh swift one, anywhere but back to my enemy, for I have no strength left to guide you."

Indeed, Faris was reduced to the extreme of having to hold on to the pommel, as a tiny child just learning to ride might do. It bothered him, even though there was no one to see. But the horse stepped along confidently, as though it were used to such useless burdens.

It carried him through the woods, until they began to thin, and Faris saw a blur of golden light ahead. Saw light and heard men singing. A beautiful chorus of voices, in a perfect blend of pitch and cadence.

The grey took him closer. And closer. The voices grew clearer, and louder, even as Faris's eyes grew impossible to keep open. He heard the clop of iron-shod hooves on stone. The sound changed, then echoed, and the courser came to a halt. The singing stopped. He swayed.

"What is that horse doing in here?"

"Look! A Moor! God save us!"

"He is hurt. Get Brother Percy, he knows about wounds."

"Nay! Not Percy—you know what the Saracens did to him—"

"Shh! Here he comes, be quiet."

Faris opened his eyes as strong hands pulled him down. Candles. Gilt. A crucifix. His heart caught in an instant of fear. He was in a church. These were monks. Christian monks.

Then he remembered. He, too, was a Christian. Surely these men of God would recognize that. But perhaps he should help them.

"Jesus, Mary and Joseph," he choked out in a haze of pain. "Hallowed be thy name. Forgive my horse, he knows not what he has done by this trespass."

Someone chuckled. "It is all right, brother. Be not concerned, I understand. We are Cistercians, not grim, dirty Dominicans."

The soft words, in Norman-French-accented Arabic, were spoken by one of the monks as they carried Faris through the cloisters and laid him on a bed.

"Brother Percy, you need not attend him. We can make ourselves understood well enough. And—"

The soft-voiced monk replied, "I will attend him. Just bring me the usual things—hot water, clean cloths and the salves and unguents."

Faris looked at Brother Percy. A grown man, well made but slim, fair, yet smooth of cheek, and his voice…somehow familiar. His fingers, long and slender.

Faris swallowed. He had been around eunuchs all his life. At home they might be slaves, or hold posts of great honor and responsibility. But never had he expected to meet one face to face in an English church.

Chapter Twenty-One

Isidora tried to look demure, sitting with Larke in the presence of Lady Amelie and her companions. But it was difficult, still clad in muddy men's clothing, with Rosamunde and the other women here, and Larke looking guilty one moment and trying not to laugh the next.

Isidora nudged the girl in the ribs and whispered, "What am I to say? Does your lady-mother truly expect Lucien to marry me just because she said so?"

Larke squeezed Isidora's hand. "Lucien will do anything to please our mother."

"No matter how distasteful?"

"I did not mean it like that! He feels responsible for what happened."

"And what did happen? What Kalle mentioned? Was that true?"

Larke glanced at Amelie, whose attention was now on her sewing. "In truth, I don't know all the details, for no one speaks of it. But Lucien had a twin. Our sister, Estelle…she was as lovely as he is handsome. Many years ago, they were out riding together—of course they weren't children anymore, but they still shouldn't have gone alone—and were set upon by thieves.

"They took Estelle and…and used her ill, and she died at their hands. I was very small, but I still remember seeing Lucien return with her in his arms. He was covered in blood. I never knew if it was his, or hers, or the thieves'. But it was horrible. He has never been the same since, nor has our mother."

Isidora looked at Amelie and saw her pale, sad face in a new light. "But that is terrible. Does she blame Lucien?"

"I don't know. But she does nothing to let him think she does not. It makes me so angry, betimes. She still has us, after all. She lost one child, does she want to lose another, by driving him away with her grief?"

Larke's voice broke as she finished speaking and Isidora returned the squeeze of her hand. How ironic—Larke lived in Lucien's shadow, with their mother, just as Isidora had lived in his shadow with her own father. He was well-named—Lucien, person of light. Without trying, he seemed to attract the most attention, wherever he went.

Isidora had yet another question. "But, Larke, why has your mother chosen me? Why not insist upon Rosamunde? She is one of you, after all."

"So? It seems obvious, does it not, that you and he are meant for one another?"

"You are being absurd."

"Your lips look like someone's been kissing you rather a lot." Larke looked upward, as if pondering deeply. "I wonder who that could possibly have been?"

Isidora could not reply for the heat burning in her cheeks.

"Nay, if I can see it, anyone can, even my mother. Her acceptance of you is the one thing that convinces me she may have forgiven Lucien, that she wants him to be happy."

"But what about your uncle?"

Larke scoffed, "Oh, no matter! He will let mother have her way in any and every thing. It has always been so, ever since *Pere*—died…" She turned to stare at Isidora. "I only just realized…"

"What?"

Larke looked away. "Nothing. I am speaking of things that I should not. I wish Lucien would hurry up. It is so boring in here."

Amelie glanced up from her needlework, but said nothing.

"*Mere,* we would like to go and bathe and change our clothes, may we be excused?" Larke asked hopefully.

Amelie gave the tiniest of nods and Larke grabbed Isidora's arm. They made their escape, and as one, headed not for warm water and clean garb, but down to the hall where the men still sat around the fire. Talking, Isidora saw to her relief, and not fighting.

Around a corner by the stairway, they stood just out of sight, but not out of hearing. Lucien had given his chair to his uncle, while Lucien, Kalle and Mauger sat in lesser seats and Wace made do with the floor.

All of them had mazers in hand, but their weapons were by the anteroom entrance.

Lucien nodded to Kalle. "So, pleasantries aside, what brings you to these parts, FitzMalheury? Surely you are not here for your health?"

This brought a general round of laughter, even from

Kalle himself. "Nay, Lucien. Perhaps to see to the health of others, but not my own. Already one of my goals has been met and you hold the *key* to the other. I have an interest in your…*work,* you see."

Lucien's throat went dry and he caught Mauger's swift and unnecessary "I told you there'd be trouble!" look.

Conrad drained his cup and held it out for Wace to refill. "What work is this? Horse breeding or keeping our lands out of the king's hands?"

Lucien began, "It has to do with—"

Kalle interrupted. "Aligning worldly interests with those of God, Sir Conrad. As should be the goal of all work."

Then he smiled at Lucien, a smile of such subtle conspiracy that Lucien knew not what to think. Kalle was the last person on earth with whom he ever expected—or wanted—to be allied in pursuit of the Work.

Wace came to Lucien's shoulder with the wine ewer and murmured softly as he poured, "Forgive my intrusion, but did you know, Sir Lucien, that Lord FitzMalheury was friend to my lord Raymond's late brother, Alonso? That they were together on King Richard's Crusade, along with Sir Percy?"

Lucien's jaw tightened for a long moment, then he replied, without looking at Wace, "Nay, but it surprises me not at all. I thank you for telling me."

Kalle and Alonso. Perfect for one another. Each a master of his own form of cruelty. And to think that Raymond's younger brother, Percy, also on the crusade, had been at their mercy. He had returned, starving, mute and nearly broken beyond recovery, years after the others had long been home. Alonso had abandoned him to the Saracens.

But wicked as Kalle might be, Lucien did not think him capable of the kinds of evil Alonso had found it a joy to make habitual. Nay, his ill temper was more the sort caused by a pain of long duration, that makes the sufferer lash out unexpectedly, like an animal that has been pushed too far.

Then he caught a movement out of the corner of his eye. Near the stair. "Pardon me." He rose, bowed to the company and made straight for Larke's and Isidora's hiding place. Catching them each by the scruff of her neck, he marched them back up the stairs.

God, he was sick of females and their antics! Why could they not simply behave as women were supposed to behave? As Rosamunde behaved? Never a peep out of her, after that first disastrous evening. Indeed he did not think twice about her.

He released Larke into her chamber and considered where to take Isidora, still his captive. He dragged her off to his solar; there he could speak to her alone. With the door closed behind them, he stood between it and her. She faced him defiantly, eyes flashing, her dark hair in wild disarray about her face and shoulders. He wanted to cup her face between his hands and kiss that perfect mouth, steal her breath away, show her what he could not tell her...

"What in God's name am I to do with you, Isidora? You imperil not only yourself but now my sister? Think you Kalle is a foe easily turned aside from his goals? Think you that I can handle him with your constant interference and getting in the way?"

She stood with her feet spread and her fists clenched, but her words did not match her fighting stance. "Aye, I do think so. I think you can do anything, Lucien. It is one of the most frightening things about you. Your own blessedness, that you seem not to be aware of, but instead complain about inadequacies that in anyone else would be considered virtues. You are exhausting, my lord, to yourself and all who care for you. After a while, one despairs of being forever left behind you."

"Nay, that cannot happen. I do not know of what you speak, except that anyone who engages in the Work must strive to meet standards that exceed the ordinary. And so I must. You yourself said that unless I prove myself worthy, you will not give me the key you hold for me from your father. What is it you would have me do? Tell me, and I will do it."

At that moment with his earnest face and eloquent hands and strong, beautiful neck that moved when he swallowed, a neck that met powerful shoulders and a muscular chest and waist that went on to meet tight hips and thick thighs and—

At that moment Isidora wanted to tell him to simply take her into his arms and allow her to lose herself in his strength, in his scent, in the sound of his voice, in the feel of his skin next to hers.

Instead she bit her knuckles, felt her face turn red and wished she had fled her father's house before he had had the chance to burden her with any such gift for Lucien. A gift that would both bind him to her and forever take him away.

She squeezed her eyes shut against the sight of him. Having him was too much to hope for, and that very having would be too much for her heart to bear. She did not want him. "Lucien," she whispered, helpless to stop his name from forming on her lips.

"I am here, Isidora. Gift of Isis…"

She gasped as she found herself wrapped in his arms. Kissed soundly. Uplifted and carried to his bed. He drew back the furs.

"Get out of these clothes, Isidora. Let me see you. Let me touch you…" His voice was low and husky. He began to kiss her mouth and throat and mouth again, all the while working her dirty garb off of her, stripping her as efficiently as any maid did her mistress or any squire his lord.

Part of Isidora wanted to say no and part of her wanted to beg him to ignore any plea she might make for him to stop. Then she realized what a falsehood her protests would be, a mere show of modesty when in truth her body cried out to meet his.

Isidora held her breath as Lucien paused to survey what he had readied for plunder. She lay before him, wearing nothing but gooseflesh. *Am I pleasing to him?*

"You are a goddess, indeed." He pulled his tunic off over his head, threw it and his boots aside, cast off his leggings and braes. There was nothing left between them but a few shreds of self-restraint and the fact that they were not yet formally wed.

Then Lucien tugged the bed furs over them both. He was hot, melting against her. Irresistible. But she had to try. He deserved that much, to save his soul.

"Lucien, wait—oh—what are you doing?"

"Kissing you. Are you frightened?"

"Nay, I know you are kissing me, Lucien, it is just that—"

He lifted his head from her breast. "What?"

She could not bring herself to tell him the truth. "This is all so fast."

"I'll go slower."

He resumed his caressing of her body. She had never been touched before. Certainly not like this, and certainly not in all these places. "Nay, I mean…I mean, oh, I forgot what I was going to say…"

He shifted, so that he was on top of her, hard between her thighs, blood pulsing visibly in his neck. His eyes shone in the firelight and long, coppery hair spilled over his shoulders.

"Isidora, do you want me to stop?"

Just as breathless as Lucien, she could barely find the words to reply. "Y-you ask me about stopping, when you have not yet asked me about starting, Lucien? What am I to say…when you and your desire eclipse all else?"

He grinned. "Say, 'Nay, please, please, Lucien, do not stop.'"

Then he bent his head and kissed her mouth again, her breasts again, until she writhed beneath him, incoherent once more. Where had such wantonness in her come from? It had not merely rubbed off from Lucien, though he was generously doing his best to share his passion with her.

"Isidora," he murmured against her neck, the length of his body pressing hers. "Saying nothing is not the same as saying you want me. But I will not ask you a third time."

Why must he insist she take responsibility for her part in this? Other men did not give women such choices…. But then, Lucien was not like other men. His muscular warmth, his arms around her, great, delicious Saxon that he was…these alone were quite enough satisfaction, weren't they?

Nay, they were not. He was quivering with the effort of

holding himself back, as was she, with waiting for him. She could ease his torment and her own…and it would bind him to her, would it not?

A certain desperation possessed her. "I want you, Lucien. Now. Take me now."

He looked into her eyes, smoothed the hair from her brow and slowly, with exquisite care, kissed her lips. Then he pushed himself back, so she was between his arms, like pillars bunched with muscle, and his weight was on his hands, indenting the feather bed on either side of her.

He drew a long breath and his chest gleamed with the motion. "Nay…there is something not right, Isidora," he said softly, sadly. "Something you are not telling me, I can feel it. If this is to be, I want nothing to come between us."

Isidora might have borne Lucien's anger, his condemnation, but she could not bear his disappointment. With a small, animal sound, she twisted over and away, so she lay with her back to him, and hid her face under one arm before the tears that threatened could escape.

He stroked her shoulder with a broad palm. "Forgive me, Isidora. I have asked too much of you."

He did not understand. Perhaps *that* was what was too much to ask of him. She turned around. Sat up to face him and wiped her eyes with her wrist. Then she slid her arms over his solid shoulders and around his neck, pressing her face to his smooth hair as it fell forward across his cheek.

Isidora inhaled his scent and savored the moment. For all she knew, he might never allow her to be this close to him again.

"Lucien, I cannot give you the scrolls, or the Key from

my father, in exchange for your love." Nor could she tell him the truth. That by breaking her promise to her father—breaking one of God's commandments—she was breaking her own heart, as well.

He spoke, his chest vibrating against hers. "Isidora, is that what you think me capable of? That I would try to sell myself to you?"

"Oh, that is not what I meant!"

He pulled away from her and straightened. Suddenly Lucien was huge, blocking out the firelight. "Then what *did* you mean?"

"I cannot say. Please, don't make me!"

At that moment the door opened and Mauger stepped into the solar. "What's taking you so long, my lord? We are all awaiting— Oh! I beg your pardon. Ahem." He turned away, then looked again before directing his attention toward the floor.

"Glad as I am to know you are pursuing your duty, should this bedding not wait, Lucien, until you have the proper witnesses? And no other business to attend first?"

Isidora scooted back under the covers in an agony of shame.

Lucien looked over his shoulder at the seneschal. "I thought this *was* the business you and Conrad wished me to attend first, Mauger. Kindly get out and tell them I'll be down as soon as I may."

Mauger bowed as he exited. "Your pardon, *demoiselle.*"

Isidora brought her head back out. "You did not bar the door, Lucien? At least I suppose that proves you did not plan all this—business—in advance."

"It proves only that I am master here. I need not bar my

door, because only Mauger would forget himself so far as to enter without knocking."

"So you did plan it in advance?"

"Nay. How can one plan anything around a creature as unpredictable as a woman?" In one graceful movement he launched himself from the bed to gather his scattered clothing from the floor.

Isidora drank up the sight of his haunches, his well-muscled calves and his—

"Do *I* stare at *you?*" He tugged his tunic down and hopped on one foot to pull up a legging.

"Aye, so you have done."

"Well, then, get used to it," he growled.

"Excuse me?"

"Whether you like me, love me or hate me, it makes no difference to the fact that we will be married before Lent. That is what my elders want. It is a prospect I find tolerable, therefore it is what I will do. In addition, it is what your brother expects, I believe it is what your father would have wished, and now that I have…have dishonored you even further, it is something you yourself should hope for, as you have no other choice but to starve."

Isidora opened her mouth, then shut it again. No other choice? Did he not know she was an artist? "I can support myself, with my scribing and illuminations. I do not need you to feed me *or* to marry me!"

"But you need me, just the same." Now dressed, he returned to the bed, sat beside her and stroked her cheek with his thumb. "To protect you."

She pushed his hand away. "But who is to protect me from you?"

"Who indeed? Kalle, perhaps?"

She swallowed and wished she had the advantage of her clothes, as well. "Nay. It was not like that."

"*It?*" Lucien's voice was too soft to be safe.

Isidora raised her chin. "Aye, our bargain. The price I paid Kalle to spare your life in Acre, Lucien."

He lowered his gaze for a moment, then brought it back to rest upon her. "I feel such shame. Whatever you paid was too much, Isidora. You should have left me there to rot, if the price was so high."

"Nay, Lucien. I know what you must be thinking. Indeed, had he asked for my virginity, I would have given it sooner than what he actually wanted. Something quite different. Something worth far more to me."

"What, then?"

Isidora twisted the sheet in her fingers. "A portrait I had painted, of my mother. The only thing I had of her. It was...so painful to give it up. But I do not regret it, Lucien."

"Oh, Isidora." He lifted her hands and kissed their backs. "I will get it back for you. I swear this, upon my father's honor and the Holy Cross."

"Nay! What are you saying? You cannot. You must not try. Kalle will kill you. It is only an image. A symbol. Not her."

"But we cling to such things, do we not? Sometimes they are our only comfort when all is dark. Like the lock of my sister's hair that I keep. It reminds me of her and of what I must do. It is why I pursue the Elixir."

"Estelle?"

He nodded. "Larke told you?"

"Aye, but she herself knows little beyond what she saw.

So do not concern yourself that I know any secrets you wish to keep."

"When I have paid what I owe Estelle and our mother, then I will tell you about it. For if you are with me, you, too, will have to live with the consequences of my actions until then."

"As you will have to live with the consequences of mine."

"You mean, your withholding of what may be the Key?"

"That, and other things besides."

He rewrapped the linen bandage on his hand, which had soaked through with blotches of crimsom. "Eventually, you will give me what I want. All of it."

"You cannot force me."

"But I can persuade you. Besides, it cannot be hidden far. Don't tell me you have dropped it down the well."

"You will not find it, not without my help."

He just smiled at her. "We shall see, Isidora. Your father was not the only teacher I ever had in Outremer."

"Either let me see to your wound or go away," she said.

His lazy grin broadened. "You are dismissing me from my own bed, my own solar?"

"What does it sound like to you?"

"Very much like a wife."

"Then listen again. Go away."

Chapter Twenty-Two

When Lucien regained the all-male sanctity of the hall, the others were just draining their mazers and preparing to disperse. It was late, and it had been hours since they had met in the woods. Lucien's head and hand both ached. Among other things.

He approached Kalle. "FitzMalheury?"

The knight turned and gave him a look that might have soured milk. "What?"

"When your man and servant arrive, Mauger will see to their comfort. You and I can finish our business on the morrow. And if I find you have killed Faris al-Rashid, you had best prepare to pay his honor price."

"Very well. *A demaine.*" Kalle stalked off toward the door, a path clearing for him as he went.

Mauger sidled up to Lucien's elbow. "How went your—you know what?" he asked quietly, without a hint of lasciviousness.

Lucien crossed his arms. "It went nowhere." Indeed *it*

was most disgruntled by the whole unsatisfactory affair. "I decided she was not ready, and she told me to get out."

Mauger's broad face looked stunned. "Oh, my God, Lucien. You did not tell her that, did you? Surely you made some other excuse, to take the fault upon yourself?"

"There was no fault. What do you mean?"

"Have you nothing between your ears but quicksilver? By *you* making the decision to stop…wherever it was you stopped, and saying it was because of *her* that you stopped—can you not see how that might seem to a proud young woman?

"She would expect, and rightfully so, that her beauty would inflame you to such passion that nothing could stop you except Isidora herself. You have taken that power from her and shamed her. 'Tis a wonder she did not throw something at you instead of just asking you to leave."

Lucien rubbed his brow wearily. "You know, Mauger, Rosamunde said you had a better way with women than me, now I think I begin to understand."

Mauger frowned. "Rosamunde should mind her own business. What's that mess there? Let me see your hand."

Knowing it would make his life easier in the end, Lucien allowed Mauger to unwrap his wound and fuss over it.

"Not good, not good at all. Look at this, my lord, what your careless neglect has produced."

Lucien looked. A still-oozing wound gaped on his palm, the angry redness of its edges puffing toward his fingers and wrist. Bits of glass and silver material still glinted within it. "So?"

"So! You never washed out whatever no doubt noxious things are therein? You never had Jager or me check it. You are irresponsible, Lucien. You need to be able to fight with this hand. Soon it will be so swollen you'll not be able to hold your own mead bowl."

"Then do what must be done, Mauger."

"I will, and the more it hurts, the less I will feel sorry for you!"

The next day, by the stream where the women did their washing, Daphne draped a linen sheet over her shoulders and ran in circles, so it billowed like white wings behind her.

Bent over the shallows, her mother looked up and shouted, "What are ye doing? Are ye daft, lass? That is Lord Lucien's! Bring it back!"

Elated, Daphne laughed and merely raised the sheet in her fists, so it flew even higher as she ran. "Look at it, Mama! All will be well! There will be an heir, these lands will remain Lord Lucien's, and all of us can stay here forever!"

"Stop yer noise and bring that here before ye dirty it more than it—" As Daphne approached, the woman's eyes rounded and she covered her mouth as a slow grin grew. "I see! He's done it! He's had her! Look there!"

The goodwives gathered to examine the evidence. A red stain, in the middle of the linen. "We should not wash this. We must show it to the Lady Amelie, and Lord Conrad, if they will allow us audience. A wedding must go forward, now, as it should have years since!"

"I'll do it!" Daphne cried.

"You will not! You'll get yer bottom smacked, more like. Nay, we must give it to someone they will listen to. Someone we can trust."

"Lady Larke?"

"Nay, bless that child." Daphne's mother tapped her wrinkled, pursed lips. "I will speak to our Jager, for he eats in hall, and he can give it to them."

"I like Jager very much, I can take it to him," Daphne offered once again.

"Nay, ye sweet wee slut, he'll be as likely to tumble ye as anything. Somethin' this important to folk, we should all go. Ye did well, lassie, to show it to us."

Daphne smiled. "I told you our lord Lucien was good luck." She pressed the cloth to her bosom. "I just wanted some of it for myself, so I'll have lots of babies. Did I ever mention the time when he fell asleep in the horse barn? He was soo-oo big when I woke him!"

The women laughed and waved Daphne away. She skipped up the lane toward the castle. Maybe Jager was back from his patrolling and she could whisper the good news to him ahead of time.

At table in the hall, Isidora sat beside Lucien as the company finished supper. It was Friday, so the main fare had been cod, as it was every fast day and would be for all the long weeks of Lent. Saxon-Norman food…sometimes she would rather starve. She took a sip of ale to try to make the taste fade.

How it produced men like Lucien was beyond her understanding. Or perhaps such men were to be expected. One is what one eats, and Lucien, after all, had about as much sensitivity and insight as did a cod. He had proven that beyond a doubt. After humiliating her beyond bearing, how he expected her to hold her head up and pretend nothing had happened was also beyond her understanding.

She welcomed the distraction as Sir Jager got up, bearing some sort of bundle, and bowed deeply before Lady Amelie. The lady turned uncertainly toward Conrad. Isidora followed suit, looking at Lucien, who in turn shrugged and raised his eyebrows just as Conrad was doing.

Jager cleared his throat. "My lady, the villagers have brought something of importance to my attention. They petition you, most humbly, that you act upon their discovery, with all due haste, and bring your son to his duty…and the altar."

Amidst the growing murmurs of the assembly, Lucien jumped to his feet. "What is this about, Jager? And why have you not spoken of it to me first, if it concerns me?"

Jager turned to Lucien. "This concerns not only you, my lord, but the welfare of the entire castle and the lands around it. And a good thing, too, that it has come to light, as such things will, by the grace of God."

He shook out the bundle. At first Isidora did not recognize it. Then she saw and was certain her face was as red as the stain on the fabric. *Discovery,* indeed. Only, the villagers were wrong. Jager was wrong. How…? She thought back.

The only blood shed that night must have been from Lucien's hand, when he'd leaned over her. The memory of him, strong, beautiful, ready for her—but ultimately finding her lacking—rushed through her senses in a hot, painful wave.

She would happily wring both his and Jager's necks, if afterward she could run and hide, so mortified was she. Beside her, apparently oblivious to her distress, Lucien caught her shoulder and squeezed it for a moment.

Amelie and Conrad remained as if frozen to their seats,

their faces unreadable. Then, with barely a glance toward Isidora, they both looked at Lucien and smiled.

"Of course we shall regard this as being under the honorable assumption that Lucien has merely made formal his intent to marry," Conrad said. "The wedding can take place at once, with just the family present. Then may the celebrations be arranged, once our friends have been invited. The question remains, of course, as to precisely whom he has chosen, though Lady Amelie looks favorably upon Isidora, here."

Lucien stood as if struck dumb, breathing rapidly, through his mouth. Just like a cod, Isidora thought. One out of water. Well, she would not help him in his plight.

She, too, stood and inclined her head to those gathered. Amelie and her ladies, Conrad and his men, Mauger, the Welsh cousins of Lady Ceridwen, Rosamunde, Larke, Wace and any number of others of varied rank. Though God may have revealed the sheet, she had Him to thank that Kalle refused to take his meals with them, preferring his private cook and pavilion to Lucien's hospitality.

"I beg your pardon, my lords and ladies," she said. "But I must assure you that the blood you see on that cloth is not of *my* body."

The sudden intake of multiple breaths was the shocked reaction that should have taken place when they first saw the stain, Isidora thought. But these folk were completely obsessed with the furthering of their line, no matter how it came about or, apparently, with whom.

"Then what virgin has Lucien been swiving, if not you?" Conrad roared.

"I have not been—swiving—any virgin, my lord!" Lucien protested.

Conrad's face began to darken toward an unhealthy purple.

"Oyez!" called a clear voice. All heads turned as Rosamunde got to her feet, pale and solemn. "My lord, I claim that blood as mine," she said, and fixed her gaze not upon Lucien, but Mauger.

Another cod! Isidora noted, as everyone watched Mauger begin his own gasping imitation of a fish. A clever move upon the quiet Rosamunde's part. She could make that claim, without telling a lie, for she had not said the blood came from her person, only that she claimed possession of it.

Which indeed, having once been betrothed to Lucien, she had every right to do, had she known it was his.

Then Isidora's eyes filled with tears as the innocent Mauger looked helplessly at Rosamunde, went down on one knee—and proved himself a true knight and faithful lover.

"I crave your forgiveness, my lady."

"As well you should!" exclaimed Conrad. "I see we have much to do, and perhaps little time in which to do it. Given the apparent fecund air of these premises, I insist upon vows being taken forthwith, before Lady Rosamunde's father descends upon us with his men-at-arms. And that goes for you, as well, Lucien. Enough has been said. It is time to act."

Mauger was still kissing the hand that Rosamunde had triumphantly offered him. Larke stood by, looking almost as furious as did Lucien, who joined her in glaring at Rosamunde.

"How dare you twist this situation to your own advantage?" he demanded, but softly.

Rosamunde tossed back her flaxen mane. "Would you have preferred that I made you keep our original bargain?"

She smiled at his stricken look. "I thought not. This way, I get what I want and Mauger gets what he wants."

Aye, the poor man! Isidora narrowed her eyes at the maiden, but was glad for Lucien's sake. She would not wish Rosamunde upon anyone.

Mauger lumbered back to his feet, and leaving Rosamunde to her wait-women, grabbed his mazer and headed for the nearest pitcher-bearing maid.

Isidora saw that Lucien was cradling his arm as his mother came up to him. Amelie drew his face down and kissed his cheeks, right and left. "You will make me happy, Lucien, I know it," she said, barely audible, then she left the hall in the company of her ladies.

Isidora's heart ached as Lucien followed his mother with a pained gaze. It struck her how alike Amelie and Rosamunde were…both of them as manipulative as they were beautiful. Perhaps it was more than coincidence that Lucien had chosen Rosamunde out of all who sought his favor.

A welcome distraction, Gawaine whined at his master's side. Lucien patted the dog's head, then turned to Isidora. "Help me," he said, his voice thick.

"All right, Lucien. I can see your uncle will not leave until this thing is done. Your desire is to please him and your mother, who will never be happy until she sees you wed."

Lucien blinked slowly. "Nay, Isidora. I mean help me with this hand."

She looked at him in alarm. He was sweating, which she had attributed to the spicy food and the emotion of the moment, but now she saw that he was in pain. "We'll see to it in your solar. Larke, come with us."

After having a basin of hot water brought up and shutting the door, Isidora unwrapped the caked bandage. The wound was ugly, festering, and Lucien's hand was alarmingly swollen, with a red streak climbing his forearm.

"This is more than cleansing herbs can remedy, Lucien. How did Mauger deal with it?"

Lucien closed his eyes. "He dug out the bits of glass and quicksilver that were in it."

"What did he use?"

"His eating dagger."

Isidora closed her eyes, too, and prayed that she did not beat Mauger over the head when next she saw him. These English knew nothing of the kind of physicking with which the Arabs had great skill. She examined the wound again. "He did not wash the knife first, I take it?"

"He wiped it on his tunic. It looked clean enough."

Isidora looked Lucien in the eye. "My lord, I must bring FitzMalheury in to see this."

"Nay. Why? I'll not have him touch me."

"And you yourself will be touching things only half as much, if this hand has to be cut off!"

"Nay. I'd rather die."

"Do not be absurd, Lucien. It has not come to that— yet. But if you insist upon being stupid, it may. I do not even know if I can coax Kalle to come up and help. But you will be fortunate if he does, Lucien. Believe me, I know he is cruel and dangerous, but he also has great knowledge.

"If the hand must be taken, that is better than dying. Whatever you think you may prefer at this moment, I assure you, even should you lose it, you will feel quite different about the loss in a few months' time."

Lucien covered his face with his good hand for a moment, then shoved his fingers back through his hair. "All right. Bring him if you can. If you cannot, then fetch Jager. He has some experience with limb-lopping. It will serve him right, for bringing in that sheet."

White-faced, Larke watched and listened, without saying a word. Then she turned on her heel and marched toward the door.

Lucien called after her, "Larke?"

Isidora was struck by the grim determination in the girl's face.

"Brother, I will return. Make no decisions about your hand until I do." She whirled out of the solar.

"Oh, God, what is she up to now? Isidora, have someone go after her, will you?"

When Isidora made no move, he started to get up himself, but she shoved him back to his bed. "Lucien, she is ten and seven. Nearly a grown woman. You must let her find her own way. She has a great deal of sense. More than you, at times. Do not worry so much."

Isidora did call for Mauger, but it was to have the seneschal come up and prevent Lucien from leaving the solar. She ordered a warm rosemary poultice and some hypericum ointment. Then she descended the stairs herself, put on her mantle and, with a heavy heart, went in search of Kalle FitzMalheury.

"Faris al-Rashid…"

Faris opened his eyes. The monk they called Percy stepped closer, then sat on the edge of the infirmary bed. The room's fire snapped comfortingly, the linens cover-

ing Faris were pristine, and the singing of the monks put
him at peace. He felt weaker than he had ever been in
his life.

Percy held a cup to Faris's mouth. "Of the host of Salah
al-Din, I remember your name as being one of renown, despite your youth at the time."

Faris swallowed the bitter liquid, grateful that the worst
was over. Thanks to the deft hands of this monk, the arrow
was gone from his body and he yet lived. "No doubt such
praises were an exaggeration."

"Do you not now have a Christian name, to which you
were baptized?"

"That detail must have been overlooked, *effendi.* But
what were you doing in the east? You do not seem the kind
of man who would join a Crusade."

Percy smiled ruefully. "If you knew the sort of family I
am from, you'd understand. They lust for blood, one and
all, whether knights or clergy. I went with Richard Coeur
de Leon, and regretted it in the end." He grew quiet for an
instant, then continued. "But more to the point, how is it
you are here? In England, I mean, for I know horse sense
brought you to this particular place. And he is being well
taken care of, by the way."

"That I am glad to hear. I came on an errand, to escort
a kinswoman to see Lucien de Griswold."

"Indeed! He is a good friend of my brother Raymond.
Not a brother here, mind you, but my actual brother. In fact,
I am expecting him any day now."

"He lusts for blood, you say?"

Percy smiled again. "Oh, he does, at that. But he is
much more selective nowadays about whose blood he

sheds than he once was. And, he never went on Crusade with us. He'll have nothing against you, mark me."

"I believe his squire Wace is already at Lucien's hall."

Percy raised his brows. "Is he? They've started early this year, then."

Faris waited politely for Percy to explain his statement, but the monk did not. "You've been very kind, my lord. I thank you."

Percy rose and inclined his head. "God grant that you be well soon. Rest now. *Adieu.*"

Faris relaxed against the pillow as the monk departed. Having found such a place of dignity and kindness as this, he felt reassured to be leaving Isidora in England. Perhaps it was not completely barbaric, after all.

Chapter Twenty-Three

Isidora hesitated at the castle gate. Beyond Lucien's walls, Kalle flew blue-and-yellow striped banners from his lances. His grand horses casually nibbled at the bedraggled dead grass of the practice grounds. It looked as though he was settling in, playing at a siege encampment, she thought.

But a tiny one. Apart from the dark man and the cook she'd met in the wood, he had no more than a half dozen warriors with him as his personal cohort. He was the only one with a pavilion, however. The others had to make due with what shelter they could find.

She picked up her skirts, walked across the field and approached Kalle's guard outside his tent. "I would speak to your master."

The guard, who smelled as though he had spent a hard night drinking, narrowed his reddened eyes. "Who are you?"

Before she could reply, Kalle's deep voice rumbled from within the pavilion. "Let her in."

The guard lifted the heavy cloth door and Isidora

stepped through into the sumptuous private world of Kalle FitzMalheury. Instead of rush matting, thick carpets intricately woven in reds, blues and gold were layered on the floor. A brazier glowed and he had candles lit all around.

He had even brought a bed and mattress, complete with a stuffed coverlet and tasseled pillows. Isidora knew, however, that Kalle was as tough a man as she had ever met. This opulence did not reflect his inner being. It was merely for show and, perhaps, to put potential enemies off guard.

She had witnessed how her father had beaten him without mercy. At first, Kalle could have easily stopped the older man or even killed him. But he had allowed the awful battering to go on, and on. She had always wondered why, and thanked God that Deogal had stopped short of murder.

Kalle's forbearance on that long-ago night was the only reason she was willing to have any dealings with him at all.

She squared her shoulders. "My lord. Apart from our meeting in the forest, it has been quite some time."

Kalle did not smile as he gazed at her; his eyes shone cold and steady. He held out the goblet he just been drinking from and only spoke after she had declined it. "*Oui,* so it has. What do you want, Isidora Binte Deogal?"

Despite the warmth in the tent, Isidora hugged her mantle closer. She might as well take full measure of the man while she had the chance. "Why did you not fight back when my father came after you?"

Kalle set his drink down upon a small, carved wooden table. "I did not want to kill him in front of his wife and child."

"You could have run away, but you did not."

He sat on the edge of his bed and crossed his arms. "Your father was once a Templar, you know that, of course."

"Aye."

"Such a distinction does not fall away with either age or changing fortunes. I was the stronger, but I had to remain, and yield, for as long as it took Deogal to feel honor was satisfied."

"But my mother…she never…she was innocent!"

"*Oui.* But I was not." Kalle paused, his eyes glittering. "I decided that if he wore himself out on me, there would be less anger to vent upon her. But…he still managed to kill her in the end. And for that, I hope he is burning in hell right now and for all of eternity."

Isidora covered her face with her hands. "Do not say such things!"

"It is the truth, Isidora. Is that not what you came to me for, the truth?"

She looked at him at last. "Aye. Did you kill Faris?"

Kalle did not flinch from her gaze. "I have little doubt that I gave him a mortal wound. He vanished into the mist."

Isidora bit her lip to keep herself from weeping. "Why?"

"He disobeyed me, he betrayed me. I cannot tolerate that, from anyone. But why do you care? Did he seduce you? Capture your heart?"

"He is a good man, Sir Kalle. One with purpose and morals and honor. Do you not know that Ayshka was his mother, too?"

Kalle went pale. "Nay…I did not. You mean, he is your brother?"

"Half brother."

Kalle examined his tented fingers for a moment and his face regained its mask of hardness. "Now you think I owe you compensation?"

"Nay. But you owe me a favor, at least. Look at a wound Lucien has—"

"*Non.* Lucien can die and rot in hell along with Deogal, for all I care."

Isidora balled her hands into fists. "You have taken from me everyone I ever loved! Now you take him, too?"

Kalle smiled, a chilling prospect. "You love him, do you?"

"Nay—"

"Do not deny it. You've already saved him once. Now you want to do so again? Is he truly worth it?"

Isidora stopped the protest that came to her lips. "Worth what?"

Kalle stood, towering over her in the small space. "I do not believe you came here empty-handed, Isidora. Tell me what you have to offer."

Kalle had such skill to make people talk, he must have been privy to many secrets when he was a priest. Despite that, a great knot of refusal threatened to bind her tongue. But she must do what had to be done. "I have some items, from my father's workshop."

Kalle's demeanor subtly changed. He could not hide it from her.

His jaw knotted. His pale eyes darkened and gleamed at the same time. She knew that look—of men who lusted after impossible things. Of alchemists.

"Where are they?"

Isidora drew back from Kalle. "Hidden."

"Does Lucien know of them?"

"Aye. But he has not seen them."

Kalle paused, then took a step toward her, his head slightly tilted. "Does he not see *you?*"

"I know not what you mean…"

"You have the look of your mother." Kalle frowned and brought himself up short. "Bring me these…items, and I will decide if it is worth my time to help your Lucien."

Isidora raised her chin. "Nay. The exchange will be as simultaneous as is practical. But Lucien must be improving, first. You will accept my word of honor upon the matter and you will give me yours."

Kalle's white grin spread slowly. "Spoken like the Templar's daughter you are. Very well."

He retrieved his sword from where it lay on his bed, put its tip into the exquisite rug on the floor, and knelt with his big hands on the hilt. "I, Kalle FitzMalheury, Knight of the Cross, do swear by life and limb, by heart and hand, and by my soul's salvation, to attend Lucien de Griswold in his time of need." He genuflected, kissed the rounded pommel of the sword and got back to his feet. "Satisfied?"

"I had better be, my lord Kalle, or your soul will be in peril. We shall expect you." Hoping he could not see her trembling, Isidora turned and departed, brushing past the dark man who was waiting outside.

Earm, still tired from his muddy ordeal, watched her go, graceful and proud. Kalle's voice startled him. "Keep an eye on her, Earm. She needs looking after. Indeed, before this is through, she may even be coming home to Acre with us."

Home? Earm sighed. He had none, not that he could remember, at least. But, in Acre was also the rare and beautiful Lina. If he won her heart, he would need call nowhere else home.

Chapter Twenty-Four

Larke cantered through the forest, with Wace hard on her heels. She could not lose him, even if her horse had been the faster—which it was not—because of the poor footing, low branches and failing light. But she could stay just ahead, because her mount was nimble and she herself was a skilled horsewoman.

"Larke! Befuddle and confound you! Stop!"

Over the wind rushing past her ears, Wace sounded quite angry, Larke thought. In that case it would be a mistake to stop. Best to push on. There was a clearing ahead, she could see the pale, early evening sky above the trees.

Then, quite unexpectedly, he thundered past her on his big, elegant courser, spun it on its haunches and forced her palfrey to a splay-legged stop that nearly put her over its head.

Wace grabbed Larke by the back of her jerkin and saved her from falling. But he did not let go and when her mount shied away from his, Larke dangled for an instant before Wace heaved her facedown before him on his horse.

"Leave go!" she gasped, her head filling with blood, and her behind awkwardly sticking up.

"This presents a most tempting opportunity to teach you a lesson, Lady Larke," Wace said. "But it is not my place. Not yet."

"*What* did you just say?" she demanded, outraged.

"You heard me."

"Put me down and prepare to defend yourself!"

"As you wish." Wace leaned down, easing her to her feet with one arm, and she was amazed at how strong he was. She smoothed her clothes back into order and put her hands on her hips. "Well? Are you going to get down?"

"You said to defend myself. I think I am safer up here than down there. I know you certainly are safer with me up here, too."

"From you, you mean?"

Wace shrugged, grinned, and said nothing.

"Look what you've done. My horse has run off!"

"Oh, dear. I guess you'll have to walk home then, will you not?"

"Wace du Hautepont, when next I see Lady Ceridwen, I shall tell her of your behavior this day."

This threat made him take pause, as she knew it would, more than anything she might tell Sir Raymond.

He shook his head. "Larke, what you are doing out here again? If you must go on these nocturnal expeditions, you simply cannot go alone. How many times must I tell you?"

"Nay, Wace, first, you tell me what you are up to here at my brother's keep. No good, I warrant, and not just to torment me. Why is your lord not with you?"

Wace studied her. "Why should I tell you?"

Larke met his gaze and saw that affection glimmered behind his arrogance. "Because, I will ride on your horse's rump and embrace you from behind if you do."

Wace smirked, as if her offer meant nothing to him. "Well, knowing you, you'll find out sooner or later anyway, since you cannot seem to keep your nose out of anyone's business. My lord Raymond and I are running horses to the Cymraeg."

It took a moment for Larke to fully realize what Wace had just said. Her jaw dropped. "You are smuggling horses into Wales? Why?"

"Get up here behind me first. We'd best be moving on to wherever you were headed before your horse gets home and everyone comes looking for you." He extended his arm for her to jump up and ride behind him. She settled on his mount's warm haunches and slid her arms around his solid middle.

Wace was wearing a felted haqueton, the under-padding for mail, though he had none on, with a leather outer layer strengthened by metal studs. His double-wrapped belt bore his sword and dagger. A tiny shiver ran through her. Despite the bulk of his attire, Larke could tell that the squire was fit, indeed.

He exuded an air of confidence that only came from actual experience in battle and she knew Sir Raymond trusted Wace with his life. Under the circumstances, she could do no less. "I am sorry, Wace, for causing you worry."

"I am beginning to think that is your sole purpose in life."

"I am only trying to get to the Cistercian abbey, to see if Sir Percy—I mean, Brother Percy—can help with Lucien's wound."

"Ah. I should have thought of that myself. Very well."

"You were saying? About the horses?"

"Aye. The crown is rather strict about horse-breeding, as you must know. A lot depends upon the quality of a knight's mount. The lords of the Cymraeg appreciate fine horseflesh, and they are willing to pay handsomely for it. So, Raymond and Lucien—"

Larke was shocked. "*My* brother?"

"Aye, of course. We can't do it without havens along the way. Lucien, and others, loan their stallions out to stud with certain sympathetic owners of broodmares. When the likely colts and fillies are yearlings, we take them in small groups across the border. Just to keep the bloodlines fresh."

"But is that not treason?"

"Not when one has been betrayed on the scale that Raymond and Percy have been."

"Percy is involved, too?"

"The Cistercians cannot support themselves only by singing, can they?"

"I want to help!" Larke exclaimed.

"Absolutely not!" Wace reached back and thumped his gloved hand onto her thigh, as if in emphasis. Then he hurriedly withdrew it, as if he had only just realized where it had landed. "We'd better hurry, if we are to get back before midnight. Your brother may have me drawn and quartered as it is."

"I think not. I think he would be relieved to know anyone at all besides him was willing to put up with me."

Wace laughed, his voice rich and low. "Oh, so you think I do this willingly?"

"Of course. Indeed, I think you harbor a certain fondness for me, Wace."

"What makes you think that?"

"Because…" She found an edge and slid her hand inside the warmth of his haqueton and around to his chest.

"What are you doing!"

"Your heart beats faster when I touch you, Wace. That is how I know you like me."

"What rot. I am ticklish, that's all."

"I don't believe so. But there is one way to find out."

"What way?"

Larke smiled. "It will have to wait. You might topple from your horse, otherwise."

"You'd do well to see that you yourself stay on. And if you cannot behave, I will put you on a lead and make you run beside me."

Larke's smile just widened. The more vexed he got, the better she felt. "I shall just hold on to you a bit tighter, then, so I do not fall off." She hugged Wace from behind and there was not a thing he could do about it.

At last Mauger had dozed off, and Lucien made his escape from bed. He fumbled with the lock on the door to the *laboratorium*. It was ice-rimed. His wounded hand felt like a hot brick and was about as useful.

There was a soft crunch of footsteps. "Lucien?"

He jumped. "What are you doing out here?" He turned to see Isidora walking toward him. The moon was just rising and it shed a silver light upon her. She had pulled her mantle up over her head and it framed her lovely face in soft, crimson folds.

"I might ask the same of you. Give me that key." She held out her hand.

Still no gloves! He hesitated.

"I won't keep it, Lucien. Let me help you."

He held out the great iron key.

She took it and wrestled with the lock until it gave way. Then she handed it back to him. "What do you plan to do?"

Lucien pushed the heavy door inward. "I come here to think. It is more of a church to me than the chapel. I am so far behind in the Work…there is a phase of the moon coming up, that is necessary for— I've done nothing, for weeks and weeks. It is a great lack in my heart. And I am starting to feel it is an endeavor beyond hope." He picked up the oil lamp he had set down before the door, set fire to a twig, and started lighting the candles in the chamber.

"Let me do that."

Lucien allowed Isidora to take over the task. He picked up a handful of kindling from a basket in the corner, laid it in the stone-lined aperture of the athanor with some wood, and dribbled oil over it. The flames burst into life with a satisfying whoosh, glowing from the niche in the wall.

His skin was wet with sweat and he felt cold and hot by turns. He dragged his chair over to the fire and collapsed into it. "You should go back to the hall, Isidora."

She moved to stand before him. "Kalle will come. He promised. If you do not want to receive him in here, you, too, should return."

"I need to think. Alone." As if he could think about anything with the throbbing he was enduring.

"About what you'll do with only one hand?"

"Nay. About my purpose, in this world."

"Ah."

"You sound angry, Isidora."

She sighed. "So I am. Why are you so stubborn?"

He looked up at her. "Oh, and I suppose you are not?"

"There is a difference between stubbornness and stupidity. Unfortunately, some people display both qualities at once. You should be in bed. You should be conserving your strength, to better serve your people in future."

"I do not trust Kalle. He may cure my hand, and yet introduce some agent that will lie within me, slowly working poison, until I am rendered useless."

"Nay, I do not believe he would. He would not betray the daughter of Ayshka."

"He already *has* betrayed her! The moment he compromised your mother, he betrayed you both, as well as Deogal, and Faris. And we have yet to see how he has truly rewarded Faris."

Isidora's eyes shone bright with tears. "We have no choice! Kalle has the skill, the herbcraft. Things that do not even grow on this side of the world, he has! Knowledge of medicine that was thought lost when the ancient library of Alexandria burned, he has!"

Lucien had to smile. "Isidora, it is not some rare disease that ails me. It is but a simple wound gone bad. It happens all the time."

"And folk die of such wounds, all the time!"

"Oh, so now we've gone from me losing my hand to losing my life."

"I could not bear it," Isidora whispered, sinking to her knees.

Lucien wiped his damp face with his sleeve. "And I cannot bear seeing you this way."

"Then accept Kalle's help. You said to bring him. Do not put the effort I made to waste."

A chill struck Lucien's heart. "I should not have asked you to do such a thing, for any reason. What has he demanded of you this time?"

"N-nothing. He is doing it as a knightly gesture."

"Oh, do not insult me with such a story! Kalle FitzMalheury does nothing merely for the sake of chivalry. He left such ideals behind him long ago. But, Isidora, if you will not tell me the truth, I will not press you into a lie."

She said nothing, but stared at the fire.

"Isidora?"

At last she turned to look at him.

"I will let him look at it. I promised you as much. But if I feel any falseness from him, I shall withdraw my consent."

She smiled, then, a tender, vulnerable smile, and Lucien held out his good hand to her, to help her rise. Then he heaved himself to his feet and looked down at her. He pushed a strand of her hair back beneath the mantle's edge. "Why do you bother about me, when I have only neglected you?"

"You follow alchemy, a path of slim hope. You should know why."

"I cannot offer you spiritual bliss, physical perfection or endless wealth, though."

"I want none of those things."

Lucien did not want to ask the next obvious question. He did not want to know her desire, which, even if she told him, he doubted his ability to fulfill. He had begun to feel queasy, light-headed, indeed, quite ready to tip over, like a tree being felled.

"I think, Isidora, that perhaps you are right. I should be in bed." He did not want to fall on top of her, as he had in Acre, when she had helped him out of the pit. Or the way he had been just the other night. Poised to enter…oh, God, if any more blood drained from his head, he would have to be carried from this place.

"Come, Lucien. Let me help you outside. Then give me the key and I'll put out the candles and lock the door after us."

Isidora put her shoulder beneath Lucien's arm and steadied him until she had him propped against the exterior wall. She ran back into the *laboratorium* and took a swift look around as she extinguished the candles. As she moved toward the athanor, she spotted what she was looking for.

A space, beneath one of the stone-topped worktables. The slab rested on a ledge built into the wall. There was a gap, between the slab and the wall, about a hand span wide. She took the small bundle from where she had tucked it under her belt and stuffed it in the crevice.

It was not obvious, but still in plain sight from the correct angle. An earthenware urn rested on the floor. She tugged on it and rocked it sideways, so that it blocked the view of the hiding place.

Then, with all the fires dead but the athanor's, she ran back out, heaved the door shut and clicked the iron lock into place like a manacle. Lucien was standing with his eyes closed, looking like a ghost.

Isidora wondered if she had the strength to get him back to the hall. "Done. Shall I fetch Mauger?"

"Nay. Just walk beside me. Act as though nothing is wrong, all right? If anyone shows concern, scoff at them."

It was one of the longest walks of her life. To be beside Lucien, knowing he was slipping farther from her with each passing moment. The stairs would be the worst of it. If he lost consciousness there, there was nothing she could do to stop him from breaking his head on the stone steps.

As they entered the hall, Mauger came to meet them, looking like a storm cloud. "Where—"

"Say nothing, sir," Isidora whispered. "Just get him to the solar. Laugh, as if you are jesting with him. Then we will wait for Kalle."

Mauger nodded and for once did not argue.

Chapter Twenty-Five

"How does it feel, Lucien?" Isidora asked. Sitting next to Lucien in his bed, pinning the covers with her weight was the only way she could keep him from getting up, short of sitting *on* him.

Lucien glanced at his hand, elevated on a pillow. "As if it were in labor, about to give birth to something twice its size. It could not feel any worse, I think, unless you poured boiling oil over it."

Mauger poked his head around the bed curtain. "Fitz-Malheury is here."

Lucien grunted in response, his expression surly.

"Bon soir, mes amis." Kalle's bulk filled the doorway. He had brought the dark-haired man and his cook, as well. "You have not been introduced to Earm, your fellow countryman, Lucien. I picked him up off of a battlefield in the Holy Land. He remembers nothing of who he is. So I brought him with me to England, in case he sees something that looks familiar."

Kalle slid a sideways look at Earm, who nodded, but

seemed worried. "He is going to hold you down, Lucien, while I work. Isidora, you should leave. Lucien will not want you being privy to his screams."

She bit her lip. "Nay. I will stay."

Lucien raised himself on one elbow. "Earm, if Sir Kalle is your lord, I would not have you disobey him, but be warned—do not handle me. If you, Kalle, require me to be still, then I will be still."

"Whatever you say, Lucien," Kalle replied in a bored tone as he unrolled a velvet cloth that held instruments of various sorts. Knives, scissors, pincers—

The cook had set a pot of something to heat on the brazier coals. Kalle pulled a stool up to the bedside and motioned to Earm. "Bring more light. Lucien, I am going to touch you now. If you fight me in any way, I will have you tied down, do you understand?"

Lucien looked as furious as Isidora had ever seen him. His eyes were mere slits, his jaw clenched. "Be certain you want to cure this hand, Kalle, because if you accept my challenge, I will use it against you in single combat."

"Of course. As you wish, Lucien. May I proceed now?"

"Shite," said Lucien.

"I take that as permission." Kalle pressed Lucien's neck, counting his pulse. He put the back of his hand against his forehead. He examined the fingertips of the affected hand. "Can you bend your fingers and thumb?"

Lucien bent them, but the swelling did not allow much movement.

"Good. The tendons are intact, then. But your blood needs cleansing, to balance the humors. Cooke has a potion for you to drink. You must take it as often as you can stand, at least four times a day, for a sennight. It is a pity the moon is waxing, but that cannot be helped."

Kalle shifted his seat so that his back was to Isidora. Lucien's hand lay on a towel on a board over Kalle's knees. "Now, hold still."

Isidora did not know what would be worse: to look at what Kalle was doing or to have to watch Lucien suffer. But when she turned to him, he gave her a reassuring grin. "It will be all right, Isidora."

Then whatever Kalle did next made Lucien go quiet. He stared up at the beams of the ceiling for a long time, without blinking. He breathed slowly, in regular, deep breaths.

Kalle cursed in Arabic and flung something down that clanked onto the floor. Cooke hovered, offering various bowls and pots. "Earm, more light!" Kalle demanded. "Isidora, pull my damned hair back out of my eyes, will you?"

She did not want to touch Kalle, for any reason. But from behind him, she smoothed his blond hair away from his face and braided it for a few turns, to keep it collected. His cheek was rough with the stubble of two or three day's worth of beard.

It was strange. Doing him that small, intimate service, for Lucien's ultimate benefit, made Kalle seem more human.

Kalle was intent upon Lucien's hand, as if he truly cared. But then she remembered. She had agreed to betray her father's trust to save Lucien. And to that same end, deny Lucien his heart's desire.

She slipped from her seat and came around to see Lucien's hand. To see what her betrayal had bought. To her surprise, though there was a lot of blood, the edges of blackened flesh were gone. A small, jagged piece of green glass rested on the linen next to the instruments.

Kalle was drawing the wound closed with a needle and silk thread, around a slender, rolled up piece of fine linen that stuck out from Lucien's palm.

"What is that, Sir Kalle?"

"A wick. A drain. To keep an abscess from forming again. You can pull it after two days. You can cut the stitches after a fortnight. Make him keep this clean and dry. If he does not follow my instructions, do not bother asking me to return. He can chop his hand off himself."

Kalle wrapped Lucien's hand in fresh linen and positioned it back on the pillow, above the level of Lucien's heart. "See that he drinks the potion."

"You need not speak as if I were not here, Kalle," Lucien said.

"You took that rather well, though it was minor."

"Deogal taught me how to endure things. It is how I survived your treatment in Acre, Kalle. You may live to regret that you did not slay me when you had the chance. But, I do thank you for using your skill on my behalf this night."

Kalle shrugged. "I try my best, whatever it is I do. But I would not have taken the trouble, if I did not consider you an opponent worth saving, Lucien. Even if only so I may slay you later."

Lucien offered Kalle his right hand. "Until we meet again."

Kalle clasped hands with him. Then turning to Isidora, he gave her a look, as if to remind her of her promise, then he bowed. She nodded to him and he departed, taking Earm and Cooke with him.

She shut the door with relief. Even Mauger was not in the chamber. But for Gawaine, resting by the fire, she was alone with Lucien. And her guilt.

"Come lie beside me," Lucien suggested.

"That is not proper, you said so yourself."

"Well, I am delirious just now, so you have an excuse."

"What if I do not want to lie beside you?"

"Then lie on top of me. Would that be more to your liking?"

"You certainly *are* delirious."

"You won't know until you try."

"Go to sleep, Lucien. Have you finished the medicine?"

He grimaced. "Bah. It tastes like stale pig piss."

"And of course you are intimately familiar with that."

"Don't ask."

She took the cup away from him and sipped a bit of the liquid. It was black, pungent, bitter. Isidora wiped her mouth and shuddered. "It tastes worse, I'd say. Now, finish it. If you do not, I will ask Mauger to make you."

"I am not a child, Isidora." Lucien took another swallow. "I don't know why I am trusting Kalle not to poison me. *He* certainly does not trust anyone else."

Isidora perched on the edge of the bed. "He respects you. As a fellow alchemist."

Lucien gave her a long, sideward look, then closed his eyes. It struck her that she had not seen him eat in days. His flushed skin was still beaded with sweat. He seemed utterly exhausted.

She got a cloth, dipped it in a bowl of the fresh water that had been provided for Kalle's ministrations, and wiped Lucien's hot face, his neck and upper chest. He had blue shadows around his eyes and hollows in his cheeks. She thought perhaps he was dozing at last, but he spoke.

"It is a pity all this bother should be over such a small wound, especially one not even honorably taken, in battle. I might as well have been washing crockery or something equally demeaning. Indeed I was, wasn't I...but I never managed to break any of your father's alembics."

"That is because he would have thrashed you for it."

"Nay. Knights do not lay hands upon fellow knights. Blades, aye...but only peasants use their fists on one another."

With an inner tremor, Isidora pondered this. Her enraged father had bloodied his fists on Kalle, but the younger knight had not fought back. Now, with Kalle's explanation, it made a kind of dreadful sense.

Deogal should have challenged Kalle to an honorable single combat instead of simply knocking him down. Kalle had tried to lessen the shame of it—perhaps for both of them—by not retaliating in kind. And, he had said he wanted to draw Deogal's wrath upon himself. To spare her mother.

But she had not been spared, after all.

Men. When would she ever come to understand their simple minds? As if to prove her point, Lucien sat up and caught her about the waist. Apparently he was not as exhausted as she had thought.

He smiled. "You look good enough to eat."

"I can bring you food."

"Bring me water. And bolt the door, please."

"All right, but I think we are safe from Kalle for the moment, if not Mauger." She poured water into a goblet and he drank deeply.

"Now you have some." He held out the goblet.

"Why me?"

"Because, Isidora, I am going to kiss you, and you have the same pig piss still in your mouth that I just washed out of mine."

"I will gladly drink the water, but you are not going to kiss me." She took a few swallows.

"Better?"

"Aye. Now I should—" She stopped as Lucien's right hand found its way into the side lacing of her gown. So that is why they call it a "devil's hole," she thought.

"Just for a while, Isidora, I want you next to me. Then I'll drink the rest of that potion and you can be about your business."

Isidora looked at Lucien and a profound tenderness welled up in her heart. "But what business have I to tend, other than you?"

"Only you know the answer to that, sweeting." Then with his arm around her waist, he pulled her close and kissed her mouth, her neck, her cheeks and ears and brow, then back to her mouth again. By the time he returned there, she was ready to accept him.

It was as though some inner floodgate had been released. As though she had been primed for years, and it took only this one last kiss to trigger all of her pent-up desire. She ached to have him inside her. "Oh, God. Lucien, what have you done?"

He smiled. "What I have wanted to do for some time now. Don't fight it, Isidora, please, let it happen, let us have this time together, just for us—not for my family or any other purpose…" He tried to bring his other arm around her.

"Nay, Lucien, keep your hand there. I will come to you, you do not have to come to me. Oh, God, this is such sin!" she moaned even as she tugged her laces free and pulled her gown and chemise over her head.

"Aye, is it not? Delicious, golden, beautiful skin." He cupped her breast and took a mouthful of it.

"That—oh!—is not what I said. *Sin* is what—I—ohhh…mayhap it is not sin after all?"

"Of course not…I would never allow you to sin. I am your husband, for all intents and purposes."

"This is for us, remember? Not for church or parents or the village—" Isidora climbed beneath the sheet and found him there, warm and willing, and by all the signs, more than ready. She ran her palm lightly over the muscled ridges of his abdomen.

"All right, I am your lover, then."

"You are not at all ticklish, Lucien."

"I know. You can touch me anywhere you like."

Lucien pulled her astride him. He was solid, firm. All male. She felt vulnerable with her thighs spread, and yet to be on top gave her a certain sense of control. "You've not been with an Eastern-bred woman before, have you?"

He tipped his chin back, exposing his throat to her. "Do not tell me that the Circassian wench let slip any tales of my prowess!"

For an instant he had her fooled. But the laughter in his eyes gave him away. She decided to play him one better.

"Marylas told me, all right. How she had you on your knees, night after night, begging for mercy, pleading with her to spare you, to allow you to rest, to unlock your chain and let you crawl back to your own bed. Oh, aye, I know all about it!"

Lucien raised an eyebrow. "But did she not mention the parade of her friends she had in tow? One after the other, all weeping and fighting to be first—though of course it made no difference, they were all equally pleased in the end."

Isidora rolled her eyes. "Well, the only one you must please now, is me. Can you do that, Lord Lucien?" She squeezed his ribs between her knees.

His gaze darkened and grew serious. "I can but try, *demoiselle*... Indeed, I can feel that you...you are already halfway there..."

She felt her cheeks flush, that he should be so aware of the private wants of her body. Then, without warning, with both hands he caught her—as if the wounded one were pain-free—and lifted her and lowered her, and met her with himself, until they were as one.

"Oh, my God." The pleasure of him filling her was intense. Deep. Satisfying.

Lucien's eyes were halfway closed. "You keep calling upon God, Isidora. But we need no miracle, for *you* are the miracle. We need no salvation, for you have saved me twice over—and we need no absolution, for you are absolutely the only heaven I crave..."

She smiled, and moved.

Lucien shut his eyes. "Oh, God, mayhap you were right to call upon Him."

She moved again.

His eyes opened wide and focused upon hers. "Methinks I should take charge of this, sweeting, before you

get any more of God's help." In a twinkling, he had rolled
her onto her back, without leaving her.

Then, he moved.

Now it was Isidora's turn to open her eyes wide, then
shut them tight as fresh sensations rippled through her.
Lucien smiled. Kissed her. And moved again.

And again…until she was caught hard in his rhythm, in
his breath, in the pounding of his heart against hers. She
was spinning, rushing in a torrent of liquid fire, headed for
an unstoppable conflagration. For something she knew
would be much, much more explosive than she had ever
imagined possible.

"Look at me…" Lucien growled.

Isidora opened her eyes. His were dark, gleaming, pas-
sion-filled. They were her whole world. He drove into her.
Her world burst into rapture. He lifted her and came again.

She cried out. Arched forward and bit his neck.

Lucien caught her hair and pulled her head back, then
covered her mouth with his as his life essence pulsed into
her. He held still, for many long minutes, and she was glad
of that. Lucien stroked her hair, kissed her tenderly and lay
back beside her.

Isidora snuggled up against his body, still in wonderment at what had just taken place between them. It had happened so fast. She had not resisted. It had felt…so good.
The coals in the brazier had burned down to a comforting
red glow that made the damp skin on his chest glisten.

"Lucien."

"Aye?"

"Nothing. I but wanted to say your name."

"Not God's?"

"I'm afraid not."

"Don't be afraid. I am here with you."

"I'm glad."

"And so you should be, for this was just the first course." He grinned at her.

"Very glad," she admitted.

"Me too."

"Truly?"

"Aye. I would never lie to you, Isidora. About anything."

A chill crept into her heart. Lucien was a pure-hearted soul. And she, by withholding the truth from him, did not deserve him.

Chapter Twenty-Six

The Cistercians refectory was a place of quiet beauty, Larke thought. Arching stone buttresses, stained-glass windows and carved, smooth oak tables and benches. She spooned the warm, savory soup into her mouth with relish, dipped some bread into it and stuffed it after.

Raymond de Beauchamp sat across and up from her, talking with his younger brother, Percy. He had arrived not long after she and Wace. She had heard a great deal about Sir Raymond's exploits, and had met him several times, but had not actually ever said an intelligent word to him, being too young for such a feat, until now.

He was every bit as handsome as a living legend should be. Thick, shiny, dark-blond hair, a perfect, straight nose and those blue eyes—a pity he was already married and madly in love with his Welsh wife, who, according to Lucien, had once been betrothed to Percy. How that had all come to pass, she did not know.

Someone—Wace, of course—gave her a rude nudge in

the ribs. "You should stop staring and mind your sop, there, milady."

"What?" she said, her mouth still full. Then she felt the rivulet cooling on her chin and hurriedly wiped it. To her horror, this exchange had drawn the attention of Sir Raymond. She gulped down the sodden lump of bread.

"Wace, go find another bottle of the Rhenish I brought, will you?" Raymond said mildly.

Wace bowed and went on his errand immediately.

Raymond leaned toward Larke conspiratorially. "If he gives you any trouble, Lady Larke, I can show you some moves to keep him at bay."

Larke smiled. "It seems that someone has trained Wace rather well, my lord, for I find that a few choice words usually do the trick."

A pair of creases formed between Raymond's brows. "Ah, so he *has* been giving you trouble."

"Nay—truly, my lord, he is a perfect example of chivalry, em, that is, when he is not correcting me."

"I see. Shall I have a word with him?"

"Oh, nay, please, my lord—that is not necessary." Larke did not want to imagine what it would be like for Wace to stand before Sir Raymond and be subject to any "word" he might have with him.

"What brought you here, in such a hurry, so late, milady? Percy says Lucien is injured?"

"Aye, it is but a cut gone bad. I fear I have worried overmuch. I thought Brother Percy might help."

"Sometimes we must do as we are moved to do, no matter what," Raymond replied with a small smile. "And if it is a mistake, we learn from it. I much prefer boldness to dithering."

"Aye," Larke said, relieved to find in Sir Raymond a kindred spirit.

Percy turned to her. "I meant to ask you, Lady Larke, do you know of a man, one who brought his relative from the Holy Land to see Lucien?"

Larke's heart caught unexpectedly and her eyes stung. "Why, indeed, that would be Faris al-Rashid, brother to Isidora, the lady Lucien is about to wed."

"What! You don't say!" Raymond grinned and looked quite pleased with himself.

Larke continued. "It is true, my lord. H-have you seen Faris, Brother Percy? We feared he might have been killed in the woods."

"He is here, Lady Larke, and you may visit him, if he is awake. He has an arrow wound and is improving, but I hesitate to leave him just yet."

Relief flooded Larke at this news and the tears that had threatened began to fall.

She was glad when Percy seemed to misunderstand her reaction—indeed, she herself did not understand it—and asked, "Has Lucien been taken so very bad?"

"Lady Isidora was worried enough, she was going to fetch Sir Kalle Fitz-I-know-not-who to help. But it is Sir Kalle we suspect tried to kill Faris."

"How can that be?" Percy threw a questioning look to Raymond, then back to Larke. "FitzMalheury?"

Larke was taken aback by the intensity of Brother Percy's gaze. What if she said the wrong thing and started some kind of war, right here in England? "Aye. He is encamped on our practice grounds."

"Why?" demanded Raymond.

"I do not know," Larke admitted.

Percy rubbed his chin. "Well. Kalle is a fine physician. If he agrees to help, Lucien is better off with him than me. But if—"

Raymond leaned toward his brother. "Parsifal," he murmured. "Leave it. Wace and I will go. Physician or no, Lucien cannot be left alone with such a wolf at his door."

Percy frowned. "Raymond, you ever seem to forget that I am a…a man now. I can make my own way in this world."

Raymond caught him by the shoulder. "Indeed, you are a man. But of God, not of this world. And you know what *I* am."

"Aye. You are a hero."

Raymond shook his head. "Nay, brother. I am a killer. A fate you have been spared. Be glad of it."

Percy and Raymond exchanged a look then, of such depth that Larke felt both privileged and shaken to behold it. It was as though she had a glimpse into a secret world, one few women were allowed to witness.

No doubt these men did not count her as a woman, because of her youth. But, in case they had forgotten her presence, she thought it best to speak up. "We should leave right away," Larke said.

"You will stay here, where it is safe." Raymond stood, ready to move on, as if his word was law. Which, whether she liked it or not, it was.

Larke, too, rose. "My lord, nothing will keep me from my brother's side."

Wace appeared in the doorway, a brown, earthenware

bottle in his hands. "Sir, I fear she means what she says. It is why I am myself here and not there with Lucien. The necessity of following her, I mean."

Raymond assessed Larke from beneath dark brows. "If you ride with us, you will obey me and you will obey Wace, do you understand?"

"Aye, my lord. My thanks."

"Then get ready."

As Raymond and Wace left the refectory, Larke tugged Brother Percy's sleeve. "May I see Faris? Then I can report to Isidora."

Percy's face creased into a charming smile. "Let us check on him."

Larke followed the monk out and around the perimeter of the cloister to a chamber not far from the chapel itself. In the infirmary were a few beds, all empty but for one, Faris being the only patient. She walked across the stone floor, her footsteps echoing in the high-ceilinged room.

It appeared as though he had not stirred since being placed there. The linens were perfectly folded and smooth over his chest, his arms lay at his sides, his long, black hair fanned across the white pillow. He looked much paler than he had the last time she'd seen him. Indeed he looked barely alive. Beside the bed, a young cleric was praying, but at the approach of the visitors, he rose and bowed.

"Many thanks, brother," Percy said, dismissing him. "Do you want to be alone with Faris, Lady Larke?"

Suddenly she found that prospect overwhelming. "Nay, please stay." Percy stood near the foot of the bed and Larke sat on the edge. "Sir Faris? Are you awake?"

At first he did not open his eyes. Then when he did, they

were that same, deep, melting brown that she remembered. He favored her with a small smile. "Greetings, Lady Larke, fair flower of Ainsley. Forgive me, that I do not rise to honor you as you deserve."

Larke felt a blush creep over her cheeks. "Please, do not tire yourself by such elegant speech. I am so very glad to see you mending. And Isidora will be beside herself with joy to hear of it."

A pained look crossed his face. "Lady Larke, not for me, but for the sake of these holy men, you must not tell Isidora that I live. If Kalle should learn his arrow failed…" Faris paused to catch his breath. "He will come here to finish what he started, and all these innocent men will be in peril. Isidora is not very good at falsehoods."

"I know," Larke said.

"So let her grieve. I ask God, and you, to forgive me for hurting her this way."

"But, Sir Faris, when she realized Kalle had made this attempt on your life, she tried to stab him with her dagger. I do not believe that allowing her to think Kalle succeeded will produce any milder result."

Faris closed his eyes again for a moment and coughed a little. "Isidora could not possibly kill Kalle. And he would not harm her, for reasons I prefer not to explain. It is more important that he believe me dead. And if it is only you who need playact, so much the better."

Larke started to ask about Wace, then she realized that he had been out of earshot when Percy had told of Faris being yet alive. He, too, needed to be kept in the dark, and Sir Raymond would need to agree to the secret.

"If this is your wish, my lord, then so shall it be. Brother

Percy, will you speak to Sir Raymond for me? I dare not approach him on such a subject."

"Brother Percy," Faris began, "I cannot ask you to lie. But I ask that you pray we be forgiven."

Percy looked down upon them solemnly. "I understand your position. And indeed, I will not lie. But I will ask our Abbot to give you and Lady Larke absolution in this. And I will tell Raymond what he must do. It will be a good thing, Larke, if you are not entirely alone in such a deceit."

"And, it may turn out not to be a lie," Faris added with a tired smile. "We do not know God's ultimate will in this. I am not yet so far removed from heaven's gate as to give up the thought of entering it. In that prospect I can find some joy, as may you on my behalf, though this is not the same as dying in battle."

Larke swallowed hard, unable to accept such a possibility. "Yet, once you are healed, surely we can tell Isidora the truth? Surely by then Kalle will have gone home to Acre?"

"Let us hope it will be thus." Faris coughed again. His chest sounded thick. He groaned and coughed some more.

Larke looked to Percy. "What is wrong?"

The monk shook his head gravely. "I will see to him. You should go now, get ready to leave." His lips were set in a firm, grim line.

"I thank you, Brother Percy." Larke took one last look at Faris as he struggled to breathe, then fled the infirmary. As she ran, she remembered with a pang that the good-luck charm she had made for Faris was still around her own neck.

Chapter Twenty-Seven

At last Lucien slept. *Riding on the bosom of an angel.* Like one dead. Isidora was certain she had tasted opium in Kalle's potion, but that would ease Lucien's pain as well as help him rest. As long as there was not too much of it.

Now it was time for her to keep her part of the bargain. She descended the stairs, expecting to have to go out and find Kalle, but he and Earm were still in the hall. Mauger stood by, fidgeting nervously in the absence of Conrad, who had gone to find a priest to perform the wedding sacraments.

Isidora still had the key to Lucien's *sanctum sanctorum.* "My lord FitzMalheury, a word?"

Kalle rose, overshadowing Mauger, who looked not a little dismayed. Isidora tried to give him a sign to stay away, but he came ahead anyway.

"This is private, Sir Mauger, forgive me," she said.

He narrowed his eyes. "If it has to do with Lucien in the least way, then it is my business, as well."

Kalle stood by, with his arms crossed. "I hope this does not take long, Isidora."

She raised one hand. "Please, a moment more." She drew Mauger aside. "Listen to me, Mauger. You want Lucien to cease his pursuit of alchemy, do you not?"

Mauger glanced at Kalle, then nodded.

"Well, I am doing my best this night to see that it comes to an end. I cannot explain quickly. But you must trust that I am doing this out of—out of love for your lord. And he must not know that Kalle was a part of it. Please."

Mauger nodded again. "But you will not go anywhere alone with FitzMalheury. I will go with you."

Isidora looked into Mauger's eyes. "Trust me. You must say nothing. Promise me this."

"I promise."

"All right." She turned to Kalle. "I thank you for your patience. Sir Mauger will accompany us on our walk outside."

Kalle smiled in his feral way. "I am confident that Mauger will not cause me a moment's hesitation in any decision I may make."

They proceeded outside into the frigid air, with Earm carrying a torch. Isidora's heart felt as cold and heavy as the stones beneath her feet. What she was about to do felt as large and irrevocable as tipping a boulder over a cliff— one that would crush her ideals and dreams as it tumbled, as well as Lucien's. One that could never be put back into place once it was set into motion.

"This way." She led them to the courtyard by the chapel and stopped. "I will be back in a moment."

Earm followed her with the light. She took the heavy key from inside her tunic, hung on a cord around her neck. Once the door to the *laboratorium* was unlocked, she turned to Earm. "There is still light, from a fire we had earlier. Stay here."

He nodded, peering wide-eyed into the chamber. Indeed, if Isidora had not seen it in daylight, she, too, would have been frightened. With the shimmering light of the athanor's dying fire, Lucien's fantastic drawings upon the wall seemed to dance and writhe as if the creatures had come to life. The translucent alembics along the shelves took on an eerie glow, the bubbles in the thick green glass winking like so many eyes.

She made her way to the niche and sighed with relief to see the bundle was still here, though she had no reason to think it would not be. But it would be best to check it once more. Untying the silk cord that bound it, she unrolled the protective leather.

The scrolls, three of them, wound around wooden dowels, each one with the head of some strange beast intricately carved in red stones set at either end.

She felt a warm presence at her back, looked up and had to stifle a scream. A monstrous shadow loomed before her on the wall, casting Lucien's figures into darkness. A heavy hand came down upon her shoulder.

"Cerebus," Kalle said softly, and his hand slid down her arm's length to ease one of the scrolls from her fingers. "The Key..." he breathed.

Isidora began to tremble and her teeth chattered with fright.

Kalle continued in his smooth voice, as if giving a lecture. "Each scroll bears one of the three heads of Cerebus, the dog who guards Hades. And opposite them are another three—the Fates. And this..." He reached around her with his other arm, so she was trapped between him and the table's marble edge. He was a solid wall of menace and she had never felt so helpless in her life.

Kalle unwrapped the final treasure. She felt a tremor go through him as the object slid into his hand. "I cannot believe you would give this to me, and not to your darling Lucien. Perhaps you do not understand its true significance."

She looked down at what he held. She had felt it before, through its wrapping, but had not actually looked at it. Indeed she had been afraid to. But it was a simple sphere, perfectly smooth, that would fit in the palm of her hand. It was of a mirror-bright, red-gold color. *Like Lucien's hair in the sun,* she could not help thinking.

"I am glad you are with me to savor this moment," Kalle whispered, and she could feel the pounding of his heart at her back. "Though I wanted it to be Ayshka."

"Lord Kalle, she would not have savored any such moment, and neither do I. I bear no love for alchemy, nor did she. It is what killed my father. It is what would kill Lucien, if I gave him these things. It is what will kill you, too. I know now what caused it—father's mind and body were poisoned by the concoctions of dreadful airs and powders from boiling acids and molten metals."

To her surprise, Kalle agreed, as if it mattered not. "*Oui.* That is why alchemists feel they are racing against time. Your father was also running a race—indeed, that was the whole point of his pursuit of alchemy—after he threw Ayshka out. To find the touchstone that would have cured her. And to think I was sitting on the solution the whole time. In ignorance. Until you happened upon it. Indeed, Isidora, you have some kind of magic about you. The Fates pulled your hand to the scrolls. And now they are returned to me, as God intended."

She had found the key to her mother's cure? But too late? She had kept these texts hidden away…from her father. From Lucien. And now she was giving them to an enemy? To get rid of him, she told herself. Kalle had to be wrong. There was no Elixir, no touchstone. It was all a delusion.

That was the only conclusion she could bear. She stared at Kalle's powerful hands, still holding the scrolls. He wore an irregular-looking ring on his left heart-finger. It seemed an incongruous ornament for a man of such malice. "Where is Mauger?" Isidora asked, suddenly afraid for him.

"Out. Cold. He should have known better than to try me one on one."

Isidora swallowed and said a silent prayer for Mauger. "You have what you want. Let me go. Leave us in peace."

Kalle deftly rewrapped the bundle and stepped back from her with it in his hand.

She spun around to face him, pressing her hands on the table edge to support herself so that she did not beat her fists against his chest. "I had intended to apologize to you properly, Kalle, for striking at you with my blade, but now I wish I had bitten you with it, right to the heart."

Kalle laughed. "Why? For telling you the truth? The truth, Isidora—there is nothing left for you here. Only heartbreak. You must come back with me, to Acre, to your home. I know you miss it."

"And Faris? I am supposed to simply forget you murdered my brother?"

"Hmm, I do wonder if he is dead. I think my aim was skewed when my horse jigged. Elsewise I would have brought his head back as proof. As for him being your brother, well…who knows?"

Kalle was mad. And cruel. And right about Lucien. A horrible, unbearable combination. "Go away, I beg of you. Please, just go away!" Isidora heard her voice rising toward a scream and bit her lip hard to keep the sound inside.

Kalle stared at her, as if she had just slapped his face. An act, no doubt, no one else had ever dared commit. He seemed to fold in on himself—not shrinking, but as though he had grown more dense, more opaque. Darker.

"As you wish," he snarled. "But you will have no peace now. Not once Lucien finds out you have betrayed him. An alchemist's nightmare…like a dream one has of drowning in blackness, of swimming with one's last breath and bit of strength toward the surface, toward light and purity and bliss, only it is too far, and the swimmer is too slow, and he awakens, gasping for air, knowing he has failed yet again, only this time it is forever, because this was his very last chance. That is all he will ever see in you, Isidora, from this day forward."

There. She looked up at him, white-faced, as though her heart had been poleaxed. Kalle felt a pang of remorse. If that had not been a death blow, he did not know what was.

"Should you change your mind, Isidora, you can find me on the other side of the river, but only until two days hence, at the nooning. After that, I will have gone."

Kalle turned and strode out of the *laboratorium*.

But he had to force himself not to run. The little bitch. *Just go away!* The words still echoed in his mind, after all these years. Ayshka's last words to him. Even from the dark pit of her life as a leper, she had refused him. Preferred shame and starvation and filth and death to any help he had to offer. Preferred them to him, to the love he bore her.

In that instant he had wanted to strangle Ayshka. To crush her slender neck with his bare hands. And with that same horrific impulse, he saw that she was right to refuse him. No matter that he had lost everything important to him because of her. His priestly calling. The respect of Deogal. His honor. The fact remained that his love was not pure. Not good enough for her. For anyone.

But that was going to change. He had the key to the Elixir. Right here in his hand, that even now shook with the incredible significance of what it held.

It would render him perfect. In every way. All-knowing, all-powerful. He would rule Acre. Then Antioch, then Constantinople. All of Outremer and beyond. It might require a sea of blood, but in the end he would have the respect, nay, the obeisance, of the world. He would be the Beloved. Feared and adored by countless millions. Invincible. He would be like a god to them. Their god.

The God.

Chapter Twenty-Eight

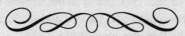

Lucien opened his eyes. Where was he? What day was it? His head felt like a toadstool, big and fluffy; his limbs unwieldy, as though they belonged to someone else. He pushed himself up in bed and as pain shot through his arm from his hand, it all came back.

He looked at the bandage. Stained with blood, but not soaked. Better yet, nor did it stink. Kalle had done his work well. And Isidora had…ah. He shivered and smiled. Now that was something he could not possibly forget. He looked about. A faint glow shone from the eastern window of the solar. Dawn. Why was his lady not here with him?

Lucien put his bare legs over the edge of the bed into the cold air, waited a moment, then staggered to his feet. Just as soon as he found a pot to piss in, he would seek Isidora out and marry her.

Mauger, his head bloodied but not broken, had been laid out on a table in the hall. He had regained consciousness shortly, and Isidora sat with Rosamunde as the young woman tended him, dabbing at the lump on his head with a warm poultice.

It should have been a cold one, Isidora knew, but she hadn't the heart to correct her. And, Mauger did not seem to really need any tending, no thanks to Kalle. Or to Isidora herself. He certainly did not want it.

"My thanks, Rosamunde, but I am well enough, you may leave me be." He tried to sit up, but she leaned on his chest with her elbow, and for one awkward moment, Isidora feared the lass was about to kiss him.

"I want to help you," she purred.

"I need no help."

"Of course you do," Rosamunde insisted.

Isidora fought the urge to catch the girl by the hair and drag her off of Mauger. But he needed to fight his own battles when it came to this particular female. And, if the glint in his eye was any indication, Rosamunde needed to learn to heed certain warning signs.

Like a whale reaching the surface of the sea, Mauger heaved himself upright, an unstoppable force. Rosamunde, apparently not believing his defiance, did not shift her weight. Mauger shifted it for her and she slid with a bounce to the floor, landing on her rump amidst the rushes.

"Ow!"

"I beg your pardon, *mes demoiselles*." Mauger bowed, though it obviously pained him, and marched in dignity out of the hall.

Isidora held out a hand to Rosamunde to help her up. The girl churlishly refused and scrambled to her feet. "This is *your* fault, anyway! Half the men in the keep are wounded or gone!"

"You are right, lady," Isidora agreed quietly. Nothing Rosamunde said could make her feel any worse than she did already. Since last night's encounters, first with Lucien, then with Kalle, her shame and misery went bone-deep, almost paralyzing in their intensity.

She forced herself to function, for she was not one to lie abed and languish. But they rested like a thick pall over her, slowing her thoughts and her actions.

She heard a sound and turned. Lucien was on the stairs. What was he doing up? She was not ready for him, had no chance to flee. But she faced him, faced his inevitable discovery of her treachery, as a deer must face the hunter's fatal arrow.

He smiled at her. He did not know. She had to tell him herself; he should not find out any other way. But not here. She wanted to do it in private. No one else should have to witness his grief but her.

"My lord, shall we take the air for a while?"

"As you wish. Is…something wrong?"

Rosamunde gave her a daggered, gleeful smile, one that was not lost upon Lucien. He turned to the girl and inclined his beautiful head. She froze, with the smile still on her face.

Lucien approached her, paused, and drew the back of his forefinger along her rosebud cheek. With his touch, as if created by it, a tear trailed after his finger. He wiped it away with his thumb, but another took its place.

"Rosamunde," he said, his voice filled with velvet sorrow.

Isidora trembled, praying that he never used such a voice on her.

"This was all wrong," he continued. "It should never have been. I think it best that you go home to your parents now, deny any rumor about the sheet from my bed, and see if Mauger comes to speak to your father. Give him some room. If it is for the best, then it will happen. But I apologize to you, yet again."

Rosamunde swallowed, and sniffed, and rubbed one eye with a delicate knuckle. "No need, Lord Lucien. You have taught me…some—some things, as has Sir Mauger. And Isidora. I thank you all for that." She curtsied and drifted up the stairs.

Lucien threw his mantle over his shoulders and held out his hand to Isidora. "Let us see what else the day has in store, eh?"

She gave him her hand and a tentative smile. Oh, this was too hard! Through the anteroom and down the outer stair they went, the cold seeping up under Isidora's skirts. Immodest and impractical creature that she was, she had not put any leggings on. But that hardly mattered.

Built on a hill, from the upper bailey they could look out over the battlements, chest-high, to the valley below. The sky glowed pink and golden as the sun crested the horizon. Small dabs of gray dotted the land.

"The ewes will soon be lambing. Are you looking forward to that?" Lucien asked.

"Not being a ewe, I don't suppose I am."

He turned so his back was to the stone wall and pulled her before him. "What troubles you, Isidora? Is it something about last night?"

"I don't know why you are not still in bed. You cannot have recovered so quickly."

He shrugged. "I would prefer to be lying down, it is true. But one cannot always give in to such inclinations.

More's the pity." He drew her closer still, so they were thigh to thigh.

She touched his forehead with the back of her hand. As Kalle had done. "Your skin is damp. But cool. The fever has broken, thank God."

"I drank a whole cupful of that vile, disgusting potion, last night, you know, after…after ravishing you."

"It is a wonder you are conscious at all then."

"It is a greater wonder that I kept it down. But I do not want to talk about that. There is still something you are not telling me."

"Oh, Lucien. I hardly know where to begin."

"Just start. Anywhere. This is very uncomfortable. And soon you'll get a chill, if we are not careful."

Isidora took a deep breath. "Lucien…"

Coward that she was, she could not bring herself to tell him. Could not bring herself to spoil the fragile happiness they had shared.

Lucien waited, gazing at her. Then the sound of shod hooves on stone broke the quiet below. Isidora felt his attention shift, his body grow taut. Relief swept her that she might have time to think of a way to tell him that would not make him hate her.

"Pardon, my lady. I am not expecting anyone."

They got to their feet and looked below. The gate had been opened for the day. A riderless horse wandered into the courtyard.

Lucien's brow knit. "That is Larke's mare. What deviltry is this?" He turned and ran toward the stairs, then halted and spoke over his shoulder. "Get back into the hall, Isidora."

She ignored his command and followed him down, her

own heart pounding. What could have happened? A groom held the animal while Lucien examined it.

His brow was still furrowed, his hair fell across his cheeks as he crouched to feel the horse's legs. When he saw Isidora, he gave her a look of frustration and concern.

"There are no wounds, nothing missing or broken from the harness. She is not winded, but it looks as though she has been walking home for some time. See, the bits of grass on the bit? She's been grazing along the way. But where is Larke?"

He stood up and glowered at the groom. "Do you know anything about this? Did you saddle this beast for her?"

The young man shook his head emphatically. "Nay, my lord. I noticed it was missing, but Squire Wace's mount was gone, as well, so I thought they…" He faltered.

Lucien chewed his lip and stared at the youth. Isidora knew Lucien was not really seeing him, but the groom squirmed and fidgeted. At last Lucien spoke again. "Rouse Jager and get Caflice ready." He turned to Isidora. "What did I tell you? Larke is enough to drive even a saint mad. Let us hope she is indeed with Wace. And why are *you* still out here?"

"I cannot bear to sit by and watch. I can ride as well as anyone else. If the mare is not too tired, let me take her out with you. Or wait till my horse is readied."

"Aye, you have demonstrated all too well your propensity to ride out. But I cannot allow it. Kalle may be still in the area. I do not want you caught in any fighting."

"I will follow you anyway."

"Not if I have you confined."

"You would not dare!"

"What is to dare? All I have to do is tell Mauger, 'Keep her here.' And so help me, he will!" Lucien advanced upon her like a storm cloud, but instead of catching her arm or pushing her before him, he caught her up and carried her as though she were a child in his arms.

It was so unexpected Isidora did not struggle. Indeed she wrapped her own arms around Lucien's neck and relished his closeness, the power of his body…the fact that he cared enough to be angry.

He climbed the stairs, then shortened his strides as they neared the anteroom to the hall. In the shadow of the curtain he put her back on her feet.

"Isidora, do you not see? I need you here, to ease my mother's fears, to keep an eye on things. When I go, there is always the chance I will not return. In which case some-one should deal with the *laboratorium,* make sure the elements are hidden or destroyed, and my books locked up. You still have the key. I won't take it from you. Guard the Work for me."

Isidora looked up at him. Lucien…person of light. "You ask a great deal of one who wishes the Work did not exist."

He drew her up against him and her knees nearly buckled. "I will make it up to you," he said.

Lucien was warm and solid and smelled of fragrant smoke and sandalwood. Isidora pulled together the last shreds of her resistance. "I will wait four marks of the hour candle. If you do not come back by then, I will ride after you. With Mauger or without him."

"I shall return in good time. Now, kiss me goodbye."

She stood up on her toes and put her lips to his in a ten-tative, delicate touch.

He gave her a wry smile. "You call that a kiss?"

Isidora let her feet go flat on the floor. "Come back, and I will try again."

Chapter Twenty-Nine

In the early morning light Larke trotted Faris's horse—formerly Lucien's—along the forest path, headed for home. She did not care if Wace or Sir Raymond didn't like it. In fact, she wanted to go even faster. As the path widened, she urged her mount into a canter.

Percy and Raymond had decided that to return the extremely valuable gray to Lucien would be a more convincing support to their story. To her surprise, Raymond joined her, his big courser's long, relaxed strides effortlessly keeping abreast of her.

At least the muck was not too slippery. They splashed along through muddy puddles, leaving Wace covered in brown splatters behind them. Raymond glanced back, then grinned at Larke. *Oh, my!* She felt herself blush to have such favor bestowed upon her by the legendary Raymond, and smiled shyly back. "Not far now," she said.

"Thank God," he replied.

They passed a group of crofters gleaning fallen branches from the forest floor, but Larke did not stop to greet them.

Lucien would be worried as it was, and furious, no doubt. She would be lucky if all he did was forbid her to leave the women's quarters for the next month.

But the hardest part would be to tell Isidora the lie about her brother. Wace, who had been given no reason not to believe Faris was dead, was still in the dark.

Larke worried that Isidora would try to get to the Cistercian abbey, to visit Faris's grave. Lies had such a way of complicating things!

The morning gave way to noon and Raymond turned his horse off the path. They cut across the fallow fields toward the castle, to rejoin the lane where it met the bridge. They slowed to a walk as they approached, for a group of riders was already halfway across it. Larke's heart leaped.

"Oy, Lucien!" Raymond called.

He was up, out and about! Had a miracle healed his hand? She hurried to meet him. "Lucien! You are well! Praise God!"

Lucien gave her a dark look, mixed with relief. "Larke, I swear, you deserve a hiding for causing so much worry! You can praise God and Kalle FitzMalheury, for he took care of my hand. By the way, my right one is in perfect health," Lucien added, loud enough for all to hear. "Fully capable of rendering your backside into a state of abject contrition."

Larke felt herself redden yet again, to be so chastised in front of not only her brother's men, but Wace and his lord. It was not like Lucien to be so harsh. "Oh, Lucien, you know I am sorry."

"I know you *should* be!"

Larke tried again. "I can explain, Lucien."

"I doubt that. Get yourself through the gates. Isidora is also worried for you. Greetings, Raymond. I am sorry you've been dragged into this. And you, Wace, I am grateful to you for returning her. But…" Lucien paled as Larke's mount pawed the ground. "That is the horse I gave… What does this mean?"

Raymond cleared his throat. "Your friend Faris was badly wounded. He barely made it to the abbey alive, and although Percy did what he could… We thought it best to bring you back the gray."

Larke marveled at Raymond's skilful avoidance of an outright lie. Of course it still was a falsehood, but by implication only. Then she saw the pain on Raymond's face, caused, she was certain, by that on Lucien's.

"How will I tell Isidora?" Lucien bunched his good hand into a fist against his thigh. "She cannot know. Not yet. Keep it to yourselves, please, for a time."

"Where is FitzMalheury?" Raymond asked.

"Gone. Now that Larke is safe, I can seek him. He has something of Isidora's that I would regain for her. And, since I am sure he is responsible for Faris's death, he owes wergild to Isidora, if not his life."

"Don't be hasty, Lucien. You should return to the hall with us and we'll talk about it first," Raymond said.

"I cannot lose Kalle now, it is imperative that I retrieve this thing. I swore an oath."

Raymond put a gauntleted hand upon Lucien's arm. "It is imperative that I speak to you before you leave. If you are meant to find Kalle, you will find him in good time. Please, listen to me, Lucien."

"All right. You ride with me and we will talk on the way."

Lucien glanced to Larke, as if to question why she remained. Reluctantly she reined her horse toward the gates.

Stranded between her and the party of armed men, Wace called to Raymond, "My lord, what would you have me do?"

"Escort Lady Larke the rest of the way in. Stay and help Mauger guard this place."

Wace nodded and brought his horse alongside Larke's as the others headed out. She saw the tightness of his jaw and his expression of annoyance—with her, no doubt.

"I am sorry you missed the riding, Wace."

He glanced at her, and with the swift cut of his eyes, tempered by understanding, the lean, determined look of his face, she realized Wace was no longer a boy. He was a man.

Ready for anything.

"Well, Larke, it is not as though Raymond is punishing me by having me stay here with you." Wace gave her a small quirk of his mouth and she felt more chastened by his remark than by Lucien's ire.

"I would like to see Isidora straight away, Wace."

"As you will, milady." He led the way across the bridge and to the gatehouse. Before entering the bailey, Larke looked back. In the distance, Lucien and Raymond rode side by side, the men-at-arms trailing after. She wondered if Raymond would tell Lucien the truth.

"Do not concern yourself. Your brother is more than capable of taking FitzMalheury. And with Sir Raymond along, there is no question of defeat."

Larke did not reply as they clattered into the courtyard. She abandoned her horse to Wace's care and ran up the stairs, through the hall and on up to Lucien's solar.

As she had expected, there stood Isidora, looking out the

narrow window toward where Lucien and Raymond were still just visible. Her hip-length, black hair flowed in loose waves down her back. Not for the first time, Larke envied Isidora her smooth, opaque complexion.

At the sight of Larke, Isidora ran to her and embraced her fiercely. "Thank God you are safe. I did not come down—it would have been that much harder to let them leave without me."

"Don't worry. Sir Raymond is with Lucien."

"Tell me what happened."

Larke hesitated. She had not thought of what to say, only of what not to say. "Em, well, Wace convinced me of the folly of my quest. My horse got frightened during our argument and fled. Then we were caught by a rain storm. Then we took shelter, in a…a barn and made our way home."

"But I saw you riding in."

"Oh, well, Wace is very resourceful. He managed to borrow a mount in a village along the way."

"I see."

Oh, God, she knows I am lying! And I told her I was good at it… Larke thought furiously how to distract her friend. "I was sent back in disgrace, Isidora. Lucien even threatened to beat me! Wace is staying, though, so I feel well protected, here. Perhaps too well protected."

"What do you mean?" Isidora drew Larke to sit with her on the bed.

"Wace looked at me…almost as though he *owned* me. Or as though he thought that to be a definite possibility. I am used to Lucien ordering me about, since our father died, God rest him, and because I love Lucien so much, I let him think he has control of me...but Wace...I have only ever thought of him as a boy.

"As of today I realize he is no longer that. And now I find him a bit frightening. He has not known me and loved me my whole life, as has Lucien. He is not thinking only of me and my welfare, as does Lucien. He wants something else, as well, a desire I have seen in the eyes of other men when they look at other women. I have even seen Lucien look at you that way, Isidora."

Isidora's cheeks turned a becoming pink. "Well, I suppose he might, considering how long..."

Larke smiled. "Uncle Conrad should be back soon with a priest, then we can get the formalities over with. You and Lucien, and Mauger and Rosamunde, I suppose."

"Lucien has sent Rosamunde home, Larke."

"How so? Not that I am over-sorry to see her leave."

"He feels it all was rather sudden, and that Mauger should have a chance to think upon the matter."

"Excellent. A relief, indeed," Larke said.

Isidora took Larke's hand in her own. "Milady, forgive me, but I know there is something you are withholding from me."

Larke swallowed. "Lucien has bade me keep silent until he returns. Please do not ask me to tell you anything more."

Isidora searched Larke's eyes. "Just tell me if you saw any sign of Faris. Can you say that much?"

"Nay. I can say nothing. I am sorry, Isidora. Perhaps I should go now."

Isidora sat up straighter. "I told Lucien he has four hours to return. Then I shall come after him. I have lost everyone who was dear to me in life. Nothing will get in my way this time to let it happen again."

Larke looked upon Isidora in wonderment. Women had vied for her brother's attention for as long as she could remember. But this was the first time she had seen a lady so protective of him. Or he of her.

"That is not much time for him to accomplish anything, Isidora. But on the other hand, a half a day's ride could put him leagues away in any direction."

Isidora stood, grave and beautiful. "Then I think that I should not try to follow Lucien, but Kalle. Lucien may indeed find him, but if I get there first, I may be able to avert a bloody fight."

"But Kalle is too dangerous—and besides, how do you know where he is?"

"He told me."

"What?" Larke exclaimed, disbelieving.

"It is true. He wants me to return to Acre with him."

Larke realized her mouth was open. "Kalle Fitz-Malheury desires this...but why? Is...is he in love with you?"

"He is in love with my mother, who has been dead for years, God keep her. Perhaps he believes I will provide some sort of link between him and her. And, I think, if he can take me away from Lucien, that would please him in some perverse way, which might keep him from doing worse things to Lucien, should he provoke Kalle. At this point I hardly know if Lucien would even mind my leaving, with or without Kalle."

"Of course he would mind!"

Isidora shook her head. "You say you allow him to believe he controls you, Larke. But in truth, he *does* control you. It is he who allows you to think you have a say in anything. He told me himself that this is the proper order of things, when it comes to men and women. So if he minds my going, I do not know if it is out of a sense of possessiveness or out of love."

Larke frowned. "I like this not at all!"

Isidora shrugged, a gesture which belied her intense tone. "Why do you think so many women go to convents? Would you not rather be subservient to God by your own choice, instead of being forced to do the will of an imperfect man?"

"Well…I see your meaning. But there must be some middle way…"

"It is rare to see it. Nor is it easy. Because when the woman loves the man, then she may choose to place herself at his mercy…and God help her, in that case."

Larke realized that Isidora was trembling. "You do love him."

Isidora met her gaze. "I wish I did not. Indeed, I wish that I had never met him."

"You can't mean that!"

"It may be you have not felt the pain I feel. And I hope you never do. But even as you have seen fit, out of your own goodness of heart to withhold something from me, Larke, so do I think it best not to share certain things with you."

"But you have to stay. You have to marry Lucien. Elsewise Mother will never be satisfied."

"Your mother needs to find out what she can do for herself, to make herself happy, instead of looking to Lucien to do it for her."

Larke, too, had felt that, but not dared voice it, for quite a while. Amelie…and Conrad. What if love of him was the source of her mother's misery, and not Lucien at all? How could they have been so blind? She bit her lip. "We have all encouraged her to behave this way, I trow."

Isidora looked down at her hands. "As I did my father, by ever doing his bidding instead of speaking my heart. It is not a loving act to allow people to destroy themselves unchallenged, however slowly or subtly."

"You must not go alone."

Isidora smiled grimly. "Familiar words, are they not?"

"Aye, but this is different."

"I do not wish to drag others into my sad tangle of events."

"It is too late, Isidora. We love you."

"You are right, it is too late, Larke. I have made my decision, and though one promise will be broken, another will be kept. If I can do no other service to Lucien, I will do this, though he will no doubt curse me for it."

Approaching footsteps sounded and Isidora jumped. She whirled about, to the formidable sight of Lucien standing in the doorway with a fair-haired, stern warrior at his side, and behind them, both Wace and Mauger.

"Isidora, this is Sir Raymond," Larke squeaked, and took a step backward.

Isidora nodded to Raymond, who inclined his head to her. *"Enchanté, demoiselle."*

"My lords?" she managed to ask. "How is it that you have returned so swiftly?"

Lucien, his hair in tangles and his cheeks shadowed, looked sorely in need of bed and board. "Isidora, I turned back from my pursuit of Kalle just now, because I thought you might provide me with a clue as to where he is, to save me time."

Isidora raised her chin. "Surely you do not need so many hands to bring me to heel, Lucien."

"Convince me otherwise, then."

She stood firm. "It is a matter of honor."

"Indeed, Isidora, what is there of importance that is *not* a matter of honor?"

"Pray tell me, then, Lucien—what has become of Faris? I think you know, and I must know, too." A lump formed in her throat, making it impossible to swallow.

Lucien looked down at his hands and began to ease the gauntlet from the wounded one. "He will not be coming back, Isidora." He glanced at Raymond, whose brilliant blue eyes flickered for an instant.

What are they hiding? Isidora thought, unwilling, unable to believe Lucien's words.

Raymond stepped forward and placed a large hand upon Isidora's shoulder. "When I left Faris, he looked not long for this world, *demoiselle*. But he was content. Indeed, he seemed happy."

Lucien stared at his friend.

Isidora shrugged free of the blond knight's hand and he moved back. "I must go to him!" She longed to flee the keep, to ride like the wind and find her brother.

"Nay. You must not." Lucien's voice was firm, his resolve upon the matter clear. "Let Faris go, Isidora. It was difficult enough for him to say goodbye once. Do not make him do it again."

Larke made a sound, as if she were weeping, and an

empty desperation filled Isidora. Nothing mattered now. She had lost too much, and too much of her loss was her own fault. She gazed at Lucien without blinking. "Then I will go to Kalle. And make him pay."

Lucien's fists clenched at his sides. "Don't be stupid!"

"I am no more stupid than you or any other man who would seek vengeance!"

"You are not me, nor are you a man."

"Aye, and I thank God for that every day!"

"Lucien." Raymond began to advance toward his friend.

"You're right. You will need my help to find Kalle," Isidora declared.

"What do you mean?" Lucien demanded.

"He is waiting for me." Isidora watched in dismay as Lucien's face drained of what little color it had.

"You…are close to him…in more than just enmity?"

"I made him a promise. I told you it was a matter of honor. That does not mean I cannot take my revenge, as well."

Raymond held up his hand. "As Lucien said, Kalle can pay wergild for Faris, you need not begin a blood feud."

"Gold does not satisfy such a debt!" Isidora bit her lip. Once Kalle had the Key, he would have all the gold he could ever want. An honor price would mean nothing to him.

"Isidora." Lucien's voice remained soft, but carried a core of iron. "You must tell me where Kalle is, and you must trust me to resolve this on your behalf, to act as your champion."

"I will show you, but I will not tell you."

Lucien moved to stand close before her, his presence warm and commanding. "Are you going to be my wife or are you not?"

Isidora wanted to run from him, to run from herself. He had not said it, but she knew that as far as he was concerned, to be his wife meant to give him her complete obedience. She could promise no such thing. "That is up to you, my lord, once this is finished."

"You have no preference on the matter?"

"My preference does not have any bearing upon it, in fact. If I wish to wed you, and you do not wish it, then my desire is of no account. But if you wish to wed me, and I do not wish it, you can still have me, if you so choose, and yet again—my desire is of no account. Is that not the way of the world, as you have described it to me and indeed, as I have experienced it? That the will of men is the will of all?"

"Nay, Isidora, you stubborn, stone-pated female! I want you. But I will not have you unless you want me, as well. That is the way of *my* world."

"You *want* me, Sir Lucien? You do not declare love nor ask for it in return? Perhaps the presence of your comrades prevents any such vulnerable admission. Or perhaps there is no such admission to be made, because of other things that consume your heart. Let me say this to you, then, Lord Lucien, before your friends and mine."

Isidora put her hand over her own heart. "I profess my love for you, Lucien de Griswold. You may accept it or reject it. Nothing you can do will change the way I feel. It remains to be seen if you feel the same about me. So do not tell me you love me, even if it be true. Say nothing until Kalle is gone from us, one way or another."

Lucien grabbed two fistfuls of air. "God in Heaven, Isidora, you weary me with your riddling and your convoluted logic and your cryptic words! I showed you full well that I loved you, the other night. What more proof do you need? Think you I share myself with just anyone who asks?"

Isidora could only stare up at him.

Raymond cleared his throat, but Mauger was the one who spoke. "Lucien, our Isidora is overwrought, as are you yourself. You need food and rest. There is no need to race off on the instant to look for FitzMalheury. Lady Isidora, think you Kalle is in a hurry to depart?"

"He awaits me, as I said. He will not leave until my business with him is done. Tomorrow is soon enough."

"There," Mauger said, his relief evident. "Sleep upon it, and on the morrow the proper course will be easier to discern."

"Aye." Lucien caught Isidora's arm. "We will have supper, and you will be spending the night with me, then, my lady. You love me? Well and good. I give you a new opportunity to demonstrate that as you see fit."

He marched her past his sister, Mauger, Sir Raymond and Wace. All of them stood red-faced and astonished except for Raymond, who looked the sort of man who would have done the same if in Lucien's place.

And, had she the least bit of pride left, she would have fought her way free and refused to cooperate with such a gesture of ownership. But she had none. For all she knew, these could be their last hours together, forevermore. She would take them, take whatever she could of him, to hold tight against the future.

The sun had set early. In the solar, with the door shut, Lucien cast off his clothes, throwing them to the floor as if challenging an opponent to some sort of combat. Isidora could only watch and marvel at what a beautiful creature he was. His sculpted face, his broad shoulders, his skin, golden in the firelight. He slid under the bed furs and sat with his muscular arms crossed, looking at her expectantly. "Well?"

What little composure she had, left her as self-consciousness spread. Her legs felt as though they could not hold her weight. "Please, Lucien, do not be cruel."

He closed his eyes and leaned back against the bolster. "Oh, Isidora. Just come here, I beg of you, and be with me."

"I can see that you are exhausted, my lord. But I will be with you." She clambered up, still fully clothed, and lay down beside him.

"Are you comfortable?" he asked, still with his eyes closed.

"Not particularly," she replied truthfully.

"Then make yourself thus."

"I don't know if that is possible."

"Take off your overgown, for a start. That would make *me* more comfortable, if I were you."

She did not allow her initial hesitation to gain a foothold, but undid her belt—then she froze. Isidora looked helplessly at Lucien. She wanted to feel free of pressure, free of guilt, free to live the moment, without thought of the past or what was to come.

Lucien said nothing, but handled her gently as he tugged off her overgown. Then he flung it out of reach, drew her close and covered her with the bed furs. He was warm and solid through the thin linen of her chemise.

"That's better," he murmured.

"What would you have me do now?" she whispered.

Lucien opened his eyes and slanted his blue gaze to her. He leaned down, cupped her face with his palm, and kissed her mouth as if she were still a virgin, still an innocent, as if he had an obligation to be careful with her. "Go to sleep, Isidora. Know that you are safe with me."

"I know," she said, a fresh tumult of conflicting feelings welling up inside. *I am safe, but my heart is not, for you are perilous fair, Lucien de Griswold.*

Chapter Thirty

Lucien woke to a moonbeam shining in his eyes from the solar's tall, narrow window. He sensed a warm presence at his side and remembered he was not alone. Isidora…dark and exquisite…outspoken and stubborn…brave and intelligent…she was here, now, her bare skin next to his, with nothing to stop him from kissing her awake.

Nothing but the certainty that she was, if not lying outright, withholding something from him. The knowledge Deogal had given her to deliver to him, for one. But beyond that, she withheld her trust. She did not trust him to use the knowledge wisely or judiciously. To guard against alchemy taking hold of his life, of his very being, the way it had her father.

He looked down at her, at the silver light spangling her hair. She breathed evenly; her breasts gently rose and fell. Then, as he watched, her eyelids fluttered, her brow knit and she began to push away some foe in her dreamworld.

"La—la!! Effendi…" she cried. *Nay, nay!! Learned One…*

"Shh, wake up, it is but a dream, Isidora." Lucien

stroked her hair back from her face and rubbed her arms. She stopped fighting and slowly opened her eyes. He pulled the furs up over her shoulders. "You've not been covered, you're cold."

"I had a nightmare."

"So I gathered. What was it?"

She squeezed her eyes closed. "Kalle. Kalle was there…I don't want to talk about it."

FitzMalheury again. Lucien made an effort to reply in a soothing voice. "Go back to sleep then."

To Lucien's surprise, Isidora turned to him and slid her soft arms around his middle. "I've slept long enough." She held him tight, her cheek to his, her eyelashes brushing his skin as she blinked.

She touched something within him that began to melt away his resistance and his anger, his sense of being trapped in his duty. "Isidora, I have not asked your permission to wed you, but I ask it now. Indeed, I should be on my knees before you, not lying here in your arms as if you were mine already."

When he started to sit up, she pushed him back. "But I am yours already." She made this profound statement, her voice soft, like the touch of an angel's wing. "I would—"

Lucien slid his hands through the skeins of her black hair and drew her face to his, capturing whatever she had been about to say in a kiss. A devouring hunger rose in him, as nothing he had ever felt before. A desire beyond possession, beyond the physical, one that simply burned for ultimate union on all levels.

If there was anyone in the world who could comprehend him, it was she. If anyone could challenge him and get away with it, she could. If anyone truly loved him—if no one else at all loved him—he hoped and he prayed that Isidora did.

He wrapped her in his arms, rolled her onto her back, and tried to show her how he felt before he himself was overcome. "Be at one with me," he breathed. "Let go of your fear."

"Lucien." She arched against him.

He slid her chemise up as her weight shifted, until her moist heat met his body, and he was lost in her.

The morning came all too soon for Isidora, and with it, the harsh reality of facing Kalle once again. Why could the night with Lucien not have lasted forever? Was she doomed to have only a few moments of happiness? She looked at him, and the soft, filtered light coming through the drawn bed curtains made him seem ethereal. Indeed, she had slept on the bosom of an angel, if ever there was one.

Her angel opened his eyes and slid his hand over hers. "What are you thinking, Isidora?"

She had to tell him the truth. Now. "First of all, let me say that…that anything I have done, is out of the love I bear for you. The other night it was necessary for Kalle to come to your aid. I made certain he did by promising him the Key."

Lucien's countenance darkened. "And what key might that be?"

"The…the thing my father sent me to deliver to you. The Key—to the Elixir. And the scrolls that I found that go with it."

"The Key," Lucien said slowly, as if in a daze. He stared at her. Then rubbed his brow. Then stared at her again. "Let me see if I understand what you just said. In return for my hand's recovery, you promised Kalle FitzMalheury the key to the saving of mankind from damnation? To wiping out famine and plague and war and ignorance for all time?" He sat up and brought her with him, catching hold of her arms, hard. "You've promised *him* the key to the divine power of the One God?"

Isidora could not breathe. Her heart felt as though it would burst. If she could escape Lucien's iron grip, she would run to the window and throw herself over the edge. What was he saying? *That the Elixir held the power of God?*

Her words tumbled out. "I thought it was a means to transmute base metal to gold. And, as you explained, to cure ills. I did not realize that—"

"You promised him this. Do not tell me you actually gave it to him, Isidora. Please." Lucien's voice was tight with quiet, desperate fury.

"I—I had to!" she sobbed, wishing the heavens would open and carry her away.

"You had to give it to him—but not to me. When?"

"Afterward— After we…oh, Lucien." Isidora's misery compounded. She had accepted Lucien's gift of himself, knowing that she had no right to such joy, because it had been an act of thievery on her part, as surely as was handing the Key over to Kalle.

His eyes full of pain, Lucien looked at her and did not speak.

"But, Lucien, what choice did I have? You were not with my father at the end. You did not have to mop up his flux and vomit and listen to his ravings. That was his ignoble death, my lord! Nothing sublime about it. And the Work was to blame—these operations you perform, the cooking of mercury and lead—it creates pure poison!

"How could I give those things to you? Send you rushing back into the greedy maw of the Work, with fresh, false hope? Your future, ours, your life and happiness, damned by the certainty of a horrible death!"

Lucien shook his head. "You had the scrolls even then, Isidora, did you not? Long before he died. You had no regular habit of visiting the bowels of Kalle's dungeons. You had them when you came for me. And yet you did not give them to Deogal?"

Isidora felt like a cornered animal. "I did not give them to him straight away. I did not know they were so important. I wanted him, for myself! Just once, I wanted my father to see *me*, Isidora—not Isidora who reminded him of Ayshka, or Isidora who prepared his food every day, or Isidora who was willing to sacrifice her life for him, because, after all, was that not what any dutiful daughter should do? I wanted him to ask me if I was happy and to tell me he loved me."

Lucien looked into her eyes for a long, long moment. She thought she might shatter beneath the intensity of his gaze.

He was a generous, noble soul. But no matter how well-mannered he was, he would not forgive her this. And she could not fault him.

"Lucien, I have one more thing to say… I see a great pity in this, a t-terrible irony. For you need nothing beyond what you already are. You are a fine man. Why do you want more than you have in yourself, more than is either reasonable or natural?" She bit her lip to mask the pain in her heart.

At last his hands relaxed and slid from her arms. "Isidora, it is not all for myself. It is too much for any one person to have such power. But it could have been guarded, until the time was right, the right kings and bishops and pope, men of intelligence and integrity. It is true, I had a selfish motive. I wanted to cure my mother of her melancholy, just as your father wanted to cure your mother. And just as he contributed to her condition, I was the cause of my mother's."

Isidora swallowed. "You mean, the death of your sister, Estelle? But that was not anything you could help."

Lucien ground his fist into his forehead. "It was my fault. I should tell you, I suppose, so you know the truth, before you hear some other version of it. She fancied a young man, you see. Robert de Clairvaux. One of my foster brothers. He was my best friend. My parents sent him away when they suspected her attachment. I was so angry with them. And with her. But she begged me to take her to meet him. Just once more. I could refuse her nothing. Nor him. She knew this, of course."

He took a ragged breath, drew up his knees and hugged his legs. "We rendezvoused near an abandoned cottage. A landmark we all knew. But we did not know a band of outlaws had taken shelter there. I should have considered that possibility, taken it into account. I was the eldest, if only by a few moments. But I was too worried about my father's wrath to think clearly.

"They came at us like wild animals. They took Estelle. Robert and I became separated as we fought. There were three or four of them attacking him at once. And others already had her—had her down... I was forced to choose. Him or her. Both of them were screaming my name. Each begging me to save the other."

His voice had dropped to a whisper and he looked down at his hands, crossed before him. "I hesitated. For an instant. Then…I left Robert to his fate and went for Estelle. But it was too late. *I* was too late."

Lucien raised his head and Isidora had never before seen anything so terrifying as the fierceness in his gaze.

"So I killed those men. Every last one. I cut off their heads and planted them in a circle, stuck on their own lances. I left them staring at each other's ugly faces. Then I rode home, with Estelle and Robert."

"How old were you?" Isidora asked, Lucien's pain making her own voice barely audible.

"We all had fifteen winters. My father sent me away after that. As far as he could. I spent the next six years in France. From there I went to Outremer. And in Acre, the farthest place I had ever been save Jerusalem, I found you."

Lucien still sat on the bed, his powerful arms now resting across his knees. He gazed at Isidora, who knelt beside him, and took a deep breath. "So, my lady, who am I to question anyone else's judgment? All I know is, a single mistake can grow into a huge calamity. I have made such a mistake already in this life. I cannot afford another. And you wonder why I seek perfection?"

She looked at him, her eyes stinging. "Oh, Lucien. No one else expects it of you."

"But there have been those with such expectations of me. And the Work demands it."

A spark of anger flared within Isidora at the unfairness of this, at the burden it placed on lives that might otherwise be spent loving others instead of alchemy.

"Then, my lord, the Work is futile! There is no such

thing as perfection, outside of God. Who are you to insist you are capable of it, when no one else is?"

Lucien's gaze softened and she felt as though he had touched her in kindness, even though he still sat by himself.

"Who are you, Isidora, to insist that I, or you, or anyone else, is outside of God? Is that not what we seek? Not just union with the Divine, but a reunion? Have you considered that perfection might be there all along, hidden, and we catch glimpses of it from time to time? Even within ourselves?"

Isidora's heart caught yet again, but this time in yearning. *This is the kind of thing he and my father must have spent hours and days and nights on end discussing. Apart from me.* "But to look for it by torturing metal, Lucien?"

"If it is in one thing, then it is in all. But metal can be worked. Flesh cannot. Mortification is not the way."

She sighed and shivered as a breath of chill morning air passed through the open bed curtain. "Then, neither is guilt."

Lucien was silent for a long breath, then opened his knees and held out one arm. "Come. You're cold."

How could this be, when she had torn from him his life's goal? "The saving grace of the world," he'd said. Why did he not throw her down in anger, as even a reasonable man might?

But such an invitation from him might not come again. Isidora crept into the warm circle of his embrace and he enveloped her in the thick folds of the bed furs, with her back to his chest. "Isidora, listen to me." Lucien put his cheek to hers and together the skin heated between them.

She knew she did not want to hear whatever he was about to say. She wanted the moment to last, just the way they were, with her surrounded by his strength and solidity. But he continued, as she knew he would.

"Kalle cannot be allowed to return with the Key to Acre."

His words struck like a hammer blow to her heart. "Nay, Lucien, how can you? He would kill to keep it, or die before giving it up. Either way—"

"It must be retrieved. Or he must be stopped. One way or another."

"I do not see how it can be done! He—" She fell silent as her mind came to a point of clarity and remembered the strange ring her mother had sent with Faris to give her. Ayshka had told him Isidora would know what to do with it when the time was right.

She thought back to Kalle's hands, in the *laboratorium.* He, too, had a ring. One that had looked curiously incomplete. And now she knew what she must attempt.

Lucien spoke again. "You must understand, Isidora, that while it is true I want this Key, I would not try to take it from him were he a man of sound principles. As it is, he is much too dangerous to have such power."

"But how can you do this? If something should happen to you…I will feel responsible…and I could not bear your loss…"

"You made a choice, the best you knew how to make in the moment. Now I am making my own. What I choose is not your responsibility. And if 'something,' as you put it, happens to me, then that is God's choice. But I have to try."

Isidora refused to think about what his effort might entail. "How does your hand fare now?"

"It pains me. But it is better. Kalle is full of surprises. Indeed, I wish he was not my enemy."

"I wish he had never darkened our door. He brought nothing but suffering to my father's house. What are you going to do now?"

"I ask that you tell me where to find Kalle."

"I cannot. I am sorry, Lucien. You sound calm, but I know I have made you angry. And I will not put you in harm's way."

"You *will* tell me. I command you in this."

"But don't you understand? Now that he has the Key, he will go back to Acre and leave you alone, leave *us* alone."

Lucien drew her from his embrace, turned her about and caught her by the hands. "Isidora, consider what is at stake. Think you Kalle will be content to sit by, concocting batches of the Elixir? Think you he will sell it as medicine in vials at the *souk?* Nay, he will *use* it himself, to become as powerful as any one man could ever be on this earth. He will try and rule the world, Isidora. And if he is determined enough, he can succeed. If that happens, then God help us all."

Isidora felt faint, as though she might keel over. "I am the ruin of the world, then?"

"Nay. You can help me get it back. You *must.*"

Isidora nodded, her defeat complete. "It seems I have no choice. But I will take you there, I will not merely tell you. I want to face him one last time, for Faris's sake. Do you understand, Lucien?"

"Aye, I do."

She rubbed one of his hard, taut thighs. "Lucien?"

He raised an eyebrow.

"Will it ever be again, as it was with us last night? Or has that been lost, along with the Elixir?"

"I do not know, Isidora. Only God knows what lies in store for us."

At these words of little hope, her tears flowed at last. She turned away from Lucien, knowing how awful she must look, red-eyed and red-nosed, and despising herself for even caring at such a time.

Chapter Thirty-One

In a secluded spot across the river, Kalle's encampment lay shrouded in mist. The day was cold and gray, and his horses stood with their heads low as his men readied them for departure. He emerged from his pavilion as Lucien and Isidora approached, his fur-lined mantle hanging loose about his shoulders.

Isidora stood before him, her heart hammering her ribs, with Lucien at her side.

"You came," Kalle said to her. "But not alone. Will the Lord of Ainsley act as your champion, then? Does he plan to try to best me?"

"To reason with you," Lucien replied. "We have an exchange to make."

"I made no bargain with you! It is Isidora to whom I swore, no one else."

"But you owe me a debt of honor, Kalle."

"So satisfy that later, instead of hiding behind a woman's business with me now!"

"There is more to it than that."

"*Oui.* More than you know."

Isidora turned to Lucien. "Please, my lord. Allow me to speak to Kalle first, in private, before you do anything further."

"What have you to say to him that cannot be said to me?"

She clasped her hands before her. "Lucien, I ask this of you now, do not make me beg."

He grimaced, as if her words pained him, and stepped back. "Very well."

Isidora walked to Kalle, her limbs trembling. "Ayshka—" she began.

Kalle's gaze sharpened. "What about her?"

"Faris brought me something of hers, which she gave to him before she died. I think you may want to see it."

Slowly, as if he was being bled, Kalle's face turned white. He wrapped his mantle closer about himself. "*Non*…I have no wish to see anything."

"I believe it is something you gifted her with."

"I gifted her with nothing. And if I had, how dare you use it—a piece of my heart—against me? What kind of woman are you? A conniving one, just like every other woman, I suppose!"

"You have a heart, Kalle? I thought you prided yourself on going without," Isidora said.

"Your only interest is that it might be a place you could stab."

She reached into a pouch at her waist and withdrew a small object. "Here, Kalle. See for yourself."

Kalle's eyes narrowed, as if what she held in her palm emitted a bright light. "That could be any bauble. Why should I look at it?"

"You know what it is," she insisted. "I wager it fits the ring on your own finger, curve to curve. Do you not see? Her keeping it proves that my mother cared enough about you to guard your gift, even beyond death. It meant something to her. *You* meant something to her…"

Kalle's jaw twitched. "And you would sell it to me, for the Key?"

"Aye," Isidora admitted, hating to degrade her mother's offering in this manner, and ashamed to be throwing the one decent part of Kalle back into his face.

"I should simply take it from you. I can, you know."

"I know. But I tell you this—Ayshka Binte Amir is watching us from Heaven, right now. And she will either smile upon you, or curse you, according to the choice you make."

Kalle stared at the ring a moment longer, then looked away. "I am already cursed. Take it. Take this." He wrenched the matching ring off of his own finger and stuffed it into Isidora's hand. "Lucien! Let us finish."

Lucien strode over to stand between Isidora and Kalle. "Keep the scrolls, Kalle, for they came from your own abode. But as Deogal was my master, you will give me the Key and return Ayshka's image to Isidora. It is not right to have taken them the way you did. Indeed, to have procured them in such a dark manner can only produce your ultimate downfall, should you use them for ill."

Kalle laughed. "You forget Deogal was my master, as well! But the scrolls are useless without the Key."

"I have sworn to retrieve these things from you. I am prepared to give you what you paid for them."

Kalle smiled without humor. "First your hand? And then your life?"

Lucien replied without hesitation. "Aye."

Isidora felt unsteady, as if the earth had shifted beneath her feet, as it had on occasion in the Holy Land. "Oh! Please, nay!"

Kalle looked at her. "You see to what foolish lengths men in love will go?"

"Women in love can be just as foolish," Lucien said.

Isidora looked from Lucien to Kalle. "There is nothing foolish about love. But what Lucien proposes is not about love, it is about pride."

"It is about honor!" protested Lucien.

"And why is your honor of more import than mine? Why can it not be my choice to give up what I will, to help you? Can you not accept that help graciously? Is it because you do not consider me your equal?"

Lucien and Kalle both stared at her in silence. Then at each other.

"Kalle and I are equals. We must fight it out," said Lucien, and Kalle nodded his agreement.

"But what are you fighting over?" Isidora nearly shrieked.

"The victor will take all," Kalle replied.

"All," confirmed Lucien, his gaze devouring her.

"What do you mean? Including…me?"

Kalle snarled, "Of course, including you. One or the other of us will be dead, so whoever is left must take you in hand. Now get out of the way!"

"But—this was about the Key. The Elixir. Not me!"

"It is now."

"I'll have neither of you, in any case!"

"It is not up to you."

Isidora could not believe Lucien had made such a bald statement. She turned around and began to run toward the river, leaving them both behind.

"What are you doing?" Kalle bellowed. *"Beteuse!"*

She flung the words over her shoulder. "I will give to the river what you claim you do not want!"

They pursued her and raced each other. Isidora dared glance behind her but once. Kalle had tossed away his mantle and was surprisingly nimble, Lucien was the younger and faster, but she saw that neither of them would catch her before she reached the river.

She teetered at the brink of the embankment. The water ran dark and swift before her. She held the two halves of the ring over her head, one in each hand. "This is your choice, Kalle. Do you wish to have these back, and with them your chance at redemption? Or will you have me cast what is left of your heart into these depths?"

"You witch! Give them to me!" Kalle roared and lunged toward her. She staggered backward, and Lucien charged. The men met like stags and Lucien's head butted Kalle's chest, knocking his breath from him.

Isidora took a step to regain her balance, her foot met with a slimy stone and she fell from the edge into the rushing torrent.

Chapter Thirty-Two

She bobbed and floundered in the icy water. Her clothing wrapped around her legs, as if she had been bundled in a rug and tossed into the sea like a harem girl who had committed some crime.

"Isidora!"

Lucien's voice, wild with rage and grief. But she could not call out, for the cold robbed her of speech. She struggled to keep her head above the roiling surface as she tumbled along, scraping rocks and tree limbs. Then there was no sound but the river, no sight but the gray sky and the turbulence surrounding her.

A small hill of water rushed toward her. Before she had a chance to decide what it was, she was swept up and over it, of no more consequence than a twig to the surging flow. She took a last gasp of air, then dropped. Her downstream journey ended as the water sucked her deeper. It churned around her, tossing her body. Captured by the water's strength, she was in a hole at the base of a huge boulder hidden below the surface.

Isidora caught a glimpse of a hoof, an antler…she was not the only one to have been trapped here. Her lungs ached with the need to draw breath. A prayer flashed through her mind, for Lucien to enjoy a long and happy life…and for she herself to be with her mother again at last, bringing her Kalle's ring….

Lucien plowed through the icy water. He knew this river, knew its moods and fury and awesome power. The water tried to overwhelm him, and was close to succeeding. He fought its weight, its speed, and his own inability to breathe it.

The great stone lay before him. In summer it reared up like a sea monster sunning itself. He willed himself to reach it, to reach Isidora before the current swept him past. Kalle was carried nearer, fighting his own battle with the river's spirit. The fool! It was obvious he could not swim.

The deceptive, smooth hump of water that marked the boulder's presence was just ahead. Lucien prayed for strength. For a miracle. He had only an instant to find something to hang on to before he rushed past the rock. He clawed his way closer, deeper. His fingers caught a submerged jutting of wood, he kicked hard and the back of one knee met with a snag.

Pain screamed through his leg. But using the branch as an anchor, he plunged his upper body farther into the river and reached blindly down. The cascade of water caught him, battered his head against the stone. Dazed, he reached again.

Something brushed his fingertips. A hand. She was here! Hope and joy lent Lucien renewed strength. He grabbed it and pulled. But it was not Isidora's face that emerged, but Kalle's.

The knight must have gone straight over the top of the stone and under, just as Isidora had. In the ensuing wave of disappointment, Lucien wanted to release his enemy's hand. Let the water sweep Kalle away. Be rid of him. But a small voice within bade him hold on.

Kalle caught Lucien's right arm and exerted a huge force, as if trying to pull Lucien from his precarious, agonizing leghold. Lucien resisted, his body at the brink of exhaustion, his lungs about to inhale whatever they could, even if water was all that was to be had.

Then Kalle brought his other hand up from the depths. In his fist was a skein of black hair…still attached to Isidora. Kalle held Lucien's wrist, wrapped the hair around it, and let go.

He vanished.

Lucien hauled Isidora upward with his arms, and himself back with the excruciating leverage provided by his leg around the tree limb.

He boosted her until her face was clear of the water. Her head lolled to one side. Her lips were blue, her eyes closed. He had her, but he could do nothing except hold on to her. He gasped for breath and became aware once again of the frigid water pounding his body, of the pain in his leg. It would not take long before he, too, would have to let go…

"Oy, Lucien!"

He turned his head, tried to focus. Raymond stood on the bank, with Wace and Mauger and Kalle's man… Raymond launched a spear. It sailed through the air, a rope trailing behind it. Lucien's hope faltered as it fell short and the current carried it off. But then Raymond mounted his horse and hurled a second lance as Wace reeled in the first.

This time Raymond's aim was true and the lance sailed overhead, upstream. The line slapped the water and when it reached him, Lucien wrapped the rough, blessed rope around his arm. He fumbled for his dagger and cut the lance free.

"Ready!" he shouted, and prayed through the numbing cold that he could hold on long enough. He clasped Isidora around the ribs with one arm and put himself beneath her, to shield her head and back from the stones.

He made ready to launch free of the snag. But his leg was in agony. It was stuck. Indeed, at last he understood how he had not been swept away. His leg was not merely hooked around the tree limb. A broken branch impaled his calf, by his own weight and the force of the water tugging at him.

With a final effort, Lucien pushed with his other foot and freed himself. Once he had shoved off, the river washed them farther downstream. But when the line grew taut, the team of men ashore acted as a pivot, and Lucien and Isidora swung closer and closer to the shallows. At last an eddy swept them into a calmer spot and Lucien was able to struggle far enough out of the water that he might collapse upon a bed of pebbles.

He lay for a moment, to breathe, with Isidora draped over his chest. He had got her, thanks in no small part to Kalle…but what was the use of having his own life, if she had lost hers? He heaved himself upright, cradling her body in his lap.

A clatter of feet and hooves met his ears above the rush of the river and the wail of misery rising in his own heart. He looked down at her. Strands of wet hair drizzled across her cold, white face, and a hank of it remained entangled about his wrist.

Raymond jumped down from his horse. "Is she…?"

Lucien met Raymond's gaze and saw his own anguish reflected in his friend's eyes. "I'm taking her home." Lucien struggled to his feet, lifting Isidora as he came. His wounded leg threatened to buckle, but he forced it straight. Then the weary muscles in his arms quivered and, fearing he might drop his lady, he slung her over his shoulder.

Her head flopped against his back. Dead weight. Dead…*dead!* Just like Estelle, just like Robert…

Then…her body spasmed. She coughed and warm water splashed. Lucien staggered with her off the rocky strand and lay her on the grass. She gasped, choked and gasped again.

"Isidora…" He stroked her face, chafed her arms and refrained from shaking her by the shoulders for being so rash. "Are you all right?"

After a final bout of coughing she opened her eyes, her lashes in wet, black clumps. "I—I think so…"

"You're shivering." Lucien's own teeth chattered as he accepted Raymond's mantle and picked up Isidora once more, wrapping her securely in its folds. He had nearly lost her…he would not let her go again.

She stirred and whispered, "I'm sorry for causing this trouble, Lucien. I thank you for saving me…and enemy or no, I would thank Kalle, as well, though I lost his ring."

Lucien kissed her cheeks and forehead. "Think upon it no more. But, Kalle…is gone."

To his dismay, Isidora stared at him dumbly, then began to weep. He looked to Raymond, who shrugged and murmured in an aside, "Who knows what goes on in their minds?" Then, more loudly, "I will send men to search the banks, milady. But, Lucien, you both need warming and we must see to your leg. Let us return to Ainsley."

"What is wrong with his leg?" Isidora demanded through her tears.

Lucien gave her a squeeze. "Shh, woman. 'Tis of no import. Be still."

She buried her face against his chest and was silent.

At the hall once more, with Isidora in the care of Larke, Amelie and Ceridwen's cousins, Lucien sat before the fire with Raymond, Wace, Mauger and Kalle's man, Earm.

Lucien's leg throbbed and had swollen to the point where to stand upon it made him clench his teeth so he could not speak. His head ached, he felt sleepy and could not remember much of what anyone had been saying. But he remained in the hall, though he longed to go upstairs to his solar. "Where did you find the rope, Raymond?"

Raymond looked in the direction of the dark knight. "Earm, here. His quick wits provided it from Kalle's horses' picket line."

Lucien inclined his head in a solemn nod. "Glad am I of your strong arm, Raymond. And, Earm, I will gift you with anything you desire, be it in my power to bestow."

The knight shifted and glanced from Lucien to Raymond and back. "I would only ask leave to remain, to try to find Lord Kalle's body. But I fear his people in Acre will not believe me when I tell them he drowned by accident."

Lucien rubbed his brow. "If we find him, he will need to be buried here, and we will give him the honor he is due.

We'll provide you with letters, and put our seals upon them as witnesses to what happened. None can fault you, Earm. Indeed, if you wish to stay, I can always use a good man."

Earm shook his head. "Many thanks, but I feel I must return. Someone awaits me in Acre. I will make a fresh start there…"

"There is news of another's death that should be delivered to his kinsmen." Lucien stared at the red glow of the coals.

"Em, Lucien," Raymond began. "I should tell you, it is not certain that Faris is dead. He asked us to allow you and his sister to think so, to keep Kalle from going after the Cistercians to find him. I am not convinced Kalle would have bothered, but the risk…"

Lucien swung his head around—regretted the sudden movement—and glared at Raymond. "You approved this? You partook of this lie, and created such suffering in Isidora's heart, as well as mine? And you allowed Larke to further it?"

"It seemed the lesser evil at the time, Lucien, and could well be the truth. But I humbly beg your pardon."

"Go beg it of Isidora!"

Raymond stood, his gaze even. "Right. So will I do. But she'll have more courtesy than thee, I trow."

Lucien realized he had gone too far. He got to his feet, as well, though only one leg bore his weight. "Raymond, please, forgive me. Take your rest here for as long as you will. I do not doubt your good intentions."

"Aye. Sit down before you fall down, Lucien." Slowly, Raymond retook his own seat. "But Wace and I should be heading home soon. We have some horses awaiting us, up the vale."

Lucien settled back into his chair with relief. "When you reach Rookhaven, tell Lady Ceridwen to make ready to attend a wedding."

Raymond raised an eyebrow. "Indeed? You'd best ask the bride before you make any further plans, Lucien. These things are not so simple as you seem to think."

"And a few things are more simple than you know, Beauchamp. Help me upstairs, will you?"

Isidora woke, but darkness surrounded her. Too much like the suffocating darkness of the cold, churning water. She shivered, then felt the reassuring warmth of a body at her back. A familiar, comforting hand slid down her arm, hugging it against her chest from behind.

"Lucien…where are Larke and the others?"

"I sent them away. Are you feeling better?"

She hurt all over, but her heart ached the most. "Aye."

"What is the matter, Isidora?"

She swallowed against the tightness in her throat. "I feel that I have been the death of Kalle. Taunting him like that…it was wrong."

Lucien sighed. "No one forced him to jump into the river when he could not swim."

"You offer little comfort, Lucien."

"I seemed to be running afoul of everyone this night."

Isidora turned in his embrace and felt his forehead. It was hot and damp. "I've caused you to suffer, as well. You have fever. Would that Kalle were here to attend your leg!"

"I thank God he is not. I am fine. I'll go to the monastery tomorrow, for Faris may live yet, Raymond says."

Brilliant, unexpected hope leaped in Isidora's breast. "Oh…I pray it is true! I will accompany you. And so will Larke. Make no attempt to stop us, Lucien."

"Heaven forbid that I even try! Raymond's brother there has some skill with wounds. He saw to Faris's, so I understand."

She turned back around, so Lucien was melded against her once more. "Good. He can see to yours, as well, then."

He gave her a little squeeze. "Isidora…I am…tired. I have been harsh with you. I—"

"Lucien, you are only trying to do your duty. Do not apologize for that. I understand."

"You understand…but do you want *me,* and all that I entail?"

"You mean, your pursuit of the Elixir?"

"Aye."

Isidora shrank inside. "I cannot compete with the lure of alchemy, Lucien. No woman can, unless she herself is part of the process."

"Earm has handed over the Key and the scrolls to me. He confessed that Kalle told him he would be cursed if he tried to steal them or profit from them."

"You did not even hear what I just said."

"I did. You cannot compete. But you need not, Isidora. I am returning the Key and scrolls to you, to do with as you see fit."

She could not believe she had heard a-right. "You are?"

"My wedding gifts to you."

"Your what?"

"You know what I said."

"Oh. Were I standing, I'd need to lie down!"

He murmured into her ear, "Well, you are not, and of that I am glad. The question remains…will you have me?"

She could not suppress a small wriggle of pleasure, which produced a groan from Lucien. She smiled. "Indeed, my lord, that I will."

Epilogue

The pure, clear voices of the Cistercian monks soared into the night, the song carrying with it their love of God. Isidora breathed in deep to savor the beauty of the sound, and held the Key and scrolls in a tight bundle as Brother Percy approached.

"My lady, you have summoned me?"

"I have something to give you in trust, brother. I cannot bring myself to destroy these ancient things, yet I want them kept in secret." She explained to him what she understood the power of the Key and scrolls to be and how she feared them, for Lucien's sake.

Percy listened in silence. "A heavy burden, indeed. The Elixir, a panacea for mankind, or the power to rule the world…no wonder Kalle was so sorely tempted by it."

"Not only him, but my father…and Lucien, as well."

Percy smiled charmingly. "But not you? You have no desire to be an empress?"

"Why, indeed not!"

"And Faris al-Rashid, who has become my good friend,

Elaine Knighton 297

has no claim upon this legacy? I would not want to see him suffer any further loss."

Isidora frowned. "Faris, now that he is on the mend, will no doubt seek fresh glory in battle, not by mixing metals."

"Ah, so there is some good to be seen in conflict."

"Brother Parsifal, you confuse me."

"I mean only to say that should the world be made a perfect place, it would cease to exist. An excellent reason to keep such an Elixir out of the hands of those who wish to do good with it, as well as those who would do evil. So why keep it at all?"

"Because it has been so dearly bought. My father's life and more…"

"Very well. Give it to me, then, and you will have seen the last of it. I will be its guardian."

Isidora placed the bundle into his hands and breathed her relief. "Many thanks, my lord."

Percy bowed to her. "This abbey is home to many treasures."

"You are chief among them, I trow," she said sincerely.

Percy laughed out loud at this. "Go to your husband, lass."

Husband. Warmth spread through her at the thought of Lucien. They were wed. Informally, but wed nevertheless. Although Conrad had still not returned with a priest of his own choosing, the Cistercian abbot had given them his blessing in the meantime.

She turned, to see Lucien leaning in the doorway, carved stone kings on either side of him and ancient knights above. He smiled, though he was pale and, she knew, in pain.

"You should not be using that leg in such a manner, my lord."

"If not for this, then what would you have me do with it?"

She went to him, close, but not touching. "It should be in bed."

"Ah, would that it could, and me along with it. But it is time to depart for Ainsley. Larke is anxious to get Faris back to where she can keep a close watch upon him."

"And what will Wace think of that?"

"Wace is herding horses with Raymond, there is nothing he can do, except get wounded himself, to gain her sympathy. Besides, he is much too young."

"He is a stout lad and Faris is not about to allow Larke's fantasies to get the better of her. Or him. But she should be wed sooner rather than later," Isidora added.

"Well, it will have to be later, because I have not yet chosen a husband for her."

"If you do not make certain it is a man to her liking— she will do it for you, one way or another."

"At least my mother is pleased with the choice I made in you."

"And if she had not been?"

"Then she would have had a long time to regret not appreciating my wisdom."

"You are not wise, Lucien."

"Nay. I am a besotted fool." He caught her in his arms and put his lips to hers.

A monk walked in, saw them, and hurriedly turned around and fled.

Isidora squirmed. "We are being improper in this place."

"Nay, this is but the remainder of the kiss of God the

abbott bade me bestow upon you. In fact, there is a good deal more of it left. Indeed it may take the rest of my life to deliver the whole of it to you, in divine increments…"

"Oh, well, I thank you for being so thorough."

"Aye, I intend to be."

She pulled back. "Lucien, I—I have given the Key to Sir Parsifal, I mean, Brother Percy, for safekeeping. But if you—"

"That is good."

"You are not angry?"

He searched her eyes. "Isidora, have you no idea of the truth of the matter?"

"What truth?"

He put his hand to her face, cupping her cheek. "That *you* are the true Elixir. You are the touchstone. All fire and innocence. Devotion and love. Nothing more perfect exists for me."

"Oh, Lucien. You please me beyond words…."

His mouth hovered above hers and he smiled. "Then stop using them, Isidora."

* * * * *

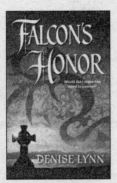

Harlequin Historicals®
Historical Romantic Adventure!

ESCAPE TO A LAND LONG AGO AND FAR AWAY IN THE PAGES OF HARLEQUIN HISTORICALS

ON SALE APRIL 2005

THE VISCOUNT
by Lyn Stone

Lily Bradshaw finds herself in a dire situation after her husband's death and seeks out the only person she knows in London: Viscount Duquesne. Guy agrees to marry Lily to protect her and her young son from harm's way. Will their marriage of convenience turn to one of true happiness and love?

THE BETROTHAL
by Terri Brisbin, Joanne Rock and Miranda Jarrett

Love is in the air this spring, when Harlequin Historicals brings you three tales of romance in the British Isles. *The Claiming of Lady Joanna* features a beautiful runaway bride and the man who is determined to claim her for his wife. In *Highland Handfast,* a Scottish lord agrees to a temporary marriage with an old childhood love, but plans on convincing her to make it permanent! And in *A Marriage in Three Acts,* a noble lord finds himself enchanted by a beautiful actress when her troupe of traveling players arrive at the lord's estate.

If you enjoyed what you just read,
then we've got an offer you can't resist!

Take 2 bestselling
love stories FREE!
Plus get a FREE surprise gift!

Clip this page and mail it to Harlequin Reader Service®

IN U.S.A.	IN CANADA
3010 Walden Ave.	P.O. Box 609
P.O. Box 1867	Fort Erie, Ontario
Buffalo, N.Y. 14240-1867	L2A 5X3

YES! Please send me 2 free Harlequin Historicals® novels and my free surprise gift. After receiving them, if I don't wish to receive anymore, I can return the shipping statement marked cancel. If I don't cancel, I will receive 6 brand-new novels every month, before they're available in stores! In the U.S.A., bill me at the bargain price of $4.69 plus 25¢ shipping and handling per book and applicable sales tax, if any*. In Canada, bill me at the bargain price of $5.24 plus 25¢ shipping and handling per book and applicable taxes**. That's the complete price and a savings of over 10% off the cover prices—what a great deal! I understand that accepting the 2 free books and gift places me under no obligation ever to buy any books. I can always return a shipment and cancel at any time. Even if I never buy another book from Harlequin, the 2 free books and gift are mine to keep forever.

246 HDN DZ7Q
349 HDN DZ7R

Name	(PLEASE PRINT)	
Address	Apt.#	
City	State/Prov.	Zip/Postal Code

Not valid to current Harlequin Historicals® subscribers.

Want to try two free books from another series?
Call 1-800-873-8635 or visit www.morefreebooks.com.

* Terms and prices subject to change without notice. Sales tax applicable in N.Y.
** Canadian residents will be charged applicable provincial taxes and GST.
   All orders subject to approval. Offer limited to one per household.
   ® are registered trademarks owned and used by the trademark owner or its licensee.

HIST04R   ©2004 Harlequin Enterprises Limited